Can Norrie stop a murderer's reign of terroir?

The descent of winter on the Finger Lakes means it's time for the Wine Trail Association's Chocolate and Wine Extravaganza. Unfortunately, for screenwriter-turned-reluctant-vintner Norrie Ellington, her Two Witches Winery is co-hosting the festivities. Norrie's duties include wrangling the three international chocolatiers featured at the event—bitter rivals and industry influencers who can make or break Two Witches.

But the heated competition among the celebrity confectioners soon spills out of the professional arena, and before the Extravaganza is over, one of the cocoa pros is dead, last seen sipping a Two Witches' Cabernet Sauvignon. With spirits souring at the Extravaganza and her winery on the line, Norrie must hustle to find the uncorked killer before Two Witches' reputation is crushed once and for all.

Visit us at www.kensingtonbooks.com

Books by J.C. Eaton

The Sophie Kimball Mysteries
Booked 4 Murder
Ditched 4 Murder
Staged for Murder
Botched 4 Murder
Molded 4 Murder
(coming March 2020)
Dressed Up 4 Murder

And available from Lyrical Press
The Wine Trail Mysteries
A Riesling to Die
Chardonnayed to Rest
Pinot Red or Dead
Sauvigone for Good

Published by Kensington Publishing Corporation

Sauvigone for Good

J.C. Eaton

LYRICAL UNDERGROUND
Kensington Publishing Corp.
www.kensingtonbooks.com

LYRICAL PRESS BOOKS are published by

Kensington Publishing Corp.
119 West 40th Street
New York, NY 10018

All Kensington titles, imprints, and distributed lines are available at special quantity discounts for bulk purchases for sales promotion, premiums, fund-raising, educational, or institutional use.

Special book excerpts or customized printings can also be created to fit specific needs. For details, write or phone the office of the Kensington Sales Manager: Kensington Publishing Corp., 119 West 40th Street, New York, NY 10018. Attn. Sales Department. Phone: 1-800-221-2647.

Lyrical Press and Lyrical Press logo Reg. U.S. Pat. & TM Off.

First Electronic Edition: December 2019
ISBN-13: 978-1-5161-0950-0 (ebook)
ISBN-10: 1-5161-0950-3 (ebook)

First Print Edition: December 2019
ISBN-13: 978-1-5161-0951-7
ISBN-10: 1-5161-0951-1

Printed in the United States of America

For Mary Jane Sbrocco,
You will always be in our hearts, and your kindness will never be forgotten.

Acknowledgments

Not a day goes by without my being thankful for our incredible support team of friends and family who give their time so willingly to ensure our books are "reader worthy." These tireless folks continue to push us forward, lend open ears, and rescue us when our technology goes on the blink. They scrutinize our every word and encourage us every step of the way. Writing is a long and thoughtful process. Having their support makes all the difference.

Thank you Larry Finkelstein, Gale Leach, Susan Morrow, Fran Orenstein, and Susan Schwartz all the way in Australia. And special thanks to the "Cozy Mystery Crew" of authors who work together to support one another. We're glad to be part of this crew. You're the best: Bethany Blake, V.M. Burns, Sarah Fox, Lena Gregory, Jody Holford, Jenny Kales, Tina Kashian, Libby Klein, Shari Randall, Linda Reilly, and Debra Sennefelder.

Our agent, Dawn Dowdle from Blue Ridge Literary Agency, and our editor, Tara Gavin from Kensington Publishing, have been with us every step of the way. Without them, the Wine Trail Mysteries wouldn't exist. We thank our lucky stars that these amazing professionals have taken us on.

And to the phenomenal staff at Kensington Publishing, we owe you tremendous thanks. Your hard work and attention to detail make all the difference.

Lastly, we thank the booksellers, librarians, and readers for giving us a reason to boot up the computer each day.

Chapter 1

Two Witches Winery
Penn Yan, New York

I pulled the quilt up to my neck and tried to ignore the incessant sound emanating from my cell phone. Why did I ever pick such an annoying ringtone? Judging from the light in my bedroom, I couldn't tell if it was dawn or mid-morning. January winters in New York's Finger Lakes region boasted one kind of sky color—gray.

My fingers fumbled on the nightstand but I finally grabbed the phone and mumbled hello, only I forgot the o.

"Hell of a morning to you, too, Norrie. What's keeping you? Catherine Trobert's driving me insane. I don't know why I ever agreed to be on this subcommittee in the first place. It's not as if the two of you couldn't work out the details. By the way, I ducked into our tasting room kitchen to make this call. I told her I was getting some more cookies. Hurry up and get over here before I lose it completely."

"Oh my God! Sorry, Theo. I totally forgot to set my alarm clock and since I left kibble in Charlie's dish last night, he didn't bother to slobber me with those smelly Plott Hound kisses of his. I'll be right over. Give me five minutes to throw on some clothes and brush my teeth."

"I'll give you ten. Brush your hair, too. Oh, and go slow when you head down the road to our place. It's pretty slick. Even the sign in front of the Grey Egret seems to be iced over. Ugh. I hate winter."

I threw the quilt into a giant wad and scrambled into the bathroom. Of all times to oversleep. I pictured poor Theo stuck listening to Catherine drone on and on about heaven-knows-what. At least she wasn't trying to fix him up with her son, which she's been doing with me since I arrived at our family winery last June. That was right. Last June. My sister, Francine, caught me at a weak moment and begged me to oversee the winery for a year so she could join my brother-in-law, Jason, an entomologist with Cornell's Experiment Station, and chase after some godforsaken insect in Costa Rica as part of a grant. Notice they never offered you grants to write novels in Paris or sample beers in Germany, but insects? The sky was the limit.

Not that I was expecting a grant. I earned a fair amount of money as a screenwriter for a Canadian film company specializing in romances and mysteries. Not bad for someone in their twenties with no real "life plan."

"All you need is your laptop and a landline," Francine told me, insisting "the winery practically runs itself." I guess I should have paid more attention to the word "practically." In the last six months, I'd dealt with a dead body in our newly planted Riesling section, one across the road at Rosalee Marbleton's place, and one halfway between Two Witches and the Grey Egret. It was a wonder I met my deadlines and managed to keep my script analyst happy. Anyway, I had another six months before my tenant's lease ran out for my tiny apartment in Manhattan, so I was virtually stuck here. Besides, a promise was a promise. Same deal with that ridiculous subcommittee I'd said I'd join.

I threw on my heaviest socks and jeans, along with an old, lumpy, mohair sweater that belonged to Francine, and headed out the door to Theo and Don's tasting room for the subcommittee meeting.

All the wineries on Seneca Lake belonged to the Seneca Lake Wine Trail, an organization that promoted tourism along with our wines. That was over thirty wineries and a heck of a lot of businesses to promote. To further the cause, our neighboring wineries started a small, more casual group so we could support each other. Under the name of WOW, or Wineries of the West, we meet twice a month to discuss important topics of interest or, as my mother used to say, "Chew that gossip as if it was a piece of gum."

Except for Theo and Don, who ran the Grey Egret, all the other wineries, including ours, were represented by women—Rosalee Marbleton at Terrace Wineries, Stephanie Ipswich at Gable Hill Winery, Madeline Martinez at Billsburrow Winery, and Catherine Trobert at Lake View Winery.

It was one of those women, Catherine to be precise, who thought we needed a subcommittee for WOW to handle the arrangements for our role in the wine trail's upcoming Valentine's Day promotional event, Chocolate and Wine. Our six wineries were selected by the Seneca Lake Wine Trail

Association to showcase the three international chocolatiers flying over from Europe to give demonstrations of their craft and compete in the first ever Chocolate and Wine Extravaganza at the prestigious Geneva on the Lake resort. I figured the only reason our wineries were selected was that we were closest to the resort.

The grand prize for the winning chocolatier was an obscene amount of money, in addition to full-feature articles in *Food & Wine, Chocolate Connoisseur,* and *Wine Enthusiast.* Not that those artisans hadn't been featured in food magazines, but the scope of it would be enormous according to the WOW members. If you asked me, though, the real prize was a segment on *Good Morning America* and some sort of book deal. Madeline Martinez explained the details at last month's WOW meeting, but I was too busy checking my Facebook status. Then, to make matters worse, I got a terrible itch on my back and when I raised my hand to scratch it, she thought I'd volunteered to be part of the subcommittee, along with Catherine. Once trapped, I gave Theo a subtle kick in the ankle and he agreed to join the subcommittee as well.

Now I was hustling to get to our first meeting. Normally I'd hoof it down the road since it was less than a mile, but it was freezing outside and I was already late. Thankfully, my well-weathered Toyota started right up and I was down the driveway in seconds. Our driveway was really the upper portion of the hill with the Grey Egret at the bottom. We shared commanding views of Seneca Lake and the Route 14 traffic that those views brought.

Theo and Catherine were seated at a small table at the rear of his tasting room and, from the look of things, they had already finished a platter of cookies. Only crumbs remained.

"Good Morning, Norrie," Catherine said. "Don't worry about being late. Theo and I had a wonderful conversation about Steven's latest trial. That law firm of his certainly keeps him busy."

My God! Not even one foot in the door and she has already managed to bring her son into the conversation.

"Um, that's wonderful."

"Yes, he really enjoys living in Maine, but he was so disappointed things didn't work out for Christmas. Of course, there's always April. He's bound to get a vacation then and the two of you can reconnect."

Reconnect? More like wave hello and goodbye. Just like our high school days.

Theo shoved a large mug of coffee at me. "It's still hot. I brought it over a few minutes before you walked in."

The aroma hit my nostrils and, for the next ten seconds, I completely forgot about Steven Trobert, not that it was difficult. I barely knew the guy in high school and I was sure he wouldn't even remember who I was.

"Yum. Chicory flavor, right? This coffee is phenomenal."

Theo smiled. "Don's idea to try new blends. Of course, now with the Chocolate and Wine Festival coming up, we'll need to add cocoa blends."

Catherine brushed some loose strands of hair from her eyes and leaned into the table. "Speaking of which, we might as well get started. To tell the truth, this whole thing has gotten me in a tizzy. Sure, we have festivals all the time, but the wine trail has never hosted an international event with world famous chocolatiers. Allete Barrineau was in last month's issue of *Martha Stewart Living* and Stanislav Vetrov made the front cover of *Saveur.* I can't believe they're actually going to be giving presentations in our wineries."

"I can believe it," Theo said. "Don even talks about it in his sleep. Mumbling about bonbons and truffles."

I shrugged. "Guess I'm the only one around here who's fine with a Three Musketeers bar or some M&Ms. Francine was into gourmet chocolate until she discovered health foods. Now we've got a pantry with dark chocolate bars that are one step away from qualifying as laxatives."

Theo laughed. "Seriously, we need to focus on the schedule so the rest of the WOW group doesn't have our heads at next week's meeting."

I nodded. "So, what exactly are we supposed to do?"

Catherine pulled out a small notebook from her bag and opened it. "We're supposed to figure out how to maximize the time we have with the three chocolatiers at our wineries. They'll be arriving the week before the extravaganza and staying at Geneva on the Lake. Essentially, they'll be available to do small weekday demonstrations at our wineries, except for Friday. They'll need Friday and Saturday to prep for the Saturday night event."

I pinched my shoulder blades together and took another sip of the coffee. "I thought they were preparing the chocolate, not making it."

"They are," Theo said. "They're not chocolate makers, they're chocolate artists. The block chocolate has been donated by Puccini Zinest from the Netherlands. I imagine Teuscher from Switzerland, and our very own Scharffen Berger, are kicking themselves in the pants for not beating Puccini Zinest to the punch."

"How do you know this stuff?"

"I live with Don, remember? He practically oozes this information."

Just then, Catherine slipped me a piece of paper entitled, "Seneca Lake Wine Trail Chocolate Extravaganza, Important Information for Winery Owners."

"You should have gotten a copy of this, Norrie. It was sent out weeks ago. It has all the pertinent information on it."

I glanced at the paper. "Uh, I'm sure we did. It's probably with our tasting room manager."

"The important thing to keep in mind is the chocolatiers will need a workspace in your kitchens and, except for Belgium's Jules Leurant, they'll need someone to be their assistant before, during, and after the demonstrations," she said.

"Huh? Why doesn't this Jules guy need one?"

Theo leaned back and groaned. "According to Don, Jules is a regular prima donna and a bona fide germophobe. He won't make appearances anywhere without his assistant."

"Well, he won't want to make an appearance at our winery once he sees our goat, Alvin, hanging over the fence by the side of the building. And I don't even want to think what would happen if Charlie trounced over to him."

"Good," Catherine said. "We'll assign Jules to two of the other wineries. Each chocolatier will be assigned to only two wineries. That way they can get used to the setup. Less stressful for them."

Yeah, but what about us?

Theo immediately responded. "Better keep him away from Gable Hill. Stephanie's twin boys will have their little sticky fingers over everything."

"Give him to Rosalee," I said. "And Madeline. That should be germ-free enough."

Catherine took copious notes for the remainder of our meeting, while Theo and I rolled our eyes at each other when she wasn't looking. We managed to assign each chocolatier to two wineries for the demos and agreed on how we were going to use social media to promote it.

Suddenly Catherine turned ashen and put her notebook down. "Oh dear. Oh dear. We haven't even discussed which wines each of us will be pairing. We don't want to overlap if at all possible. Of course, it really shouldn't matter since it's a food pairing and not a wine demo, but still…we want our visitors to get a good sampling of what we produce in the Finger Lakes."

"Merlot," Theo said. "What about you, Norrie? Your winemaker must have shared that info with you by now."

"He did. Franz said we'll be serving our Cabernet Sauvignon, and when I spoke to Rosalee last week, she mentioned something about Pinot

Noir. At least her Pinot wasn't tampered with by that lowdown crook a few months ago."

The color slowly returned to Catherine's face. "Thank goodness. We're serving Lemberger and I know for a fact Stephanie's going to present their Cabernet Franc. That leaves Madeline. I know they produce Syrah so I'll ask her if they'll serve that. Oh my! Is that clock over there right?"

Theo nodded as Catherine rattled on. "I can't believe it's a quarter to ten already. I really should get back to our winery. I promised I'd give a hand in the tasting room. Now remember, we only have three weeks before those chocolatiers arrive and I, for one, want things to go off without a hitch."

Theo's phone buzzed with an alert and he mumbled, "Facebook or Twitter" as he picked it up from the table. None of us said a word as Catherine stood up to leave. No sooner did she push her chair into the table when Theo announced, "Without a hitch may be an impossibility."

Catherine froze. "What do you mean?"

"It's a news alert and it's probably trending everywhere. It says, 'New threats and old rivalries loom for famed chocolatiers.'"

Chapter 2

I don't know who invented the term "train wreck" when it came to describing impending or ongoing disasters, but this chocolate fest had train wreck written all over it. Somehow it didn't surprise me. I figured I'd go along with the plan, *whatever the heck we come up with,* and hope for the best. As far as I could tell, all I had to do was ensure our winery was prepared for the demonstrations and attend the bookended events that called for my presence.

The not-so-casual but not-quite-formal opening reception was to take place at Geneva on the Lake the week preceding the grand competition. I figured it would be an introduction of sorts with lots of boring speeches from the wine association. Apparently, I was wrong. My tasting room manager, Cammy, set me straight as soon as I left the Grey Egret. I parked my car next to one of the three visitor cars in our lot so it would look as if more people were there and walked into our wine sampling room. I swore my lips were blue from the cold.

"There you are!" Cammy held a duster and walked away from the gift shelf. "Did you get a chance to read that chocolatier article on Facebook? It might be from the Associated Press, but I'm not sure. Boy, talk about tabloid news. Guess this event is going to be a humdinger, huh?"

"I only got the headline from Theo. Please tell me it's nothing that's going to do damage to our winery. We've already had enough media attention this year, not to mention I'm probably on Deputy Hickman's speed dial."

"What part of the disaster do you want me to start with?"

"The part that doesn't involve us."

"Come on. Let's chat in the kitchen for a few minutes. Besides, you look as if you could use a hot cup of coffee. Glenda and Sam have the tasting room tables covered."

Cammy pulled the maroon ribbon on her French bun tighter and opened the door to the kitchen for me. A robust brunette in her thirties, Cammy had a welcoming demeanor that put everyone at ease. "I'll pour us some dark blend. Glenda just made it. Pray to the gods she didn't put any weird essences of God-knows-what in it."

Glenda was a dear soul and our resident kook, for lack of a better word. She swore by séances and spirits, premonitions, and voices from the netherworld. Don't ask.

"Sit down. This could rival one of your screenplays."

Cammy was right. I did need more coffee. I figured there was no such thing as too much caffeine in one day, so I took a good gulp. "Go on."

"Stanislav Vetrov, who, by the way, gets my vote for hunk-of-the-year, had a short-lived affair with Allete Barrineau a few years back until her husband found out and threatened to cut off the guy's you-know-what. Rumor has it, the affair got rekindled and Allete filed for divorce. She cited his erratic behavior and unrelenting insomnia as issues that destroyed the marriage. According to the article, the husband threatened to lob off Stanislav's head this time."

"Ew. Please tell me the husband isn't planning on attending the event."

Cammy shrugged. "Who knows? But I can tell you this much—all the major news networks are sending reporters. The backstories are almost as riveting as the event. Including the cannabis remedy Allete's husband tried for his sleep deprivation."

"Oh brother."

"Anyway, I've got a friend who handles the reservations for Geneva on the Lake and, even though it's confidential, she did name names."

By now I was chomping at the bit. "What names? Whose names?"

"Robin Roberts from ABC and Hoda Kotb from NBC. There's more, but she couldn't tell me—and that's not all. A few world-famous chefs have reservations, too."

"Like who?"

"No idea, but my friend said that the resort beefed up security like nobody's business."

"Holy cow. For chocolate and wine?"

"I imagine it's a bigger deal than any of us realize. Anyway, getting back to that article, the Stanislav and Allete situation is only the tip of the iceberg."

"Please don't tell me we need to beef up security. The best I can do is move Alvin closer to the entrance. You know how he gets when he freaks out."

"Uh-huh. Your poor vineyard crew can probably rebuild fences in their sleep. Listen, someone sent Jules Leurant a death threat stating if he dared to participate in the competition it would be his last."

"Terrific."

"Wait. There's more. The article also said Jules's long-time assistant quit because he feared for his life," Cammy said.

"Oh no. I'd better tell Catherine. The wineries we assigned to Jules will need to do some jockeying around and get him a temporary helper."

"No, they won't. He's bringing his nephew, some wet-behind-the-ears kid by the name of Earvin Roels. That was all over the news, too."

I took a good whiff of the coffee before putting it to my lips. "Too bad Jules doesn't have a relative who's well-versed in martial arts and real familiar with using a handgun. Did the article say what was behind the death threat? I mean, other than the obvious thing of someone else not wanting him to win."

"Nope, but it does sound all Tanya Harding and Nancy Kerrigan to me."

"Who?"

"Yeesh. I keep forgetting you're only in your twenties. They were Olympic figure skaters. Nancy Kerrigan was attacked in an attempt to knock her out of the competition."

"Let's hope no one knocks anyone out of this competition. Especially in our winery."

"Did your subcommittee work out the schedule?" Cammy asked.

"Sort of. We left it to Catherine to finalize. If I've got things straight, the chocolatiers will be visiting each of the six wineries individually to sample the wine we plan to pair with their creation. They'll be doing this the week following the opening reception."

"Uh-huh. So far so good," Cammy said.

I continued, "Monday of that week is for the chocolatiers to get acclimated. Nothing scheduled. Then the ticketed program begins on Tuesday. The full ticket includes the winery demos and the grand competition event on Saturday night. Visitors can choose to purchase grand event tickets only or demo tickets. The Seneca Lake Wine Trail Association is handling all of that."

"Good. They planned this shindig. They should be doing something."

"Judging from the internet attention, we should make doubly sure that when the chocolatiers arrive for their individual tastings with us, they don't accidently bump into each other in our parking lot or, God forbid, our building. Sounds like it could be volatile."

"Nah, it's probably a bunch of hype so we'll sell more tickets."

As things turned out, it wasn't hype and, if anything, it was understated. It didn't take one of Glenda's premonitions to tell us we were in for a maelstrom.

And while I wouldn't quite use the word "maelstrom" to describe the WOW meeting I was forced to attend the following week, words like "nerve-racking" and "tense" certainly came to mind.

A fast Alberta Clipper charged through the Finger Lakes and forced our already cold temperatures to a new level of misery. John Grishner, our vineyard manager, still managed to don his winter parka and, along with his crew, prune the grapevines and repair any falling or failing trellises. And while the landscape smacked of "dead of winter," the vines only looked that way because dormant could easily be mistaken for deceased.

I had the heat cranked so high in my Toyota that the interior of the vehicle actually condensed in the three or four miles it took me to get from Two Witches to the WOW meeting at Billsburrow Winery.

"I'd offer to take your coat," Madeline said, "but it's still cold in here. We insulated the enclosed porch, but it's not enough. That fireplace of ours could really use a new heating fan. Anyway, there's hot cider on the console along with coffee and muffins."

Stephanie Ipswich and Rosalee Marbleton were already seated at the long rectangular table that overlooked Madeline's vineyards. Both had steaming cups of liquid in their hands.

"I'm here! I'm here. Don't start the festivities without me," Theo bellowed from the doorway.

Madeline ushered him in and, within seconds, Catherine arrived. She was laden down with a stack of papers and literally plopped them on the table. "Updated schedules and information for everyone. I've been on the phone all morning with Henry Speltmore. Honestly, for the president of the wine association, the man was practically no help whatsoever. All he kept saying regarding the chocolatier schedules at our wineries was, 'I'll leave it in your capable hands.' That's a euphemism for 'you do all the work.'"

Stephanie reached across the table and gave Catherine's arm a pat. "And we appreciate it. We really do."

The next half hour was grueling. We went over the event schedule ad nauseam, pausing every few seconds so someone could add a recent tidbit of tabloid gossip to the mix. Twenty minutes later I was ready to heave—either that or bolt out of there. The latest news was that one of the chocolatiers insisted we let them choose their block chocolate, rather than subjecting them to the "blind drawing" for blends like dark, semi-sweet, or milk chocolate. The end result, which probably came after ceaseless bickering, was that the three chocolatiers would select their preferred block chocolate for their creations.

"Dear Lord!" Rosalee exclaimed. "Don't tell me they'll insist on a particular wine—because all they're getting from us is Pinot Noir. Next thing you know, they'll want us to plant a specific variety for them."

"You can relax, Rosalee," Catherine said. "That's not one of their demands."

"Demands? Are we being held hostage?" I was flabbergasted.

Catherine cleared her throat. "Maybe I shouldn't have used the word 'demands.' More like *requests,* only with a strong emphasis."

Theo kicked my ankle from under the table and mouthed "Oh brother."

I lowered my voice. "What kind of requests?"

"Nothing that we really don't expect of our own customers," Catherine said, "only we don't brow beat them. You know, like not wearing heavy perfume because it interferes with the ability to smell and taste our wines."

"What else?"

"A consistent room temperature of sixty-five to seventy degrees and a humidity level not to exceed fifty percent."

Theo laughed. "Good luck with that. Especially in some of our tasting rooms. Whenever the doors are opened, the cold air rushes in. And who the hell checks the humidity levels?"

Catherine took a deep breath and pulled out a piece of paper from the pile sitting in front of her. Her eyes scanned the sheet as if it was a train schedule. "Those are the workable expectations. I'll get to the point. Jules insists *all* surfaces be sanitized prior to his arrival. Allete only uses one-hundred percent cotton towels. And here's something new—Stanislav refuses to be in the same room as Jules. Apparently, they had words at a chocolate festival in Munich last year."

Madeline brought the muffin tray to the table and offered us second helpings. "Please don't tell me there's more."

Catherine looked at each of us and then fixed her stare on Madeline. "Only one. And oddly enough, it's not coming from Jules. Stanislav and Allete insist on complete dossiers for the staff we assign to assist them."

I rolled my eyes at least a half dozen times. "Why? I mean, I can understand Jules's concern considering he got a death threat, but the other two? What are they worried about?"

This time it was Stephanie who answered. "Someone stealing their trade secrets."

"I doubt that's going to be an issue at Two Witches. Cammy's idea of fine chocolate is a Hershey bar, and I'm not even sure anyone else cares."

"Well, these folks do," she said, "and I wouldn't put anything past them. I mean it. *Anything.* We need to be on our toes."

Terrific. Who needed Glenda's premonitions when Stephanie was doing just fine scaring the daylights out of us?

Chapter 3

I tried not to dwell on what *could* happen because inevitably whatever *did* happen made what *could* happen seem mild. Stumbling over dead bodies had a way of doing that to someone's psyche. At any rate, the two weeks that followed the WOW meeting were uneventful, except for the constant reminders from Renee, the movie producer in Toronto, that my next screenplay was due the end of February. *Beguiled into Love* wouldn't go into production for at least a year, and that was only if my script analyst didn't reject it altogether. So far, I was doing all right, but I always anguished over my work. Now, with this chocolate fest hanging over my head, I had something else to anguish over.

Cammy seemed to have everything under control in the tasting room and the same could be said for Franz and his assistant winemakers, Alan and Herbert. Yesterday, I ran into Herbert at Wegmans, of all places, and he informed me he'd just dropped off our bottles of Sauvignon at Geneva on the Lake for the casual opening reception.

We were standing near their bakery's little bistro and Herbert motioned me aside. If I didn't know he was a graduate from Cornell with a degree in viticulture and enology, I would have easily mistaken him for a professional football or basketball player. He was tall, dark, and muscular. Not to mention good looking. Besides, those sports jerseys he always wore under his lab coat all but screamed "jock." Oddly enough, he wasn't and the only reason he wore them, according to Franz, was that the cotton blends were comfortable for long days in the winery.

"The chocolatiers will be arriving in less than ten days," Herbert said. "I'm not sure if they'll all be flying in on the same day, but I wouldn't be surprised if they pop by our wineries next weekend. Franz had me buy extra containers of Clorox wipes for our office area in case Jules wants a tour of our personal workspace as well as the lab."

"I thought their official tours begin on Monday, after the reception."

"The official tours, yes, but that doesn't mean they won't get a head start on Friday or Saturday. Alan volunteered to chat with them about the filtering and blending we do in the winter."

"Good, as long as I don't need to say anything."

Herbert laughed. "You said enough at the last tour you gave when you told that group of visitors from Japan that 'something happens when juice goes into the tanks.'"

I cringed. "Yeah, well, maybe they'll blame it on a poor translation. Francine's the one who knows the ins and outs of the business. I'm simply babysitting."

"Relax. You're doing a good job."

In the days leading up to the "grand arrival," news of the chocolatiers' exploits was everywhere—on the local TV stations, social media, and my personal favorite, "gossip media." At one point, I even considered jotting down the scuttlebutt emanating from our tasting room in case I needed a plotline for my next screenplay. The customers regaled us with stories they heard and even our own workers, like Roger and Sam, who were usually quiet about those kinds of things, offered up enough scenarios to make all of us blush.

"I can't wait to get my eyes on Allete," Sam said. "If she's half as good-looking as she appears in all those photos, I may need to change my major to culinary arts and ask her for an internship."

Lizzie, our bookkeeper/cashier, pooh-poohed most of the conversations. "When you get to be my age, you focus more on character, not appearances."

To which Sam replied, "I'll keep that in mind when I get to be your age."

Only Glenda held back and that was completely out of character for her.

"Do you think she senses something ominous coming?" I asked Cammy the day before the first of the chocolatiers landed in Rochester.

"Hard to say. If she did, she'd be insistent we douse the place with sage and lavender or something else. As long as the word 'smudging' doesn't enter her vocabulary, I'd leave things alone."

So, we did. In retrospect, we should have doused ourselves with that stuff to ensure that our pores were clogged up for the next century. As far as the winery went, it was too bad we didn't put in a bulk order for sage sticks.

* * * *

Jules Leurant was the first of the chocolatiers to arrive in the Finger Lakes. It was the Thursday before the program was to begin. Stephanie called me a little before eleven to tell me that, "The crazed germophobe from Belgium is making the rounds. He's on his way to Rosalee's and then to the Grey Egret. I've already warned them. You're last on the list, Norrie. Pray he doesn't stay long."

"Was it that bad?"

"After he sent his obnoxious assistant in to make sure the place was safe and no assassins were lurking around, he came inside and sniffed around our tasting room like a bloodhound. He informed us chocolate cannot be placed near anything with an odor or it would pick up that odor. My God, Norrie! I can't do away with everything that smells. And I can't hose down our customers if they're wearing perfume."

I was in the middle of writing a heartwarming scene and, thanks to Stephanie's phone call, all I could think of were those commercials for Febreze. I thanked her, threw on a heavy sweatshirt, grabbed the parka I had thrown over a chair in the kitchen, and raced down to our tasting room. It was blustery with a few wisps of light snow—but nothing that called for boots. No need to start the car. I needed the fresh, albeit frigid, air.

The aroma of grapes and freshly baked bread wafted through the air. One of the things I really liked about Fred, our bistro chef, and Emma, his wife, was the fact that they cooked everything from scratch. I inhaled the aroma and paused. Were aromas synonymous with smells? If so, we were doomed.

There were at least twelve or thirteen customers milling around the tasting tables or checking out the wine bins and gift racks. No need to panic anyone. I looked around for Cammy, but she wasn't in sight. Lizzie was at the cash register, and Glenda and Sam had full tables. I rushed into the kitchen and threw open the cabinet below the sink where we kept the baking soda.

Immediately, I poured it into every conceivable bowl I could get my hands on and started placing those bowls all over the winery. Cammy finally appeared from the bistro—where she had stopped to grab a bite for lunch.

"What's going on? What's with those bowls and what on earth's in them?"

I told her about Stephanie's call and she groaned. "It takes hours for baking soda to absorb odors and that's for small odors in tiny places. I say we take our chances. I mean, what do they expect? This is a winery. It's supposed to smell like wine."

"I suppose you're right. I'm overthinking this."

Just then my cell phone buzzed and it was Theo. "Brace yourself. And if I were you, I'd make sure the men's room is gleaming like a fourth of July sparkler or you'll never hear the end of it. Gotta go."

"Cammy, take over for Sam and send him into the men's room now. Theo called. Disaster awaits. Tell Sam to make sure everything in there is spic and span. And tell him not to use air freshener. It smells."

Spic and span? Air freshener? Yikes! I'm beginning to sound like my mother.

I imagined Cammy saw the look of fear in my eyes because she darted off to Sam's table, leaving me standing with a bowl of baking soda in each hand.

I cannot let this get to me. They're only chocolate confectioners... chocolate confectioners whose reputations can make or break our wines.

At that instant, a short balding man entered the building and loosened the scarf from his neck. He was wearing a dark sweater, dark jacket, and dark pants. Lizzie called out a welcome greeting to him, and he gave her a cursory nod before taking out a pen and a small notebook.

Within seconds, he flitted around the tasting room like a fly at a picnic, pausing occasionally to jot down a few things. I watched as he made a beeline for the men's room, missing Sam by a matter of seconds.

"Makes you wish the food inspector was visiting instead, huh?" Cammy straightened the glasses on Sam's table.

"Shh! He's coming out of the men's room. Smile at him. Act natural."

I gave the man a wave and was about to introduce myself when he marched straight out of the building.

"Maybe that was too natural," Cammy chuckled.

Before I could respond, the man returned, only this time he was followed by a slightly taller gentleman who appeared to be in his late forties or maybe even early fifties. Unlike his counterpart, the other man had a full head of thick, dark hair, a dark moustache, and an equally dark goatee. His overcoat was trimmed in what I hoped was faux fur and his shoes were practically gleaming.

I took a deep breath and approached the men. "Hi! I'm Norrie Ellington and this is my family's winery, Two Witches. You must be the chocolatiers we've heard so much about."

The taller man unbuttoned his coat. "*I* am one of the chocolatiers. Jules Leurant from Brussels, and this is Earvin Roels, my nephew and assistant."

Jean-Claude Van Damme is from Brussels. Why can't he be in the chocolate industry?

"We're pleased you're visiting us today. Would you care to sample some of our wines?"

I motioned to Sam's table, where he and Cammy were now both stationed. Jules glanced at the table and then at me. "The only wine I care to sample is the variety that will be paired with my chocolate confections during the demonstrations."

"Um, well, actually, I believe your demonstrations will be taking place at Billsburrow and Terrace Wineries. Because there are six participating wineries, we divided up the tastings."

Jules turned to Earvin and stomped his foot. "Why wasn't I made aware of this? I told you to keep me apprised of everything." Then he said something in either Dutch or German, but I wasn't sure.

I gave Earvin one of those been-there-know-how-it-feels looks when I thought Jules wasn't paying attention.

"I'm sorry," I said. "It's not your assistant's fault. Our organizing committee should have done a better job at conveying the information."

Jules immediately buttoned his coat and pulled the fur collar closer to his neck. "I see no reason to remain. I can only hope there are no other surprises awaiting me during this exposition. Good day."

With that, he and Earvin walked directly to the door and out into the cold.

"Whoa!" I said. "That was more chilling than the weather. I wanted to tell him that all of the chocolates were going to be paired with all of the wines during the opening reception, but he didn't give me a chance."

Cammy stepped away from the tasting table and walked toward me. "Guess he'll have to get used to surprises."

Chapter 4

As the chocolate saga continued, it wasn't only Jules who would have to get used to surprises. It was me. No sooner did I return to the house for a few hours of writing when Godfrey Klein called. Godfrey was the young entomologist I kissed a while back. Long complicated story, but it wasn't so much of a passion kiss than an emotional I-don't-know-what kiss. Anyway, Godfrey was also one of Jason's colleagues at the Experiment Station and he kept me updated on my sister and brother-in-law's exploits in the Costa Rican rain forests. Cornell could afford a satellite phone. I couldn't. That was probably a good thing, considering my sister had no idea about the murders. At least up until today.

"Hi Norrie. Hope I didn't catch you at a bad time, but there's something you should know."

"If it has anything to do with insects inhabiting the house in winter, I don't want to know."

"Uh, it's worse."

After my miserable encounter with Jules Leurant, I didn't know what could be worse. "What do you mean?"

"Francine and Jason know about the murders, but there's good news."

"What? She's probably chewing her fingernails off and demanding they return to Penn Yan. His grant will go up in smoke."

"They only found out about the last two murders, not the one in your Riesling section. So far, that's been kept pretty hush-hush."

"How did they find out? And more importantly, did my sister freak out?"

"Another group of entomologists from UC Davis' Department of Entomology and Nematology joined up to work on the Global Invasive

Species Database. One of them had recently returned from a family wedding in Geneva and found out about the murders."

"Oh brother."

"According to my department head, Francine and Jason weren't all that alarmed once they were told the murders had been solved and everyone at the wineries was okay. Anyway, thought you should know. By the way, how's it going with that chocolate extravaganza? It's been all over the news."

"I met one of the chocolatiers earlier today. If that's any indication, it will be a nightmare."

I went on to tell him about my encounter with Jules and the frenetic schedule the six participating wineries had to deal with. I didn't know why, but it was easy to talk to Godfrey and pour out all my frustrations. Unlike Bradley Jamison, the super cute lawyer I was dating but not yet ready to call my boyfriend. I was always on my best behavior with Bradley. Maybe I was, in some way, intimidated by his amazingly good looks. Those cobalt blue eyes and that sandy blond hair reminded me of an old poster of one of the Beach Boys that my mother had stashed away.

Bradley was one of Rosalee's attorneys, and he and I dated on and off—usually dinners and long, languishing kisses. He was supposed to attend the grand finale Chocolate and Wine Extravaganza with me but called to tell me his boss, Marvin Souza, was sending him to Yonkers, of all places, to handle a complex settlement case in conjunction with another law firm.

"I'm sorry to hear that, Norrie," Godfrey said. "But look at it this way. It'll be over before you know it."

"The same could be said for Typhoid Fever, but it doesn't help at the moment. Say, what are you doing this week? You could come as my plus one to the opening reception and the competition. Come on. You have nothing to lose. It's not like they're pairing up those chocolates with some awful insect from your lab."

"For your information, many cultures dine on chocolate-covered insects. Ants, crickets, locusts—"

"Ew! Yes or no. Will you do it? Attend the events?"

"Sure. From what I've heard, this will be the most entertainment I've had in a long time."

Relieved I had someone to commiserate with during the festivities, I went back to my writing, only to be interrupted again at a little past six—this time by Theo, who called the landline.

"Are you watching the news? Stanislav and Allete are being interviewed by 13 WHAM TV out of Rochester. They're both at the airport. They caught the same flight from JFK. No coincidence there, I'll bet."

"Hold on. Let me turn on the TV."

I walked into the living room and grabbed the remote. "Geez! Look at that crowd. Whoever thought chocolatiers would be so popular?"

"It's all that tabloid media coverage. Whoever thought the Kardashians would be so popular? Anyway, it's great news for us. Think of all those visitors who are going to show up at our wineries. Someone at the Seneca Lake Wine Trail Association knew what they were doing."

"Hold on. I want to hear what Stanislav and Allete are saying."

Except for interrupting to ask, "Are you still on the line?" Theo and I kept still for the two- or three-minute interview.

When the segment moved to school bus safety in winter, Theo spoke. "Those magazine photos of Stanislav don't do the guy justice. He's beyond 'striking good looks,' and don't you dare tell Don we had this conversation."

I laughed. "Allete's quite the looker, too. No wonder Sam was so enamored. Guess it's those delicate features of hers and that upturned nose."

"The strawberry blond hair and those cherubic cheeks don't hurt either."

"Oh my gosh. Would you listen to the two of us? We're worse than the WOW women."

"I guess there's no love lost between Stanislav and Jules. Did you catch what Stanislav said about Jules accusing him of stealing his technique for piping the chocolate?"

"Was that what the ruckus in Munich was all about? Garnishing the chocolate? I thought it had something to do with their personal lives."

"I think chocolate *is* their personal life," Theo said. "And speaking of which, I can't believe Allete told that reporter about her and Stanislav's plan to start their own chocolate manufacturing company in Luxemburg if either of them wins the competition. They'd certainly have enough start-up monies, not to mention all the money they'd earn from advertisement contracts."

"Was it my imagination or did they both appear kind of smug about that deal? True, they'll be competing against each other, but it really won't matter in the end since they plan on starting a business together."

"At least we don't have to worry about them stopping by tomorrow. They told that reporter they intend to give themselves a day of rest before visiting a few wineries on the trail that weren't part of the festival pairings."

"Good. Means we're off the hook for another day. Guess I'll see you Sunday night at Geneva on the Lake. I invited Godfrey."

"Not Bradley? I thought you two were dating."

"We are, but he's going to be out of town. Godfrey's just a good friend."

"Uh-huh. Keep telling yourself that."

"Bite me." I laughed and then hung up the phone.

* * * *

Geneva on the Lake was an old, elegant resort designed in Italian Renaissance style. It sat on the outskirts of the city and, with its meticulously sculpted gardens, sloped down to the lake. Built at the beginning of the twentieth century, it was a private estate that later became a monastery at the end of World War II. I wasn't sure what happened, but in the early 1970s, the monks left and the building fell apart. Literally. Dilapidated and a regular eyesore on Route 14. Then it was purchased by a developer and completely remodeled with the purpose of serving as a resort. It changed hands once again in the mid-1990s and was embellished to the point of rivaling the most prestigious Italian villas. Figured. It was the perfect place for the Chocolate and Wine Festival—not to mention the three egos that would be housed there.

The Sunday weather forecast in our part of the Finger Lakes called for five or six inches of snow by nightfall. Nothing to worry about. Then, seven to eight inches. Still not a problem. However, when I arrived at Geneva on the Lake and the road looked like a holiday snow globe, I was concerned. At least I was smart enough to use Francine's Subaru with the studded snow tires and all-wheel drive. I was also smart enough to choose one of Francine's special outfits—a dark A-line dress that looked phenomenal with my black knee-high boots.

I figured if the press planned on hovering around the chocolatiers, I might wind up in one of the photos. The way things were with social media, I didn't want to look as if I planned to stomp on the grapes instead of presenting them via our fine wines.

My instincts were right. The Channel 13 WHAM van was in the parking lot, along with 8 WROC and 10 WHEC. Thank you, Francine.

Don, Theo, and Godfrey had the same idea. They arrived in shirts and ties, all set to impress. The only thing casual about the Chocolate and Wine opening reception was the fact it wasn't a sit-down dinner. Instead, it was a classy buffet in one of the ballrooms, and if that wasn't enough, they had scads of wait staff making the rounds with all sorts of canapes. White and red wines were on a separate buffet, and both tables had staff to assist the attendees.

I immediately spotted Madeline Martinez chatting with Stephanie Ipswich near the wine table and Rosalee Marbleton chewing off someone's ear by the bistro tables that were set up for the guests. Franz, our winemaker, was conversing with three or four men whom I presumed were our neighbors' winemakers. I hoped Cammy would attend, but unfortunately, she had to take over for one of her aunts and help out at their family bar and restaurant in Geneva.

Godfrey gave me a wave from across the room, but just as I headed toward him, Catherine Trobert grabbed me by the wrist. "The forecast is calling for nonstop snow. Something about lake effect. We always have lake effect. Why couldn't they have predicted this earlier?"

I shrugged. "It shouldn't matter. The chocolatiers are all staying here at the resort and those news crews probably have super studded tires. The rest of us are only a few miles away and Route 14 is always plowed."

Catherine wrung her hands together. "I suppose you're right. Even if we get two feet of snow, they'll have everything cleared off by morning. I don't know why I'm so worried about snow. Maybe it's my nerves. I've been a wreck ever since Jules Leurant came into our winery."

"Your winery? I thought Stephanie, Rosalee, Don, Theo, and I were the only lucky ones who had to endure his visit."

"Don't I wish. That dreadful man stopped by Lake View before he set foot in Gable Hill. It was horrible. Simply horrible. He didn't have one nice thing to say. No wonder he got that death threat. Or was it more than one?"

Just then, Stephanie joined us. "What a piece of work that Jules is. I hope he chokes on his own bonbons or whatever he plans to make."

Suddenly, we heard a man's voice and both of us spun around to face a reporter and his cameraman. "Can we quote you on that? Wade Gallagher, 8 WROC. We're covering this event."

Guess snow isn't going to be the only thing to worry about.

Chapter 5

"That was a private conversation, Mr. Gallagher," I said, "and if you quote anything, you'll have to deal with the wine association's attorneys."

Wade Gallagher put his hands in the air and took a step back. "Whoa. No need to get in an uproar. Guess I was being a little over-zealous covering this event. It's always a matter of having the best eye- and ear-catching stuff for our viewers."

"I don't think you have to worry about that," I said, "Take a look behind you."

Allete entered the ballroom wearing a black sheath dress with slits that practically came up to her waist. I later realized it was backless as well as side-less, if there is such a word for a dress. But that wasn't the eye-catching part. I was positive it was the plunging neckline that made everyone in the room stand at attention. True, she was wearing a lovely single strand of pearls, but I seriously doubted that was what caught everyone's eye.

Wade spun around to look, muttered something, and, within an instant, introduced himself to France's most famous chocolatier.

"No sense standing around here," I said to Catherine. "We might as well mingle. In fact, that's a friend of mine over there. I'd better say hello."

I was never so happy to see Godfrey Klein as I was at that moment. Last thing I needed was to be hounded by the press, or worse yet, by Catherine.

"This is quite the party," Godfrey said. "I've been to weddings and Bar Mitzvahs that didn't have this much food."

"Yep, the wine association knows how to put on a good show. Uh-oh. Speaking of which, do you see what I see?"

Godfrey looked around. "You mean those two men near the fireplace? Doesn't appear to be too friendly, given their body lang—Oh, my gosh! Did you see that?"

"Hard to miss. The tall one is Stanislav Vetrov and the fussy-looking one who shoved a finger in Stanislav's chest is Jules Leurant. Holy Cannoli. Do something, Godfrey. Go over there and introduce yourself. Tell them about insects. Anything. I can't go over there because I already have a strained relation with Jules. You have nothing to lose."

Godfrey walked over to the fireplace and positioned himself between the two men. Within seconds, everyone scattered. I immediately rushed over. "What did you do? What did you say?"

"What you asked me. I simply remarked that the Halyomorpha halys, or brown marmorated stink bug as they're commonly known, are bound to be lurking in the cracks by the fireplace."

I burst out laughing until tears rolled down my cheeks.

Just then, Theo approached. "What did I miss? It must be the only funny thing going on in this place."

Before Godfrey or I could answer, the sharp sound of a spoon being rattled against a glass permeated the room. Henry Speltmore, the president of the wine association, cleared his throat. "Welcome, everyone!" He went on to introduce the event, the chocolatiers, and the winery owners who were hosting them. He then bored the daylights out of all of us by dredging up the history of the wine trail.

"My God," Stephanie whispered as she approached us. "Will he ever shut up?"

"Maybe one of us needs to shove a bonbon in his mouth," Theo replied, which resulted in some chortling on the part of Godfrey and me.

Finally, Henry stopped talking and invited everyone to enjoy the food and wine. I helped myself to a small plate of stuffed mushrooms, Swedish meatballs, and tiny puffed pastries filled with Brie while Godfrey and Theo got into a discussion about the best techniques for removing cluster flies.

Other than the near altercation by the fireplace, the chocolatiers seemed to be behaving themselves. I figured it was because they were besieged by reporters and forced to endure all sorts of questions. I made a mental note to turn on the eleven o'clock news in case one of the cameramen happened to film me—as well as the real reason we were all here.

At least an hour had passed, and I wondered if the snow was still falling, or if it had fizzled away as it sometimes did. I went over to one of the long windows that faced the rear of the building and glanced across the lake. It was impossible to see anything except the falling snow. Francine insisted

I have an app for road conditions in Yates and Ontario counties. It came in handy at times like this.

According to the report, the plows were working nonstop and the roads were clear and passable. Of course, they did warn about visibility. I put my iPhone away and went back to the buffet table.

I had to say this much, the affair was animated. People enjoyed chatting it up and imbibing our wines and the mouthwatering canapes Geneva on the Lake provided. Finally, at a little past eleven, the crowd began to dissipate. Good. I could finally get home to a warm bed—complete with Charlie in it.

I thanked Godfrey for coming to the rescue and reminded him of the culminating event at the end of the week.

"Think I should bring up overwintering pests?" he asked.

"Only if there's another chance of an altercation. But somehow, I think everything will be fine. Absolutely fine."

It was a damned good thing I wasn't in the psychic readings business or I'd be broke. After Godfrey left and I was on my way out the door with Don and Theo, Madeline approached us.

"Have any of you seen Jules Leurant? No one can seem to find him. The chocolatiers were all tasting our wines last anyone knew."

I shrugged. "He probably got tired of the affair and went to his room. Did you check with that mealy assistant of his?"

She nodded. "Earvin thought the same thing and even went as far as knocking on Jules's door, but there was no answer. So, he got the house manager to unlock the door and Jules wasn't in the room."

Don elbowed Theo. "Maybe Stanislav's not the only one getting under the sheets at this party."

"I'm sure Jules is milling around somewhere," I said. "It's not like he's going to be outside in this storm. We're the only crazy ones."

Don turned to Madeline. "Norrie's right. I wouldn't worry about it if I were you. He's probably around here somewhere. Maybe a long sojourn in the men's room. That fancy food can go right through you."

I grimaced and pulled my winter scarf tighter around my neck. Seconds later, we were on our way home. Theo and Don followed Francine's Subaru to our turn-off on Route 14 and signaled when they turned into their own drive. Francine insisted I use their Subaru when the winter roads were iffy. In addition to all-wheel drive, the car had four studded snow tires and chains in the trunk. I made it up the hill with no problem, considering our driveway wouldn't be plowed until morning—when John and the vineyard crew arrived. Storm or no storm, the vineyard crews couldn't afford to sleep in.

Charlie refused to budge from his position on the bed, and I practically had to shove him off to the side. I pulled the quilt over my head, turned off the light on the nightstand, and burrowed under the covers. The sound of the wind rapping against the window was the only noise I heard...that is until I heard a loud pounding—at some ungodly hour in the morning. It took me at least a full minute or two to wake up and realize someone was knocking on our front door. I was positive it had to be our vineyard manager informing me of some weather-related emergency. Few people would be able to make it up our driveway unless their vehicles were equipped for Siberian winters. I threw on an old Penn Yan Mustangs sweatshirt and the sweatpants that accompanied it. Funny how those things could last for years.

"Hold your horses," I yelled. "I'm on my way."

Charlie beat me down the stairs, but instead of going to the door, he went to the kitchen and buried himself in a bowl of kibble. Figuring it was John, I flung the door open only to find myself face-to-face with Deputy Hickman.

"Um, is there some sort of problem I should know about?" I asked.

The snow was still coming down, and Deputy Hickman looked absolutely miserable. Large flakes of the white stuff covered his hat and eyebrows.

"Indeed there is, Miss Ellington. Do you mind if I step inside?"

I motioned for him to take a seat at the table. "I'm about to make myself a cup of coffee. I can pop in a K-cup for you, too. We have Green Mountain roast and some organic coffee from a country whose name I can't pronounce."

"Green Mountain is fine. I'm sure you've surmised by now this isn't a social call."

Gee, you think?

"The grounds crew at Geneva on the Lake gets started early in the morning. They need to have the parking lots done in time for deliveries and that sort of thing."

"Uh-huh." I put a mug on the Keurig, tipped open the little compartment and plopped in the pod of coffee. "Did they find a stolen car or something? All of our winery vehicles are accounted for."

"No, not a stolen car. A body. Face down in the snow. The coroner and the forensics team have been at the scene since before daybreak."

I caught the blue light flashing on the Keurig and pushed the start button while trying to grasp what it was he had just said. The body couldn't belong to Theo, Don, or Godfrey because they left around the time I did. The coffee began to pour and I stood motionless. The thought that it could be one of the winery owners or winemakers gave me goose bumps.

"Did you say 'body?' Whose body? What body? And what does it have to do with Two Witches Winery?"

"That's what we'd like to find out as well, Miss Ellington. The man was identified as Jules Leurant, one of those chocolate chefs. He was last seen tasting your winery's Cabernet Sauvignon, and, in fact, an empty wineglass was found in his hand. The lab is testing it now."

So much for a little sojourn in the men's room.

"Dead? My God! Don't tell me you think he was poisoned from tasting our wine. Lots of people tasted it at that event and, to the best of my knowledge, they're still breathing."

"I'm not making any accusations until all evidence has been thoroughly reviewed. That's how the Sheriff's Department works around here. For your information, all the empty wine bottles from last night's soiree have been confiscated by the Ontario County forensics department, who called us in to this case. The lab will test them for toxins."

"What makes you think he died from being poisoned? Maybe he had a heart attack or something. Did you look for gunshot wounds? Maybe someone decided the world could live without one more pompous pain in the butt."

As soon as I said that, I knew I should have kept my mouth shut.

"I take it you weren't on good terms with Mr. Leurant?"

I handed Deputy Hickman the coffee, took out a small container of milk and pointed to the table where we keep the sugar bowl. "I wasn't on any terms with him. I only met him this week but if you ask me—"

"Stop. It's too early in the day for your theories. I wanted to let you know personally about the grim discovery—since your wine was apparently the last thing to touch Jules Leurant's lips."

"How can you be so sure?"

"It's been a busy morning for my department. As I mentioned, we're working in conjunction with the Ontario County Sheriff's Department since the venue involves our local wineries. Our team secured video footage from one of the news stations. They must keep accurate time and date information on it. It appears that Mr. Leurant tasted your wine and then hastily exited the room. He was still holding the glass."

"That doesn't mean our Cabernet Sauvignon had anything to do with his death."

"Only time and forensic science will tell, Miss Ellington. But the footage was quite explicit. The server opened the wine bottle in front of Mr. Leurant and then poured it before securing the cork."

"Who else was served from that bottle? Where's that bottle now?"

"We're in the process of looking into it."

"Well, look into everything else that touched Mr. Leurant's lips while you're at it. Maybe he digested some uncooked fish."

"I'll keep that in mind. Thank you for the coffee. Much as I'd like to stay and get out of this storm, I've got an investigation on my hands."

"Before you leave, does anyone else know about this yet? Like the president of the wine association?"

"As far as I know, only the manager and morning staff at Geneva on the Lake. The manager insisted the other chocolate makers not be disturbed at such an early hour."

"Chocolatiers."

"What?"

"Chocolatiers. They don't make the chocolate. They make the confections from the chocolate."

"I don't have time for a lesson in semantics. As I was saying, only the morning staff at the resort were privy to the unfortunate discovery. No doubt the news station that shared the prior night's video with us will realize something's amiss, but that's neither here nor there. Needless to say, we'll need to interview everyone who attended that party. Expect to hear from my office later today."

"Um, I hate to say this, but news like this usually hits the scanners and it's probably all over the county by now."

Deputy Hickman groaned. "Last thing we need is a media circus. Maybe they'll hold off a bit and focus on the storm."

"In case you haven't noticed, I sort of just got up when you knocked on the door. How bad a storm is it? Or was it? Are the roads closed?"

"The roads are being cleared and schools in Yates and Ontario Counties are on a two-hour delay. Please don't tell me you intend to drive anywhere. And certainly not to the crime scene."

"Couldn't you just refer to it as the death scene until we know for sure it was foul play?"

"Preliminary indications point to a suspicious death. And there's more."

Now what?

"The wineglass wasn't the only thing found on Mr. Leurant's person. He had a handwritten list of the six featured wineries for this so-called chocolate pairing."

"And?"

"Only your winery's name had a heavy black line drawn through it. Any idea why?"

I shrugged. "People do that all the time with their shopping lists."
Deputy Hickman took a long swallow of coffee and then walked to the door. "I don't think Mr. Leurant was in the market for purchasing wine."

Chapter 6

Charlie darted out after the deputy and dove into the snow. At least someone enjoyed what looked to be at least two feet of the white stuff. The winds weren't blowing and the snowflakes were tapering off. Unless blowing and drifting were in the forecast, I expected to see the yellow school buses. Poor disappointed kids. A delay and not a snow day.

I stood by the front window and watched as Grizzly Gary, aka Deputy Hickman, made his way down our driveway. Headlight beams from another vehicle were clearly visible, and it took a moment for me to realize it was one of our vineyard workers with the snowplow. For a brief instant, I wasn't sure who to call first. Theo and Don definitely needed to know about Jules. It was only fair to tell Godfrey—rather than have him find out when he turned on the news or, worse yet, pushed some app on his phone.

While I mulled over my decision, Charlie returned via his doggie door and shook a ton of the white stuff all over the floor before sniffing at the uneaten kibble in his bowl. I was about to pour a tad more into the dish when the phone rang.

"Hey, Norrie. It's Theo. I tried your cell phone but it went to voice mail. Turn that thing on, will you? Glad you have a landline. Anyway, is everything all right? Don went outside to see how much snow we got and he saw the sheriff's car leaving your place. What's going on?"

"I was about to call you. Jules Leurant was found dead in the snow. The sheriff's department thinks our winery might have had something to do with it."

"What? Has Hickman lost his senses? Why?" Theo asked.

"Apparently Jules's body was found face down in the snow by the resort's grounds crew when they went to clear the parking lot."

"What does that have to do with Two Witches?"

"Jules was holding an empty wineglass and, according to some video footage, the last wine he tasted was ours. Cabernet Sauvignon to be exact."

"So, they think he was poisoned?"

"They don't know. The lab has to check it out. But even if he was, that doesn't mean we had anything to do with it. Anyone could have monkeyed with it. It's not as if Jules Leurant was on terrific terms with his competitors. Not to mention his nephew. From what I witnessed, he treated that guy as if he was a manservant, not his assistant."

"Boy, talk about jumping to conclusions. Big deal. An empty wineglass."

"Um, they also found a piece of paper in the guy's pocket with all our winery names written on it. Two Witches was crossed off in bold ink, according to Deputy Hickman."

"Still nothing conclusive. So now what?"

"Expect to be interviewed. Or should I say *grilled* by Yates County's finest. They're working with the Ontario County Sheriffs on this case."

"Does anyone else know about this?"

"Only the manager at Geneva on the Lake and the morning staff. I imagine the liaison for the sheriffs' departments will be contacting Henry Speltmore from the wine association for a list of attendees and their guests. Oh blast! The wine association. What's going to happen now with the chocolate and wine festival? And that competition?"

"I'll tell you what's going to happen. Earvin Roels will need to put on his big boy pants and step up to the plate. He must know how to do *something.*"

"Maybe he did. Maybe that something was murder his boss-slash-uncle. I've heard of things like that."

"Yeah, well, what about Allete and Stanislav? They had motive if ever there was a motive. With Jules out of the picture, one of them will most definitely win the competition."

"Unless the companies involved decide to cancel it. What a mess. We'd better hope Earvin is up to the task. Meanwhile, I don't intend to wait it out until the sheriff's department gets its act together."

"Uh-oh. What are you saying?"

"The roads will be clear in less than an hour. At which time I intend to do a little fact-finding on my own."

"I doubt the hotel manager will want to share any info with you. Besides, he's probably under a gag order from Hickman."

"I'm not talking about the hotel manager. I plan to see what the kitchen staff may know. I'll go in under the guise of picking up our unused wine bottles. I'll also try to find out who the servers were and see if I can dredge anything up from them."

"That place is going to be crawling with deputies."

"Maybe you should come with me. You know, like a distraction," I said to Theo.

"As much as I'd enjoy reprising my role as one of the Hardy Boys, I'm going to pass. We're shorthanded today and I'm needed in the tasting room. Two of our employees wound up with pinkeye. Talk about Don going berserk disinfecting."

"Oh no."

"Listen. Don't do anything that would give anyone a reason to think you have something to hide," Theo said.

"Don't worry. You're beginning to sound like Francine."

"Good."

It was now a little past seven, and I figured Godfrey was up by now. His phone number was on the wall next to our calendar under the list of emergency contacts my sister had written. Since June, I had added two more—Tony's pizza delivery and Rosinetti's Bar. Cammy's family owned that Geneva establishment and more than once she'd had to bail some family member out by taking over their shift.

Godfrey barely had time to say hello when I cut in. "Jules Leurant was found dead this morning in the parking lot. Not ours. Geneva on the Lake. Deputy Hickman woke me up to give me the grim tidings. Their preliminary guess is poisoning from our Cabernet Sauvignon."

I went on to reiterate everything I told Theo, including my "plan of action" to snoop around the resort.

"Are you really sure that's such a good idea? You might be better off letting the deputies do their job."

"According to Deputy Hickman, we're numero uno on their suspect list. If it turns out Jules was really poisoned from drinking our wine, I have to find out who's responsible because it sure as hell wasn't any of us."

"What does Franz say about all this?"

Oh, good Lord! Franz! Right now, he's probably on his way to the winery—completely clueless about Jules.

"I, uh, er, what the heck. I totally forgot to call our winemaker. Deputy Hickman got me so worked up I moved right into investigation mode without giving any thought to communicating with my own staff. How can I be this lamebrained?"

"Give yourself a break. Your mind is working on fast-forward, that's all. Same thing happened to me once with the classification of the lepismatidae. Of course, I was just a sophomore at the time, but—"

"The lepismatilda or whatever that thing is, wasn't lying face down dead in the snow, having just consumed a glass of our wine. I've got to get ahold of Franz."

"Take a breath and calm down. It'll be all right. I'll talk to you later. Oh, and it's lepismatidae. You know, silverfish."

Silverfish. The last thing I felt like thinking about. I wondered if Francine had to endure these kinds of conversations with Jason. I thanked Godfrey for listening and immediately dialed Franz's cell phone.

"Franz? Are you on your way into the winery lab?"

"Yes. I'm speaking over Bluetooth. Why? Aren't the roads plowed yet? Everything's pretty clear here in Ontario county."

"The roads are fine. It's just that, well, do you remember anything odd toward the tail end of last night's event?"

"Odd? What do you mean *odd?*"

"I'm not sure. Maybe some sort of a scuffle or argument near the wine table."

"Can't say that I did. Leandre from Terrace Wineries and I were talking about this year's vintage in comparison to prior years', but we weren't standing next to the wine table. Why?"

"One of the chocolatiers was found dead in the parking lot this morning. Face down and buried in the snow."

"Stanislav! I knew it was only a matter of time. Did his paramour's husband shoot him? That ongoing affair has been all over the internet."

"What? No. Not Stanislav. Jules. Jules Leurant."

"Someone shot the chocolatier from Belgium? Why? What possible motive?"

"Not shot. Maybe poisoned. Poisoned from our Cabernet Sauvignon."

"My God! That's impossible. That's outrageous. Are you certain?"

"I'm not certain of anything. It's what Deputy Hickman told me this morning. Until lab results are in, we won't know. What we do know is it appears the last thing Jules put to his lips was our wine."

"This is a catastrophe. It will be all over the news. Pray tell they won't mention the wine, will they?"

"Oh no. They might. The footage shows someone pouring that Cab-Sav into Jules's glass. And that footage came from one of the TV stations, according to the deputy. That's how the authorities found out."

Franz didn't say a word and, for a minute, I thought we had lost the connection. "Franz, are you still there?"

"Yes. Sorry. All of our Cabernet Sauvignon was bottled at the same time. And all of it came from the same barrels. If that man was poisoned, it was after the fact."

"I know. I know. At first, I thought maybe I should have Cammy pull those bottles from the shelf, but then it would look really suspicious. Besides, that wine's already been distributed up and down the state, not to mention the surrounding ones. It's been months and no news of wine-related deaths anywhere. Still, it doesn't look good for us, does it?"

"No, I suppose not. Would you like me to inform Alan and Herbert or is that something you plan to do?"

"I need to take care of some other matters, so please let them know and please tell them to keep everything hush-hush."

"Absolutely."

Hush-hush. I grimaced. Here I was telling my winemaker to keep this matter quiet when I'd all but been shouting about it from the rooftops. Of course, I had to let Theo know. And Godfrey. And now Cammy. It was business. Not gossip. Not yet, anyway.

I glanced at the wall clock and couldn't believe I'd been talking for over forty-five minutes. Cammy had to be up and about by now so I wasted no time adding one more call to my morning's "to-do list."

Cammy picked up on the second ring and, for a second, I forgot everyone had caller ID these days. "Norrie, what's up? Is Route 14 really bad at the winery?"

"Uh, no. The road's fine. Plows have been up and down. Salt trucks, too. I can hear them from the house. That's not why I called. We seem to have a bit of a situation."

"Uh-oh. What do you mean, 'bit?'"

"Arrgh. I really wish you could have attended last night's event with the chocolatiers."

"Me too. You probably had more fun than I did, but what did you mean by 'situation?' Did the power go out in the tasting room?"

"No. Someone's lights went out. Permanently."

"Huh?"

I sighed and took a deep breath. By now I could recite the scenario in my sleep. "Jules Leurant was found dead in the snow holding a glass that contained our wine. Our wonderful, now-under-suspicion-of-poison Cabernet Sauvignon."

"Holy Cannoli! How did you find out?"

"How else? Grizzly Gary paid me a house call first thing this morning. I'm still in my loungewear, so to speak."

"Please don't tell me he thinks our winery had anything to do with this."

"The winery? No. Most likely me."

Chapter 7

The road into Geneva was wet, but otherwise clear. The shoulders, however, were piled high with snow that was bound to turn yucky in a day or two. So much for a nice scenic drive up the lake. As I expected, the parking lot in front of Geneva on the Lake was plowed to perfection. I found a decent spot for Francine's Subaru off to the side of the building and walked to the front entrance.

Godfrey wasn't kidding when he said the place would be crawling with deputies. A full line-up of official Yates and Ontario County vehicles bordered the perimeter of the driveway and a few feet away, near the entrance to the ballroom, was a ribbon of crime scene tape that formed a huge rectangle in the parking lot. A single deputy stood over the spot and it appeared as if he was taking notes on an iPad.

As tempted as I was to approach him, I knew better. Instead, I went directly to the concierge desk and smiled at the middle-aged woman seated behind it.

"As you probably surmised," the woman said, "we had an incident here last night. An unexpected death in our parking lot. One of our chocolatier guests."

Unexpected or perfectly planned?

"I know. I'm one of the winery owners who attended the event. In fact, that's why I'm here. I need to pick up our remaining bottles of wine from the kitchen. I'm Norrie Ellington from Two Witches in Penn Yan."

"Oh dear. I'm not sure there's anything left in there. Those deputies have been hauling out boxes for the last hour. I have no idea about the contents, but they did come with a search warrant. Woke up some poor Ontario County judge."

"Wow. What could they possibly be looking for?"

"I don't know anything of an official nature, but I've had my ears perked up since I got here at five. The words 'substance' and 'toxic' kept coming up. Usually it's 'stroke' or 'heart attack.' Believe it or not, we've had other deaths in our resort before, but they were all due to natural causes. Nothing natural about this one."

"Um, how can they be sure?"

The woman motioned for me to lean closer to her desk. "I really shouldn't be telling you this, but it will probably be on the news at some point. When they found the body, the man's clothing was frozen and all rumpled up. I overheard one of the forensic people telling that gnarly-looking deputy from Yates County that it appeared as if the man originally fell backwards and then someone made a point of rolling him over into the snow so he would be facedown."

Wonderful. Next thing I know our winery will be accused of doing that as well.

"That's horrible. Then again, maybe he did have a heart attack and staggered around in the snow."

"Honey, if that was the case, we wouldn't have half the county deputies in here. Listen, if you really need to get those wine bottles of yours, I suggest you use the side entrance. It's in the back and clearly marked KITCHEN. I'll call and let them know. Did you bring your own cart?"

My cart? How can I be so dense? Who goes to pick up bottles of wine without a handcart?

"I thought your kitchen would have a cart. Once the carton is in my car, my staff can haul it into our place."

She nodded. "Makes sense. Drive your car around back, too. Much shorter distance."

I thanked her and did exactly as she said. Unfortunately, the moment I chose to enter the kitchen was the exact moment Deputy Hickman chose to exit it.

He took one look at me and let out a groan that could be heard in Cleveland. "Miss Ellington. I thought I made it perfectly clear you were to stay away from this investigation."

"You did. I am. Staying away."

"Then why are you here?"

"Thought I'd save our winemakers the time and pick up our unused bottles from last night."

"I'm afraid that won't be possible right now. Everything has been seized for evidence."

"Everything as in food and wine?"

"Yes. The consumables."

I pretty much figured that would be the case, but I wondered if those deputies were also busy ransacking Jules's room for clues to his death. In the movies, and my screenplays were no exception, the police were always scouring the victim's room. It was one place I needed to check out. Still, if I could get in there, the place would be picked over like Best Buy after Black Friday. Nevertheless, I'd kick myself in the pants for not trying.

"Fine," I said to Deputy Hickman. "I need to use a restroom and then I'll be on my way."

He muttered something and brushed by me. I waited a few seconds and then stepped inside. The kitchen entrance was straight ahead, but there was a stairwell a few feet away. I immediately took it to the second floor instead of the elevator farther down the corridor. I distinctly remembered Catherine telling Theo and me that the chocolatiers were all assigned deluxe suites, complete with Jacuzzis, on the second floor. Now, all I needed to do was find out which one belonged to Jules Leurant.

If anyone's timing could stink, it was definitely mine. The instant I opened the stairwell door to the second floor, I noticed Stanislav and Allete emerging from the room cattycorner to where I was standing. I pulled the door partially shut, allowing a narrow opening for me to eavesdrop as they walked past to the elevators.

"*Mon Dieu!*" Allete said. "This is all we need."

Stanislav ran his hand down her cheek. "Stay composed and be brief with your answers. Tell them how saddened you are at the loss of such a great talent."

"You mean blowhard. Is that not the word?"

Stanislav laughed. "Indeed it is."

Their voices faded as they approached the elevator, but I had heard plenty. Unfortunately, it was all hearsay as far as anyone else was concerned. Most likely, Allete and Stanislav had been summoned for questioning by one of the deputies. I wondered if Earvin had already been questioned or if he'd be making an appearance in the hallway as well.

I took a tentative step away from the stairwell and glanced in the opposite direction from the elevators. No guesswork regarding which room was Jules's. It had to be the one with the door ajar and a wooden chair in front that held the sign, "Do Not Enter." It didn't take Sherlock Holmes to reach the conclusion that a forensics crew was inside.

So much for the hopes I had of finding a threatening message or even a flash drive with who-knew-what on it. Instead, I hit a wall. At least as far as Jules's room went. However, that interesting little bit of intel from the receptionist regarding the placement of Jules's body was quite telling. *If* indeed that was what happened. And if so, why were those deputies so intent on checking our wine for possible poisons? Was this simply part of the protocol when a corpse was found holding an edible or drinkable substance? Damn. Why couldn't Jules's body be found with one of those tasteless cucumber sandwiches in his hand?

Then I realized something. Maybe someone *had* tampered with the glass of wine Jules drank but not to poison him, but to temporarily knock him out. Face it, finding a lethal poison like cyanide wasn't the easiest thing in the world, but lacing a drink? Probably more common than I could imagine.

My mind flitted from scenario to scenario as I stood by the stairwell. Was the person who laced Jules's wine the same person who messed with his body in the snow? Or maybe it was a crime of opportunity, and whoever turned his body over had nothing to do with putting him there to begin with. Or maybe he really was poisoned.

Theo would tell me it all came back to motive and everyone in this little chocolate and wine festival seemed to have one. Earvin, if he had half a brain and half the talent his uncle did, could climb to the top as Belgium's next chocolatier extraordinaire. He'd be at the right place to prove it, too. All that notoriety.

As far as Stanislav and Allete were concerned, it was a no-brainer. Eliminate the competition. But what if Jules's death had nothing to do with his skills as a confectioner? What if it was something else entirely? Was he blackmailing anyone? Did he scorn some revenge-seeking woman? I had absolutely no confidence that those deputies would expand the perimeters of their myopic investigation, but that didn't mean I had to accept the status quo.

Suddenly I remembered something—Cammy's friend handled the reservations for Geneva on the Lake. It wasn't like I'd be asking her to divulge a state secret. All I needed to know was if anyone else had arrived from out of the country. Identification was usually requested at the front desk. Driver's licenses, passports, military documents...I ducked back into the stairwell and phoned our tasting room.

Glenda answered on the first ring and mentioned something about an air purification ritual in case the negative energy surrounding Jules's death somehow managed to permeate our establishment.

"Uh, thanks Glenda. I guess Cammy must have shared the news with everyone."

"She didn't have to. I could sense something awry when I walked in."

"Give it a break," Sam shouted in the background. "It was all over the radio with the farm report."

"Never mind," I said, "put Cammy on the phone, will you? This is important."

Next thing I knew, Cammy was at the other end. "What's up? Please don't tell me you're in any sort of trouble over there. When you mentioned taking a drive over this morning, I knew I should have stopped you."

"I'm fine, but I need your help. That friend of yours who handles the reservations...can you give her a call and ask her if anyone checked into the hotel this past week from another country? Other than the chocolatiers. It's really important. I can't very well knock on the door to their business office and demand information. I already pried some juicy stuff out of the concierge. I don't want to overstay my welcome."

"Where are you exactly?"

"On the second-floor landing in their stairwell. Allete and Stanislav walked past me a few seconds ago. They had no idea I was behind the door. A forensics crew is in Jules's room as we speak."

"You can't hang out in that stairwell forever."

"Then call your friend and get back to me right away. I'm sure I'll be fine. I've been in hotels before. The chambermaids don't clean until the afternoon and the dining service will use the elevators. Hurry up. I really need to know."

Cammy moaned and told me to give her a few minutes. I leaned against the stairwell wall and fiddled around with my iPhone. Facebook. Emails. The weather app. A thud from the door below me. Crap. Someone was taking the stairs.

I shoved my phone in my pocket, exited the stairwell and made a beeline for the elevator. If I didn't turn around, no one would know who I was. Unfortunately, that meant I wouldn't know who had emerged from the floor below. I pushed the button and stood absolutely still, but didn't hear anyone. Finally, I turned around and noticed a woman a few feet away holding a cup of coffee in one hand and sliding her room card into the lock with the other. Maybe she had a fear of elevators. Or maybe stair climbing was on her fitness list. At any rate, she didn't notice me and that was all that mattered.

Seconds later, Cammy called. "You owe me."

"Give me a minute. Call back. I've got to get to the stairwell."

Too late. The elevator door opened and again I was face-to-face with Deputy Hickman.

"Do I need to place you under arrest for interfering with a crime investigation, Miss Ellington?"

"Someone was in the restroom downstairs so I had to use the one right here on this mezzanine floor. If you want to investigate anything, find out why they use such crummy bathroom tissue."

The deputy didn't say a word but motioned for me to get into the elevator. I nodded, thanked him, and waited for the door to close. At that precise second, Cammy called back.

"Norrie, she's not allowed to give out their names or she could lose her job, but she did tell me a woman arrived with a Belgium passport the day before Jules checked in. And later the same day, a gentleman from the Netherlands. She has no idea if they are part of the chocolate festival."

"Did she mention if the sheriff's deputies requested the reservation list?"

"Requested? More like strong-armed it, according to Barb. That's my friend's name. The *only* name I can give you without breaking the law."

"Very funny. I don't suppose Barb mentioned what kind of rooms they booked, did she?"

"Only that she wished she had expendable cash for a night in the whirlpool suite, wherever *that's* located."

"Did she say who? The man or the woman?"

"The woman. Geez, I was lucky she said anything. If she gets sacked, you'd better be prepared to hire a new person for our tasting room."

"The whirlpool suite, huh?"

"Aargh. I'm sorry I said anything. Watch your back."

Chapter 8

True, Geneva gets its fair share of international visitors, thanks to Hobart and William Smith Colleges, but I had a funny feeling the woman from Belgium wasn't one of them. The timing of her visit was too coincidental. The elevator door opened to the ground floor and I stepped out. A woman in a heavy winter coat, holding a bouquet of flowers, brushed past me into the elevator. "Winter snowstorms or not, we've got to make our deliveries."

I stepped back into the elevator. "Are you familiar with this resort?"

"Blooming Bouquets makes deliveries here all the time."

"Great. I hate to keep pestering the staff, but I can't seem to find the Whirlpool Suite. I'm supposed to meet a client there."

"Must be one heck of a wealthy client. That room is phenomenal. It's nicknamed the 'Chapel' because of its ceilings. Add a double whirlpool bath and a canopied bed and you've got it made."

"Um, do you know where it is? What floor?"

"You're on it. It's the first floor. The room is on your left. It has its own special entrance. You can't miss it."

I stepped out as the elevator door began to close. "Thanks. And by the way, that bouquet is lovely."

I had to find out the identity of the Belgian woman in the high-priced suite and if there was any connection between her and Jules. Too bad I didn't know how to hack into the reservations system at the hotel. In all honesty, I had absolutely no computer tech skills and my sleuthing skills were more dumb luck than anything else. Lizzie, our winery bookkeeper, kept telling me I needed to familiarize myself with the Nancy Drew Handbook. So what if the series took place in the 1930s. "Investigating is investigating," according to Lizzie, "and timing is the staircase to success."

She had a point about timing. I was in the right place, more or less, and I doubted I'd find a better time to get the answer I needed. Unfortunately, I had absolutely no idea how to go about it without winding up in the back seat of Deputy Hickman's squad car. Still, I rationalized it wouldn't hurt to meander down the hallway toward the Whirlpool Suite.

One of the few life skills I *did* learn came from middle school and not Nancy Drew. *Always act as if you're supposed to be doing whatever it is you're doing.* That skill came in particularly handy when cutting a class. I walked down the school corridor with determination written all over my face. I paused to look at my watch when an authority figure approached and then I quickened my steps. Today was no different.

I walked directly to the entrance of the Whirlpool Suite and stopped dead in my tracks. One of those housekeeping carts was in the private foyer. A few mops, a broom, lots of complimentary mini bottles of shampoo, lotions, and soaps. No linen cart in sight. I prayed my hunch was right and the maid was fast at work making the bed.

Without wasting a second, I leaned into the small trash receptacle in the suite. Whew! Nothing sticky. Nothing smelly. Nothing gross. Only papers. No time to sift through them. No time to think or I'd be tempted to change my mind. I froze for an instant to make sure I didn't hear anyone approaching. Then I gathered as many papers as I could into a giant armload, crumpled them even more than they already were, and stuffed them into my bag.

A side exit was only a few yards away, and I hurried toward it. From there it was a quick jaunt to my car and an even quicker exit out of the parking lot.

Twenty minutes later, I was back home with Charlie whining for more food and the red light blinking on the landline. Calls could wait. Annoying Plott Hounds couldn't. I grabbed a handful of kibble and put it in his bowl before clearing off the kitchen table and dumping the pile of papers from the Whirlpool Suite onto it. Francine would have had a conniption. I, on the other hand, planned to use a Clorox wipe on the surface once I was done scrutinizing the papers.

I fanned out my hands to move the papers so I could get a clearer look at them. Nothing earthshattering caught my eye—advertising flyers from local establishments, coupons for fast food restaurants, none of which I frequented, and a torn note written in what looked like Dutch or German.

With the palm of my hand, I moved the top layer away and kept looking. Squiggly lines on hotel stationary. Testing out a pen, maybe? A Walgreens receipt for Tylenol, lip balm, a bag of Lays potato chips, and a six pack of Coke. Hmm, a woman after my own heart, only she paid cash.

So as not to miss anything vital, I tossed all the ads and coupons in my trash. Then I spied the one piece of information Nancy Drew would have coveted. It was a boarding pass from Jet Blue Airlines. JFK to ROC. ROC! Rochester International Airport. It was the boarding pass from the connection that woman had made.

"Charlie!" I shrieked. "We might have hit pay dirt!"

The dog, who was intently licking his front paws, looked up and then resumed his licking.

"Hortensia Vermeulen. It's right here on the boarding pass. She flew into Rochester two days ago. Oh my God! I've got to call Theo. And Cammy."

I was so intent on rifling through those papers, I had momentarily forgotten I had a phone message. I tapped the button and listened. It was Stephanie Ipswich and she sounded hysterical.

"That swine from WROC recorded that comment I made. It was on the noon news. He knew that cameraman of his had the film rolling and he didn't stop him. I can sue the station for slander, can't I? Oh hell. It's coming out right out of my mouth. 'I hope he chokes on his bonbons.' I could be implicated in a murder. I'm calling Rosalee's attorney right now."

It was one of those moments I didn't know what to do next. Call Stephanie back and reassure her she had nothing to worry about or tell Theo and Cammy about my discovery. I figured Stephanie was likely to go off the deep end so I pushed the redial button and waited for the call to go through.

Stephanie answered on the first ring. "Norrie. Thank goodness. I wasn't going to pick up the phone but then I saw the caller ID. I'm terrified I'm going to be besieged with phone calls from the media. Or worse yet, that brutish deputy. I know they'll be questioning all of us since we were the last people to see Jules alive."

"Take it easy. You can't be held responsible for an off-the-cuff comment." *Can you?* "All those reporters want to do is drum up interest in that murder investigation so they'll get more viewers. They probably don't have anything else to go on right now."

"You sound just like Rosalee's attorney."

"You spoke to Marvin Souza?"

"Uh-huh. The secretary put me through right away. Of course, Marvin told me they're a family law firm specializing in wills and that sort of thing, but he didn't think I had any reason to be worried. Honestly, whatever happened to investigative reporting?"

"Oh, that's still going on but not by the reporters."

"What do you mean?"

I told her about the snooping I did at Geneva on the Lake, including my asking her if she knew German or Dutch.

"Sorry. Only one year of Spanish in high school. I can order tacos like the best of them. What about your winemaker? He speaks German. It's better than using one of those internet translation sites. Way too literal."

"I know. I know. I'd just have a hard time explaining to him how it wound up in my hands. You know how Franz is. Everything on the up-and-up. Still, I might not have a choice."

"Did you get a chance to check your emails today?"

"No." *And there better not be one from Renee telling me they're moving the date up for my script.*

"Henry Speltmore sent out an official letter from the wine trail. The program is going on as planned. Including the competition. Jules's nephew, Earvin, will be the third competitor. Can you believe they got all of that settled and it hasn't even been twenty-four hours?"

"Yeah, I can believe it."

"When it comes to money and the wine trail, Henry Speltmore knows how to move things along. Say, what's your take on Earvin? I got an earful from Rosalee when I called her to get Marvin Souza's number. She said Earvin struck her as a Casper Milquetoast kind of guy. I didn't want to sound ignorant so I Googled the name."

"And?"

"Casper Milquetoast was a 1950s cartoon character. I kept forgetting Rosalee's in her seventies. She's got a whole different set of references than the rest us. Anyway, she went on to say Earvin didn't seem to have much style or flair. Not that it matters, I suppose, when you're concocting chocolate delicacies, but face it, Stanislav and Allete are on top of their game."

"Maybe Earvin knows more than we think he does." *And I'm not referring to chocolate.*

"Do you think the sheriff's murder investigation is going to interfere with the festival? Madeline's all worked up over it and Catherine is her usual basket case."

"Uh, I know we're all referring to it as a murder investigation, but the official cause of death hasn't been determined yet."

"They said it was 'suspicious' on the news. That's always synonymous with homicide. The noonday news anchor said they expected preliminary toxicology results by the end of the day."

"Pray the guy died from an embolism or aneurysm or any of the isms that don't involve wine," I said.

"No kidding. And pray he didn't choke on something or I'll really need to find a good criminal lawyer."

My stomach was grumbling by the time I got off the phone with Stephanie, so I rummaged through the fridge and made myself a bologna and cheese sandwich before taking a brisk walk to our tasting room. I didn't expect the place to be brimming with activity, even though the roads were cleared. Mondays were usually slow, and a Monday following a storm was bound to be even slower.

Cammy, Glenda, and Sam were the only ones on the schedule for the day. Glenda was manning the cash register and Sam was busy with two customers when I came in. "If you're looking for Cammy," he said, "she's in the back room putting price tags on a new shipment of sweatshirts."

"Thanks. And here I thought Glenda was the only mind-reader."

"Hey! I can hear you from over here!"

I gave Glenda a wave and walked into the back room, the catch-all for storage and deliveries.

"You've returned unscathed," Cammy said. "I half expected another phone call telling me you were in lockup at the public safety building."

"Nah. I did run into our favorite deputy twice, but I think he bought my very valid reason for being at Geneva on the Lake."

"Good. I'll get Sam to bring in the wine bottles."

"Don't bother. They confiscated everything for evidence. Most of it last night, but they were still going through stuff this morning."

Cammy sighed. "Once they find out the guy died of natural causes, or stupidity maybe, for drinking too much and passing out in the snow, they'll drop the investigation and move on to the usual stuff. Pilfering at the mini-mart and graffiti on the light poles."

"You think that's what happened? Jules overdid it and passed out in the snow?"

"He was probably overheated from all that wine, went outside to cool off, and tumbled into a nice soft bed of the white stuff. He wouldn't be the first person to have done a thing like that. Every winter my aunts find some nutcase passed out in the snow behind their bar. Only those guys are usually holding beer bottles and none of them are dead. Only dead-drunk."

"I hope you're right, but I'm not banking on it. Those deputies are paying way too much attention to Jules's death. I'm positive they know something they're not sharing. Meanwhile, you can thank your friend Barb. The woman from Belgium is Hortensia Vermeulen and she took a flight from JFK to Rochester two days ago. I've got a hunch she didn't come all that way for a tour of the wine trail."

"Don't tell me you broke into her room?"

"The room, no. Her garbage, yes. I found her boarding pass. And that's not all. I've got a note written in Dutch or German and, for all we know, it could be the motive for Jules's death."

"Or it could be directions to the mall. Norrie, why on earth would you think this woman is connected to Jules Leurant? Other than the fact she's also from Belgium."

"Process of elimination. Look, we already know Stanislav, Allete, and Earvin have the same or similar motive for murder. But that doesn't mean it's the only motive. What we don't know about Jules could be the very thing that got him killed. Including a possible connection with Hortensia."

"You've been writing too many screenplays. Next thing I know you'll be climbing up a trellis to get into that other visitor's room. The man from the Netherlands."

I shook my head. "There has to be a better way."

Chapter 9

"Are you insane?" Theo asked when I called him from the winery office a few minutes later. "Routing through trash where anyone could have seen you?"

"I was careful. If natural causes are ruled out and that toxicology report shows that our Cabernet Sauvignon was the culprit, those deputies will be all over this place like ants at a picnic. And they won't be looking elsewhere. That's why I need to find out who those international guests are and if they were at last night's function. For all I know, Jules Leurant could have been persona non grata all over Europe. And the most non grata of all as far as Hortensia was concerned. Darn. I absolutely have to learn more about that woman. And what she's capable of doing."

"Yikes. Talk about going to extremes. I'm surprised you didn't launch a Google search."

"Google *and* Facebook. I had no idea Hortensia was such a popular name. And Vermeulen? It's like Smith or Jones. There's like a zillion of them. Forget it."

"You may have a point about the investigation focusing on the wineries. Two junior deputies from our county left here a few minutes ago after questioning Don and me about what we had observed last night and if we had heard any threats being made about Jules. They also had a chat with our winemaker."

"And?"

"We were no help whatsoever. I'm surprised they haven't been to Two Witches yet."

"Give them time. I'm antsy to find out who that other guest is, but I don't want to risk running into any interference."

"That's the smartest thing you've said so far. Look, Don bought a gigantic brisket at Sam's Club and we'll never eat all of it. Come over for dinner and the three of us can strategize."

"You sure it's okay with Don?"

"I wouldn't have asked if it wasn't. See you at seven-ish."

"Sounds good. And thanks, Theo."

I needed to head back to the house and tweak some of the dialogue from the screenplay I was working on, but I really wasn't in the mood. If those deputies had already questioned the guys at the Grey Egret, we were probably next on their list. Unless, of course, they decided to pop over to Rosalee's winery first. I picked up the phone and called her.

Rosalee didn't waste any time with formalities. "The two deputies they sent over looked like they belonged to a Cub Scout Troop and not the Yates County Sheriff's Department."

"What did you tell them?"

"The truth. I got cornered by Catherine Trobert at the event and had to listen to her go on and on about her son until she found another sucker she could trap."

"What about Leandre?"

"He didn't know anything. He was too busy talking with your guy."

That's right. Vintages. "Rosalee, do you know if those deputies were at any other wineries before they saw you?"

"The one who looked as if he'd recently been weaned said they'd already met with the owners from Billsburrow and Lake View Wineries and they were planning on visiting the Grey Egret before calling it a day. Short day if you ask me."

"Funny that they didn't go to the Grey Egret first and in fact, skipped Gable Hill Winery since it's on the way to yours."

"They probably couldn't read a map. That's the trouble these days. Everyone expects some computer voice from their car to tell them where to go. No common sense anymore."

I chuckled. "Let me know if you hear anything."

"The only thing I've heard is the official list of kitchen demands from that nincompoop at the wine association. When that chocolate prima donna arrives to do the demonstrations tomorrow, she better be happy with the kitchenware."

"She? Allete must be on your schedule. Holy cow. I'd better check my emails. Thanks Rosalee. I'll be in touch."

I bit my lower lip and thought about that conversation I'd had with Catherine and Theo when our little WOW subcommittee met. I distinctly remembered us insisting Jules be assigned to Rosalee and Madeline due to his germophobia. Of course, it really didn't matter now. Earvin couldn't possibly be as picky as his uncle.

It only took me a minute to boot up the office computer and check my emails. Sure enough, there was an official notice from the wine association. Blah blah…unfortunate incident…blah blah tourism…blah blah blah. There was an attachment that detailed the schedule for the chocolatiers as well as a complete inventory of the kitchen gadgetry they would need. Winery owners were asked to contact the association office if they couldn't provide the necessary pots, pans, cutlery, etc.

Terrific. One day to go and we better not need a trip to Geneva Restaurant Supply on Seneca Street.

I studied the schedule and then printed it off. There were two demonstrations slated for each of the three days. One from eleven o'clock to noon, and the other from two thirty to four. Our winery had Earvin every morning and the Grey Egret got him in the afternoon. Allete would be starting off at Rosalee's Terrace Wineries and then ending up at Billsburrow. That left her…her what? Boyfriend? Lover? Soon-to-be-business-partner Stanislav with Lake View in the mornings and Gable Hill in the afternoons. At least Stephanie would have some eye candy to watch, along with the actual confection making.

While I was certain our kitchen would have all the necessities in place, I didn't take a chance. I printed out the inventory list and marched it over to our chefs, Fred and Emma, in the bistro.

"Gosh, Norrie," Emma said when I handed her the paper, "we got that list weeks ago. Thank goodness the wine association rented chocolate tempering machines. Geneva Restaurant Supply delivered ours a few days ago, along with dipping utensils. That company must be the conduit for the demonstrations because they also brought the block and wafer chocolates from Puccini Zinest to Geneva on the Lake as well as delivered the ingredients like corn syrup and confectioner's sugar to the wineries. The email explained it. Geneva on the Lake needed a bulk amount of chocolate for the competition and they agreed to deliver the smaller blocks to the wineries each day for the demonstrations."

I must have had a sheepish look on my face because the minute Emma said that, she added, "I'm sure with all of your screenplay deadlines, that email from Mr. Speltmore was easy to miss."

"I, um, er…"

Then we both laughed.

"I have no idea what a tempering machine is," I said. "I have enough trouble learning about our own equipment in the winery."

"Well, you don't have to worry. Everything's under control here." Our tasting room was all set for the next three mornings of wine and chocolate pairings. According to the wine association brochure, the chocolatiers would demonstrate their techniques and then have the guests taste the confections paired with our wine. I was half-tempted to have Sam or Glenda pour me a sample of our Cab-Sav so I could see how it went with the Milky Way I had in the office, but I knew it wouldn't have the same effect.

Like it or not, I had to get back to my screenplay. I told Cammy I'd be in the tasting room first thing in the morning and then I darted out the front entrance. Alvin gave me a snort as I walked past his pen. The little hut was filled with fresh bedding or it would have been trampled on by now.

"Why my brother-in-law thought you'd be good for business is anyone's guess," I muttered to the goat.

He turned away and busied himself with a huge pile of hay that was off to the side. I wondered what lucky vineyard worker got to deal with the goat today as I headed to the house.

It was twenty to seven when I finally closed my laptop and refilled Charlie's food dish. I changed my top to a decent-looking sweater, fixed my hair, and grabbed the keys to my Toyota. Walking down the long driveway at night wasn't something I cared to do in the dark, but I didn't need to start up Francine's all-weather Subaru for a two-minute jaunt my sedan could certainly handle.

"It's open," Don shouted when I knocked on their door. No sooner did I turn the knob than Isolde, the Grey Egret's long-haired Norwegian Forest Cat, greeted me. She rubbed against my jeans and then scurried off to the living room.

"Those cats were bred to enjoy the snow, but Isolde abhors it," he said. "The undersides of her paws have really long, thick fur so the cold won't penetrate, but don't tell her that. She won't believe you."

"It's probably best you've made her a house cat. Too many predators out there."

"And one on this wine trail. Only he or she doesn't have four legs or wings. Have you heard anything more from Deputy Hickman?"

"Zilch."

"Nothing on the news either. Come on. Theo's in the kitchen setting the table."

"Oh my gosh. That brisket smells phenomenal."

"Wait till you taste the seasoned potatoes that go with it."

Theo gave me a wave and motioned for me to take a seat at their table. Like the Grey Egret Winery, Don and Theo's home was warm and inviting with a style that reminded me of the Pacific Northwest. Beautiful beamed ceilings with teal and beige accent walls.

"We've got flavored seltzers and Merlot to go along with the meal," Theo said. "I kidded Don about trying out our Merlot with an old Nestlé's Crunch bar we had in the pantry, but we never got the chance."

"Join the club. Milky Way and Cabernet Sauvignon. Only I chickened out, too."

"Well, tomorrow we'll all get a taste of our wines with gourmet chocolates. That is if Earvin is up to the task."

"I know what you mean." I helped myself to a second scoop of the potatoes. "He hardly said a word and acted like he was scared of the world."

Don groaned. "Just what we need. Showmanship is everything when it comes to these winery demonstrations. We had a cheesemaker two years ago who could have had his own act in Vegas."

"I doubt Earvin will come close."

"Norrie's right," Theo said. "We better hope the chocolate is spectacular because I'm not putting too much hope in Earvin's presentation."

Dinner was followed by a marvelous lattice cherry pie, compliments of Wegmans' bakery. When I finished my last sip of coffee, I insisted on helping with the dishes and cleaning up their kitchen. By then, the three of us were pooped and I was ready to head back up the hill. At that moment, their phone rang and Don took the call.

"Theo! Turn on Channel 8 WROC. Hurry up!"

Theo rushed out of the kitchen and into the living room while Don continued to yell. "It's Stephanie. She tried calling Norrie's cell but it went to voice mail. The lab report came in on the wineglass Jules had in his hand."

By now, Theo and I had cranked up the volume on the TV and situated ourselves on the couch directly in front.

"Tell her we'll call back," Theo announced.

Seconds later, the three of us were glued to the screen as Wade Gallagher, the nightly anchor, pontificated about Jules Leurant's untimely demise. "The glass that Mr. Leurant was found holding had been sprayed with the prescription drug, Ambien. Ambien is a commonly used sleep aid, but it does come with a litany of side effects. It's one of the few sleep aids that's available in a spray. At this time, the authorities don't believe the amount of the drug was sufficient to result in death, but its common side effects including dizziness, fainting, and lightheadedness may have contributed to Mr. Leurant falling in the snow where he was initially presumed to have suffocated."

I grabbed Theo's wrist and shook it. "It wasn't our wine. That's a relief, I suppose. But the drug was sprayed on a wineglass. People will be petrified to drink from a Two Witches wineglass again."

"Think, Norrie, think," he said. "Not Two Witches. Those wineglasses came from Geneva on the Lake. The problem, as I see it, is now theirs."

"Shh!" Don said. "There's got to be more. The guy said, 'initially presumed to have suffocated.' Listen."

"One more caveat to the mysterious death of noted chocolatier Jules Leurant," Wade added. "While authorities haven't ruled out suffocation as a cause of death, a yet-to-be-determined substance was found at the back of his throat during the autopsy."

Don gave Theo a poke in the arm. "Ah-ha. Did I call it or what?"

Theo and I shushed him. Then, out of nowhere, the co-anchor put in her two cents. "Wade, wasn't there some prior footage about a winery owner's comment regarding Mr. Leurant's choking to death?"

"There most certainly was, Latisha. We'll see if we can dig up that video for our viewers."

I got up from the couch and fumbled in my bag for my cell phone. "Stephanie! She must be a basket case by now."

Don shook his head. "Pray to the gods it wasn't a bonbon."

Chapter 10

"Stephanie's probably holding her cell phone and waiting for our call," Theo said as I handed him my phone. "She'd better not shriek in my ear."

Don turned the volume down on the TV and the two of us watched Theo for any sign of reaction.

A second later he said, "Calm down. Calm down. No, don't wake up your husband. What? No! It's not as if you shoved a piece of chocolate down his throat. What? Here, talk to Don."

Don flashed Theo a look and took the phone. "Hey, Stephanie, try to relax. What? Yeah, we all saw that video. Trust me when I tell you, it was an attention getting move on the part of the station. It doesn't mean a thing. People say stuff like that all the time…Uh-huh. Hold on. Yeah, here's Norrie."

Like a game of hot potato, the phone was now in my hands. "Stephanie, we've got bigger things to worry about. Whoever sprayed that wineglass with Ambien could very well try it again during one of the demos tomorrow. Who knows what kind of nutcase is running around here and if Jules was targeted or if he was merely the first person to succumb to a—"

"Serial killer? A serial killer?"

"NO! I wasn't going to say, 'serial killer.' I was going to say 'lunatic.'"

Stephanie lowered her voice and said one word. "Oh."

"Look, it's late right now, but first thing tomorrow, we need to call the other wineries and tell them to be extra vigilant about their wineglasses. Have one of their employees on the lookout at all times. I'll call Rosalee and Madeline. Can you give Catherine a buzz?" *Because I'll get stuck listening to her talk about Steven.*

"Sure thing. You're positive I don't have anything to worry about?"

"Absolutely."

Who am I kidding? We all have something to worry about, only it isn't a bonbon blocking Jules Leurant's windpipe.

Isolde followed me to the front door as I said good night to Theo and Don. Both agreed we might have a problem on our hands if Jules's death was only the beginning.

"It's funny," Don said, "that they haven't released the results of the preliminary toxicology report on Jules. Only what was found on the wineglass. I know full toxicology screenings can take weeks, but they should know something about what he ingested."

I nodded. "I'm sure they do, but maybe the sheriff's department hasn't released it yet. I know the drug was on the wineglass, but all people will hear is Two Witches Cabernet Sauvignon. I wish to heck they'd hurry up."

Theo handed me the scarf I had tossed on the little table by their entry. "You and the rest of the wine trail."

"Thanks for the great meal. Talk to you tomorrow."

The question of motive plagued me well into the night and when I woke up the next morning, I was groggy and miserable. I'd promised Cammy I'd be at the tasting room first thing in the morning, even though our entire tasting room staff would be there. I didn't actually specify the time of my arrival, but I didn't want to get there after everyone else had done all the set-up work. The crew would be on edge with the publicity and the onslaught of ticket-holding visitors. True, "Deck the Halls around the Lake," was our showcase event, but this one was proving to be a close second.

I opted to wear a dark turtleneck pullover so I could promote the winery by layering it with a Two Witches T-shirt and a colorful acrylic scarf. Usually I threw on a woolen hat and took my chances with my hair, but since I was promoting a major winery event, I didn't want to ruin it with unruly hat-hair. I made sure Charlie had plenty of food and fresh water before putting on my boots and trekking over to the tasting room.

The one piece of good news was the weather. Nothing that involved precipitation was on the forecast for the next four days. "Abundant sunshine," according to the Weather Channel, "coupled with exceedingly low temperatures." That meant clear roads and winter tourists who were apt to linger around the tasting rooms. Our huge gas fireplace with its semicircle of occasional chairs was bound to set the mood for the festivities.

Unfortunately, Earvin Roels wasn't.

When I walked in, he was standing in front of the demonstration area Fred and Emma had set up in front of the bistro. At first, I didn't recognize him. He directed our staff as if he was the conductor of the New York

Philharmonic. Oddly, he looked taller. The Earvin I remembered from that first encounter slouched. This one didn't.

With sharp black trousers and a white collared chef's jacket, complete with pearl buttons, Earvin seemed comfortable in his new role. Maybe too comfortable. He inspected the cookware and utensils, snapping his fingers every few seconds.

Cammy tiptoed behind me and whispered, "Pompous ass."

I tried not to snicker. "I'd better give him the official welcome."

Just then, Glenda appeared out of nowhere and motioned for Cammy and me to step aside.

"Do you feel that?" she said. "It's a cold aura that's permeating the room. I think it's centered on the chocolatier."

"That's not a cold aura," I replied. "It's the front door opening and closing."

Glenda shuddered. "I'm not talking physical cold. I'm sensing a spiritual one. That chocolatier, Earvin something or other, is altering the mood of the winery."

I put my hand on Glenda's shoulder. "As long as he can produce stunning confections that augment our wine, we'll deal with it. The demonstration and pairing are only for an hour and a half. Try to make the best of it."

In retrospect, I never should have told Glenda to "make the best of it," because her interpretation and mine were eons apart. Within seconds, she rushed off, muttering something about needing a ritual cleansing.

I wasted no time catching up. "Not now. We need you in the tasting room. Can't you say a mantra or something?"

Glenda shook her now pink, orange and blue hair until it fused into a greenish hue. "Do you think he'd mind if I touch his hands and infuse some positive energy into his being?"

"Oh, he'll mind all right! Don't touch anything. Especially him. And don't infuse anything either. Look around. Customers are lining up already. We need to hand out their festivity wineglass and usher them to the presentation area."

Glenda let out a long, dramatic sigh but not before touching my wrist. "I'll give you the positive energy, Norrie. You'll need it. Looks like Sam, Roger, and Cammy are all set at the tables. How about if I help distribute the souvenir wineglasses?"

Terrific. Just what we need. Souvenir wineglasses.

The wineries handed out event souvenirs to all ticket-holding patrons. Ornaments for the holidays, little cheese cutters for Wine & Cheese, and, up until this year, heart-shaped cookie cutters for the Chocolate and Wine. What imbecile on the wine trail decided on glassware this year was beyond me. We'd have to practically swear to the customers that their wineglass hadn't been tampered with.

Emma and Fred must have seen to it that everything met with Earvin's approval because when I glanced over to the presentation area, he was standing calmly in front. I could smell the enticing aroma of chocolate emanating from the tempering machine, and I wondered what kind of confection he'd be demonstrating. Then I realized it was awfully rude of me not to welcome him.

I immediately walked over to the large demo table, but before I could utter a word, Earvin held up his hands. "Please stay back. Everything has been sanitized, organized, and finalized."

"Fine." I backed off. "We really didn't get a chance to chat when you paid our winery a visit with your uncle a few days ago. I'm terribly sorry for your loss."

"My uncle was a self-centered narcissist who would walk over bodies to get what he wanted. Apparently, so did his killer."

"Uh, um, er..."

"Don't look so shocked. Those qualities of my uncle didn't detract from his extraordinary talent as a master chocolatier. No doubt someone wanted him out of the way. But rest assured, it wasn't me. I would be remiss if I didn't acknowledge that I owe my own edification to him. I wouldn't be standing at this very spot today had it not been for his tutelage."

Or the fact Ambien comes in an easy-to-use spray. "Um, yes. Indeed. Anyway, welcome. I know your uncle was originally scheduled to give his presentations at two different wineries, but the committee seems to have changed the schedule."

"A minor inconvenience. Nothing in comparison with...what do you call it? Oh yes. The red tape involving the release of my uncle's body from the county morgue."

"That's pretty usual in an investigation involving suspicious death. Did the sheriff's department liaison give you any idea of their progress?"

"None whatsoever. I *was* asked, or should I say, *told,* to remain in the area until they reach a conclusive resolution to the matter."

"That's what you were told? Those words? 'Conclusive resolution?'"

"Yes. Those were the very words that disagreeable deputy from Yates County used after badgering me well into the night. And the other deputy, the one from Ontario County, was equally abrasive. Bothering me at my hotel, no less. It's a wonder I had any sleep. And when I yawned in front of them, they immediately demanded to know if I used or was in possession of any sleep aids."

"I'm sure they explained why."

"The cause of my uncle's death, yes. I told them that if I had any desire to end my uncle's life, which I didn't, I certainly wouldn't resort to such a cowardly means."

For some reason, the expression "Death by Chocolate" popped into my head, and I had to bite my lip so I wouldn't laugh. Fortunately, Cammy appeared and pointed to her watch. "I hate to interrupt, but it's time for the demonstration to begin. I've got the Seneca Lake Wine Trail chocolatier introduction sheet to read, unless, of course, you want to do it. Henry Speltmore emailed it when he sent the schedules."

Earvin pushed his shoulders back and gave his head a shake. "I would rather neither of you read it. I shall make my own introduction."

"Um, sure. If that's what you'd prefer," I said. "For that matter, your assistant for today, Emma, can also introduce herself."

With that, I tugged Cammy's sleeve and we retreated to the back of the tasting room. In the few minutes that I'd chatted with Earvin, the room had filled up completely. Our staff arranged the chairs so everyone would have a clear view of the demonstration. Immediately following, the individual tasting tables were all set to pair Earvin's chocolate delicacies with our Cabernet Sauvignon.

Then I realized something. There was no way on earth Earvin Roels would be able to make enough chocolate so everyone in the room would have a sufficient sample to taste with our wine. An hour and a half wasn't nearly enough time. Heck, even when we made chocolate-covered marshmallows in my Girl Scout troop, we only had to create twenty-five or so, not quadruple that number.

Cammy must have seen the strange look on my face because she gave me a nudge. "What? What's the matter?"

When I told her, she broke out laughing. "Earvin's chocolates were pre-made this morning. Same deal for the other two chocolatiers. They were up at the crack of dawn using the facilities at Geneva on the Lake. The chocolates are in coolers, in our kitchen."

Theo was right. I really needed to pay more attention to my emails. Lately, if the subject line wasn't marked urgent or didn't have the word "screenplay" in it, I tended to gloss over it with the intent of returning. Unfortunately, intent and time management never seemed to coincide.

I stationed myself in the rear of the tasting room and watched closely as Earvin demonstrated his craft. I was mesmerized. He had poise, he had style, and most of all he had confidence. Today's confection was a variation of butter cream patties, only his looked rounder and more complex than any I'd ever seen.

At first, I didn't notice the tall auburn-haired woman with the calf-length winter coat as she glided past me. It was only when Earvin stopped talking to the audience and looked directly at her that I stopped thinking about butter cream patties altogether.

It was only a few seconds, but the tension was palpable. Earvin stood perfectly still, the melted chocolate slowly dripping from the dipping fork he held. Then, as if he'd been in a trance, he re-emerged. "It's imperative to dip deep down into the chocolate or your confection won't be completely submerged and will be most unsuitable."

I turned to see the reaction from the auburn-haired woman, but she had left. I all but collided with a few of our visitors as I rushed to the front entrance. Lizzie was at the cash register/computer and I all but accosted her. "Did a woman with auburn hair just leave?"

"The door opened and closed but I wasn't looking. I heard it, and, of course, I felt the gust of cold air. Sorry, Norrie. I've been busy tallying the tickets. Were we supposed to be on the lookout for someone?"

"Now we are. If a woman fitting that description comes back in, find me."

"Tsk-tsk. You need to be more explicit. Like Nancy Drew. Hair color isn't a description."

And Nancy Drew isn't a real detective! "Okay. Okay. She was fortyish. Wearing a dark calf-length coat. Material, not fur. No hat, but a light brown plaid scarf. It could have been wool."

"Much better," Lizzie replied. "I'll be on the lookout. Is she dangerous?"

"I have no idea. She might not even be who I think she is, but I need to find out."

Cold air or not, I threw open the front door and scanned the parking lot. No sign of her. And no vehicles heading down the driveway. My next stop was the restroom, but that didn't pan out either. No one could have driven off *that* quickly. Then it occurred to me she could have been a passenger in someone else's car and they had already made their way down the drive before I even opened the door.

I walked back to the demonstration in time to watch Earvin dazzle the crowd as he created a latticework of white and dark chocolate on top of the butter cream patties. Then, immediately following the applause, he excused himself and disappeared.

Chapter 11

"I thought he walked into the kitchen." Cammy was overseeing one of the wine pairing tables and had her hands full with anxious customers.

Apparently, Earvin's butter cream patties were a big hit. So much so that a few of the people at the table asked Cammy if they could pay an additional fee for more samples.

I overheard her tell them, "The wine, yes, but we only have a small allotment of chocolates for the event. Each guest is allowed five pieces."

"If you're looking for the chocolatier," one of the guests said, "he left the building a few minutes ago. I'm pretty sure that was him. Short, balding man with a fur-lined jacket?"

"That's him. It doesn't matter. He'll be at the Grey Egret this afternoon and back to our winery tomorrow morning. I was just hoping to catch him, that's all."

"When you do," she said, "tell him these butter cream chocolates are to die for."

Yep. Just the words I'm sure he'll want to hear.

I turned back to the demo table in time to see a frustrated Emma shaking her head. "I have no idea how to clean a tempering machine. It's not as if I expected Mr. Roels to be doing the clean-up, but I did expect some direction."

The chocolatey mess inside the machine was heavenly and my first thought was to grab a spoon and have a field day. It would serve Earvin right. Then again, the machine was the property of Seneca Restaurant Supply.

"Give Seneca Restaurant Supply a call," I told her. "They should be able to help you out."

Emma sighed. "These perfectionists are something else, aren't they?"

I gave her a pat on the shoulder and perused the room. Every table was full and it looked as if our guests were enjoying themselves. No one asked about the safety of our wineglasses and no one seemed the least bit perturbed about the recent death of Jules Leurant or the sudden disappearance of his nephew. However, that changed in a matter of minutes.

A tall, blond man in a chauffeur's uniform walked over to me. "I was told by the gray-haired lady at the cash register you're the owner of the winery."

"Uh-huh. I'm Norrie Ellington. Can I help you?"

"I'm with Round-About-Seneca tours, and I seem to be missing my passenger. Our company was hired to take some chefs around the lake for demonstrations."

"Not chefs. Chocolatiers. Oh, never mind. You must be referring to Earvin Roels."

"That's the name on my list. Earvin Roels. I have his schedule in front of me. I'm supposed to pick him up at twelve forty-five and drive him to Port of Call on the lake for a very brief respite. Then I'm to take him directly to the Grey Egret and ensure he arrives no later than one fifty for his demonstration. I haven't met Mr. Roels. Another driver brought him to your winery earlier today."

I was somewhat familiar with the arrangements for the chocolatiers but I wouldn't exactly bet money on it, even though I did read Henry Speltmore's email. Round-About-Seneca Limousine Company was hired to drive the chocolatiers to their destinations and back to the hotel. That much, I knew. So, where the heck was Earvin? Maybe that customer was mistaken and it wasn't Earvin she saw leaving our winery.

"Would you hold on for a moment, please? We'll look around for him. There's complimentary coffee for drivers at the bistro to your right. Help yourself. I'm sure Mr. Roels can't be too far."

What the heck am I saying? For all I know, Mr. Roels could very well have hightailed it to Calcutta!

I smiled and tried to remain calm while a tight knot began to form in my stomach. Without wasting a second, I charged over to Cammy's table and whispered, "Earvin is AWOL. We've got to find him."

She moved out from behind the table and scanned the room. "Has anyone checked the restroom? Sam or Roger can go in."

"Good idea. Be right back."

Five minutes later, our winery staff had checked the restroom, the kitchen, the bistro, and the entire tasting room. No sign of Earvin. Sam even went outside and reported back that "There's no one dumb enough to be hanging out by Alvin's pen. Too damn cold."

By now, not only was my stomach doing flip-flops, but it was as if my entire body had developed a tremor. This would be a disaster for the Grey Egret, not to mention The Seneca Lake Wine Trail. People had paid good money to watch master chocolatiers demonstrate their art and without Earvin at his designated location, we'd have at least a hundred angry customers. A veritable nightmare.

The chauffeur was now standing by the front door, paper coffee cup in hand. "Any sign of him?"

"Not yet. Can you give us a few more minutes?"

"Sure. He's my only customer. I'll wait in the limo. Here's my card with my number. Call or text me when he shows up. Okay?"

"Sure. Same deal here. You've got the winery numbers, so call us if he appears out of nowhere. You know, you're welcome to wait here or in our bistro."

"That's all right. I'll be fine. Besides, I like to make sure the car's safe. We've had problems in the past."

Problems in the past didn't surprise me. Large party groups were notorious for leaning against the vehicles and scratching them. Not to mention spilling wine or, worse yet, heaving from too much wine.

I thanked the driver and returned to the tasting room. By now it would be too late for Earvin to enjoy his little respite at Port of Call. He'd be lucky to have enough set-up time at the Grey Egret. At least Don was no stranger to food preparation, so I was positive all the preliminaries were in place.

"Any luck?" Cammy asked.

Her group of tasters had just exited the table and were now looking at the wine bins.

I shook my head. "Nope. The guy with the fur-lined jacket must have been Earvin. Geez, I'd better give Theo and Don a heads-up."

"We'll keep looking," Cammy said.

I plunked myself down at the desk in the office and used our winery phone to call theirs.

After a few rings, Theo picked up. "How was it? Did it go well? What was the customer reaction like?"

"Great demonstration. Lots of style. Delicious butter cream patties and yes, it went well until, oh my gosh, I hate to tell you this, but Earvin's missing. He literally split without even telling Emma how to clean the tempering machine."

"I'm sure he just wanted to give himself a sufficient break time between presentations. Don't worry. The limo company will get him here on time."

"Yeah, about that, Earvin never got into the limo. The driver came inside to look for him, and as of this very minute, the poor guy is sitting in his vehicle waiting. Earvin's a no-show. AWOL."

"Oh no. OH NO! This is a disaster. Ticketed customers are already lining up. Did he say anything? Give any indication he wasn't going to be here?"

"Not directly."

"What do you mean 'not directly?'"

"Maybe I'm making too much of this, but a classy-looking auburn-haired woman came in to the winery during Earvin's presentation and he froze for an instant. As if he knew her. Then it was business as usual. Except for one thing, the woman left almost immediately."

"That could have been coincidental. Earvin Roels wouldn't be the first man to succumb to the charms of a classy-looking woman."

"Theo, I don't think it was that at all. It's too coincidental that this Hortensia Vermeulen woman arrived from Belgium a few days ago and is staying at the same hotel as the chocolatiers. That woman might very well be her. Plus, I'll bet money she and Earvin have a history. Or at least an acquaintance. Cammy's friend Barb, who handles the reservations at Geneva on the Lake, told her the sheriff's department demanded a list of the guests. They should be vetting that woman instead of willow-wallowing around."

"We don't know that they're not, but right now, I've got a major problem on my hands if Earvin doesn't walk through our doors in the next ten seconds."

"I'm so sorry. I probably should call our sheriff's office and let them know."

"Good idea. If he shows up, I'll get back to you."

Before I called the sheriff's office, I had another thought and raced to find Emma. She was in the kitchen using hot water to clean the tempering machine.

"Emma! How closely did you watch what Earvin did?"

"Close enough, why?"

"Because I think you've just become the next chocolatier."

"Huh? What are you saying?"

"I don't have a whole lot of time to explain, but Earvin is still missing and his presentation begins at 2:30 at the Grey Egret."

"That's less than an hour. Norrie, I don't think I can pull off something like that."

"Do you know how to work the tempering machine?"

"Uh-huh. And at this point, I'm an expert on cleaning it."

"Dipping the chocolate shouldn't be all that hard. Did you see what stuff Earvin put in the mix for the butter cream?"

"I know the basics, but it's the technique."

"Don't worry. I'll make sure you get a topnotch assistant. Hurry! You need to get down the driveway and into the Grey Egret right away."

The look on Emma's face was a combination of shock and terror. "I'll do what I can, but that's not saying much."

"Hurry! And remember to dazzle the audience with your smile."

"Smile? I'll be lucky if I don't burst out in tears."

As Emma scurried out of the winery, I made two phone calls. The first to tell Theo I had found a replacement for Earvin and the second to Deputy Hickman.

"Emma knows what's she's doing," I told Theo, "but she'll need Don right next to her so she doesn't fall apart."

"Wonderful. And who are you going to send so Don doesn't flip out? Seriously, Norrie, we'll muster through. Of course, the wine trail will need to comp today's ticket holders since they're not really seeing a world-class chocolatier."

"No, they're seeing a class act without the ego."

Chapter 12

Gladys Pipp answered the phone when I called the Yates County Public Safety Building. She was the secretary/receptionist and the only pleasant person I'd come across in that building. She was also a good friend of Catherine Trobert and, as a result, more than willing to share information with me. Of course, it helped that I brought her lots of homemade jams and jellies my sister had prepared before venturing off to Costa Rica.

"Gladys," I said. "It's Norrie Ellington from Two Witches. I really need to speak with Deputy Hickman."

"You're in luck. He finished eating about ten minutes ago. Without food in his stomach, I wouldn't approach him even if I was wielding a big stick. Is everything all right?"

"Not exactly. The chocolatier who did the demonstration at our winery sort of disappeared."

"I can dispatch nine-one-one quicker."

"No. Better not do that. I mean, it's not as if he's been kidnapped or anything." *I hope.* "But it's important Deputy Hickman knows what's going on."

"Sure. I'll transfer the call."

The next voice I heard was becoming way too familiar. "Miss Ellington, to what do I owe the pleasure?"

"Jules Leurant's nephew is missing. Earvin Roels. He gave his presentation at our winery and then poof! It was like he disappeared into thin air."

"How long ago was this?"

"Um, maybe about thirty or forty minutes ago."

"Minutes? Thirty or forty minutes?"

"Uh-huh."

"That's hardly a reason to send up a flare. Have you checked the men's room?"

"We've checked everywhere. He's got another presentation at the Grey Egret, but they haven't seen him either. I think his disappearance may have something to do with a woman who came into our winery."

"What woman?"

"I don't know, but if I were to wager a guess, she's an acquaintance of his from Belgium."

"Tell me, how exactly do you know all of this?"

"Um, well, I don't *really* know they know each other, but it makes sense."

"And you're certain this woman is from Belgium?"

"No, I think she is. Or she may be."

"Miss Ellington, you're making absolutely no sense. Our department cannot file a missing person's report until someone has been missing for forty-eight hours. Unless, of course, it was a child or an elderly individual with a medical condition. According to my information, Mr. Roels is neither."

"But doesn't this smack of foul play? One minute he's garnishing chocolate confections and the next he's out of sight."

"I'll make a note of it for my deputies. If we hear anything, we'll let you know. In the meantime, I suggest you concentrate on facts, not fabrication."

"Earvin Roel's uncle was found dead under suspicious circumstances. For all we know, the nephew could be next."

"At this juncture in time, there's nothing to substantiate that."

Not yet, but who the heck knows? "Um, about the uncle, has there been any determination about the official cause of death?"

"Contributing factors led to suffocation. There. I've said enough. Now, if there's nothing else, Miss Ellington, I've got work to do. Murders don't solve themselves."

"Ah-hah! You said it! *Murder.* Jules Leurant was murdered. It was no accident that he drank from a drug-sprayed wineglass after consuming heaven knows how much alcohol."

"Miss Ellington, I must remind you that the case is under investigation. Not speculation. We don't know if Mr. Leurant was the intended victim of the Ambien-laced wineglass."

"No, but he was the victim of someone rolling him over in the snow."

"Where did you hear that piece of information?"

Yeesh. I can't very well tell him about my conversation with the receptionist at Geneva on the Lake. "Um, uh, er, it just made sense, that's all."

"Let me tell you something that *does* make sense. We will conduct our thorough investigation and you need to do whatever it is you do at that winery."

"If the next body to turn up in the snow is Earvin Roels, don't say I didn't warn you."

I hung up before he could answer and then I cringed. Last thing I needed was to tick him off, but I was afraid it was too late. If the sheriff's department wasn't about to take Earvin's disappearance seriously, I had no choice but to continue with my own little bit of probing. Beginning with that note I found in Hortensia Vermeulen's trash.

Our tasting room was still packed with customers as I walked to the door. Lizzie looked up from whatever she was doing at the cash register and adjusted her wire-rimmed glasses. "Are you leaving already? Must be that chocolatier finally showed up somewhere."

"Not exactly. I sent Emma to the Grey Egret in his place."

"I didn't know Emma could make chocolate confections."

"Long story. Neither did Emma. Listen, I've got to talk with Franz. When things slow down in the tasting room, tell Cammy to call me on my cell."

"Certainly. And remember, if you ask the right questions, your investigation will move much smoother."

"How did you know that's what I was doing?"

"I saw the panicked look on your face when that chauffeur came in to find Earvin Roels. That *is* what you're doing, isn't it? Tracking him down?"

"To do that, I need to find out what business his uncle might have been involved in. It could be what got the guy killed."

"And you think Franz knows something?"

"Yep—German, French, and hopefully, Dutch."

Lizzie gave me a strange look when I exited the building, but at least that was all she gave me. Glenda, on the other hand, would have doused me with some healing or cleansing oils.

Alan was the only one in the winery lab when I knocked on their office door and stepped inside. Except for a difference in height, he and our master winemaker could pass as brothers. Red hair, horned-rimmed glasses, ruddy complexions, and nonstop babbling about things like botrytis, early fermentation, and acidity.

"Hey, Alan, please tell me Franz is in the lab. I need him to translate something for me."

"A recipe in German?"

I laughed. "No, that would be more up Don's alley next door. I may have a lead into Jules Leurant's death."

"Then you should share it with the sheriff's department."

"Trust me, they're not interested."

"Well, they were plenty interested in what Franz observed the night of the event when Jules was found in the snow."

"What do you mean?"

"An assistant deputy sheriff left a few minutes ago after questioning him. According to Franz, 'it wasn't enough to be badgered at the time of the event, most likely they lost their notes and had to start all over.' I must say, finding a master chocolatier dead in the snow wasn't the best start to a wine trail event. At least the nephew was able to step in."

"Uh, yeah. About that, the nephew is missing. And the note I've got may give us a clue as to who killed the uncle and where the heck the nephew is."

"I want to hear this, too. Come on. Let's pull Franz away from racking the wines. He and Herbert have been at it all day with the racking hose and tubes. Wine must be filtered. Still, when you move it from barrel to barrel so the tannins can soften, the process seems endless."

And also like Greek to me.

At least I didn't have to hear about fermentation. Herbert gave me that lecture every few months because my brain was kind of like a sieve when it came to understanding chemical processes. Now, apparently, there was another one, although it sounded more like grunt work than anything.

Sure enough, Franz and Herbert were both bent over two of our oak-aged barrels, and the hose system they had set up reminded me of the time I ran out of gas at a party on Keuka Lake. If it wasn't for one of the boys who offered to siphon some gas from his car to mine, I would have really paid the price with my parents.

"Hi, Franz! Hi, Herbert!" I said. "I hate to pull you away from what looks like lots of fun, but I really need Franz to translate this note I came across. It may shed some light on Jules Leurant's death and the whereabouts of Earvin Roels. That's right, the whereabouts. Earvin left Two Witches as soon as his presentation was over and didn't say a word to anyone. He never got into his limo. The driver is sort of freaked out. The Grey Egret is freaked out. And Henry Speltmore from the wine trail will be *really* freaked out. Anyway, I found the note at Geneva on the Lake."

"Slow down. Catch a breath." Franz stepped away from the barrels and walked toward me. "You're going to have heart palpitations. Now, start from the beginning. Did you say you found the note during the night of the event?"

"Not exactly. I kind of did some snooping on my own the following day. Listen, can you translate it for me? It looks sort of like German but not quite."

I handed him the note and he read it out loud.

"'We hebben onafgemaakte zaken en ik durf niet langer te wachhten. Als je dacht dat deze kleine excursie van jou alles zou laten ver dwijnen, heb je het helaas verkeerd.'"

"Well? What does it mean? What does it say?"

"First of all, it's written in Dutch, not German. It's what you would call cryptic. It could mean anything."

"Franz," I whined. "Just translate the darn thing."

Franz cleared his throat and took his time reading it.

"We have unfinished business and I dare not wait any longer. If you thought this little excursion of yours would make everything go away, you are sadly mistaken."

"That's it?" I asked. "That's all there is to it?"

Franz nodded. "That's everything on this note. Where did you say you found it?"

I groaned. "In a Belgian woman's trash receptacle at Geneva on the Lake. And before you ask any other questions, I know she was Belgian because I also found her boarding pass. Listen, it's more information than those deputies have, but they refuse to widen their investigation. I think this woman might have something to do with Jules and Earvin."

I expected Franz to chastise me for letting my imagination run like crazy but instead, he rubbed his chin and let out a sigh. "So do I."

Chapter 13

Franz handed the torn note back to me. "Look closely at the top of the paper, where it was ripped. That's not a decorative design from the stationery. Those little curly loops are the bottom of letters and they spell out 'Puccini Zinest.' That's the chocolate manufacturer who provided their products for this event. And, if I'm not mistaken, and I know I'm not, Puccini Zinest is in the Netherlands, a stone's throw from Belgium."

I squinted to make sense of what I was reading. "So, you think the woman who wrote the note works for that company? And what would she have wanted with Jules Leurant and Earvin Roels?"

"You're getting way ahead of yourself," Franz said. "We don't even know who she is."

"We do! We do. I mean, I do." I was all but jumping up and down. "It was on the boarding pass—Hortensia Vermeulen. And that's not all. I found out from someone who works at Geneva on the Lake that Hortensia isn't the only international guest. There's a gentleman staying at the hotel as well, and his passport is from the Netherlands."

Herbert shook his head. "I'm surprised the sheriff's department isn't taking this seriously."

"They're not taking it at all. Deputy Hickman blew me off as usual."

Franz reached his hand out to me. "Let me see that note again."

None of us said a word as he took his time rereading it. "I've got some contacts of my own at Geneva on the Lake. No promises but I'll see what I can find out about our guest from the Netherlands."

He handed the note back to me and clasped his hands in front of his chest. "The winner of this grand competition will be walking away with enough money to start their own company. Do you know who the contributors are?"

I thought back for a moment to one of our WOW meetings when Madeline Martinez went off on a tangent about how she and her husband had to scrimp and save for years, and borrow money from her mother-in-law, to open Billsburrow Winery. And I distinctly remembered hearing her say, "We didn't have the luxury of being handed money by giant corporations and major publishers like the winner of our Chocolate and Wine event will be."

"It has to be those chocolate manufacturing companies as well as the major media publications. The wine trail provides the resources and we were the ones who had to cough up money for that."

Franz rubbed his chin for a moment. "Don't repeat this verbatim but what I'm saying is maybe Jules and his nephew were being bribed by one of those companies and something went miserably wrong."

"Bribed? What do you mean?"

"Like throwing the race?" Herbert chirped in.

By now Franz had chafed his chin to the extent his skin was pink. "It's pure speculation but a definite possibility."

I froze. "If you're right, that could be what got Jules killed and could be why Earvin took a hike. Unless, Earvin's face down somewhere, too."

"I'll do what I can, Norrie. Like I said, I have contacts at Geneva on the Lake. If there seems to be a connection between this Hortensia Vermeulen and the man from the Netherlands, they'll know. Is the sheriff's department looking for Mr. Roels?"

"No. It hasn't been forty-eight hours."

Franz groaned. "Keep us informed, will you?"

"Absolutely. And thanks."

Franz and Herbert went back to whatever it was they were doing with the racking and Alan walked with me to their office.

"Franz always keeps his word. He won't let you down," Alan said. "By the way, how did the wine pairing go this morning? Were people the least bit hesitant about tasting the Cabernet Sauvignon, even though we were vindicated?"

"I saw a few people scrutinize their wineglass and one woman actually used her own bottled water to rinse off the lip edge, but other than that, we were fine. I'm not sure if I can say the same thing about what's going on at the Grey Egret."

"Oh, you're right. The chocolatier is missing. Yeesh."

"I sent Fred's wife, Emma, in Earvin's place. It'll be a learning experience for her." *Or a disaster that I'll never live down.* "Um, come to think of it, I really should head over there. Thanks, Alan. Have a good afternoon."

Cold stinging air bit my face as I slammed their office door shut and walked the quarter mile down our driveway to the Grey Egret. Like our parking lot, theirs was packed, too. I followed a few customers into their winery and went directly to their tasting room. The Grey Egret always reminded me of a classy lodge with its high-beamed ceiling and framed photos of waterfowl. It was a much smaller building than Two Witches, but what it lacked in space, it made up for in style. With its gray and teal color combination and just the perfect accent pieces, I would have sworn Don and Theo had HGTV's Joanna Gaines design the place for them.

A crowd similar in size to the one that graced our winery this morning was out in full force, watching the afternoon's chocolate confection demonstration. With a smaller space, the event holders didn't have as much elbow room as the ones in our winery did, but their view was unobstructed with the same semicircle set-up.

Emma stood a few yards away at a large prep table, complete with the identical tempering machine and accoutrements. Don was standing to her right, and it looked as if he was poised and ready to catch her should she faint on the spot. He kept wiping his brow and taking deep breaths. Emma's voice was tenuous, but she went through the motions of showing the audience how to dip chocolate as if she'd done it a hundred times instead of once.

At least they were preparing the exact same confection as earlier in the day—chocolate butter cream patties. I glanced around the room and saw that the tasting room tables were all manned by the Grey Egret's staff. The only person I didn't see was Theo. I figured he was either in the kitchen or their office.

I positioned myself off to the side so I could watch Emma and offer moral support should she suddenly have a major meltdown. My mind reeled with all sorts of unsettling scenarios, but never once did it conjure up the actual sequence of events that took place minutes later.

Like our winery on biting cold days, the Grey Egret's entrance door sent an arctic blast through the place. I felt it immediately and rubbed my arms. Seconds later, I heard the thud of heavy footsteps and turned to see Earvin Roels charging toward the demonstration table. He tossed his outer coat over an empty chair and moved like nobody's business. The tiny hairs on the nape of his neck looked as if they had been charged with electricity, and his pristine chef's jacket was rumpled and splotched with dirt.

"Stop! Stop this instant!" Then he said something in Dutch or German before adding, "The chocolate is too hot. Too hot! I can see it running off the confection mixture. Stop! Immediately!"

Emma gasped and so did I. Running down his cheek was a thin line of blood. Don must have seen it, too.

Without wasting a second, he handed Earvin one of those fancy napkins that were on the demo table. "Your cheek. Your cheek is bleeding." Earvin took the napkin, patted his cheek, saw the blood, and patted it dry. "A paper cut, that's all. I shall require a moment to freshen up." It was one of the rare times I'd seen Don speechless. He pointed to the corridor where the restrooms were located and watched, along with the rest of us, as Earvin shot off to presumably wash his face.

Theo, who emerged from whatever he was doing in the kitchen, rushed over. "What was that all about?" he whispered.

Meanwhile, poor Emma was still standing, dipping fork in her hand, looking at the chocolate mixture. She took a deep breath, swallowed hard and spoke to the crowd. "I'm sure Mr. Roels is correct. About the temperature of the chocolate. I should have mentioned this earlier. Chocolate shouldn't be tempered if it is going to be eaten immediately afterward. That's why the chocolates you're going to sample today with the Grey Egret's Merlot were made earlier at Geneva on the Lake by master chocolatier Earvin Roels. Today's demonstration is to show you the process, and, in a moment or two, you'll be privy to a fascinating presentation. Mr. Roels was unfortunately detained but thank goodness he's here in the building to dazzle you with one of his original creations in butter cream."

The audience applauded and Emma gave a slight bow.

Then Theo addressed the guests. "While we wait for Mr. Roels to resume the set-up, please feel free to taste our other wine samples. Our staff is ready to assist you. Once Mr. Roels returns and prepares his demonstration table, we'll invite you back to watch the program."

I expected some grumbling, but there wasn't any, only the sound of chairs being moved against the wooden floor as the event holders moved to the tasting tables.

Don, Theo, Emma, and I leaned toward each other, forming a tight circle that reminded me of a football huddle.

"What the hell do you suppose happened to him?" Don asked. "And that cut was no little scrape."

Theo shrugged. "The face, forehead, and scalp bleed like crazy, even if it's a nothing cut. My five-year-old nephew once fell on the concrete in front of his house and there was blood everywhere. Looked like a massacre. Turned out to be nothing. Except for the blood stains on the concrete. I think they're still visible."

"How would that explain the smeared dirt on his white jacket?" I asked.

"A bad fall maybe?" Emma ventured. "It *is* slippery out there."

Don shook his head. "Yeah, but that doesn't explain where the heck he was or why he didn't bother to inform his driver or our winery, for that matter, that he was going to take an unscheduled break. We thought we were left in the lurch. Frankly, that was downright inconsiderate of him, to say the least."

"Inconsiderate for him," I said. "I'm the one with egg on my face. I called Deputy Hickman thinking the guy had been abducted or worse. Now I have to call back and get lectured about not jumping to conclusions. Darn it all. Where on earth was he? And what was he doing?"

"Shh! You can ask him yourself. He's on his way back. Wearing one of our aprons over that chef's jacket of his. One of our employees must have given it to him. His face looks a tad better, but that's not saying much."

Up close, I could see the cut on Earvin's face was formidable. It was just above his left eye and the dried blood almost made it appear as if he had two eyebrows. Earvin was headed directly for the demonstration table, but I blocked his path.

"That cut above your eye looks nasty. You may need to get stitches once your presentation is over. What happened?"

"I bumped into something sharp. That's all. And now, please, I must begin my demonstration."

Hmm, first a paper cut, now something sharp... "If something's going on, we should know about it."

"The only thing about to go on is my presentation. Now, please, let me begin."

With that, Earvin brushed me aside and positioned himself behind the large table. Don and Emma eyeballed each other before Don motioned for Emma to assist Earvin as she had done at Two Witches.

"Ladies and gentlemen," Theo announced, "our program is about to resume. Please return to your seats and feel free to continue with your wine tasting once Mr. Roels has concluded."

Theo and Don moved to the rear of their tasting room and I followed. When I was positive we were out of earshot, I whispered, "Do you think someone tried to kill him?"

Don stared straight ahead at the demo table. "Given his attitude, I can think of lots of people who'd want to."

Chapter 14

Prior to racing off to have Franz translate the note I found, I told the limousine driver from Round-About-Seneca that we'd call his company if Mr. Roels showed up. No sense having the guy wait it out for nothing. "You probably should call the limo company," I said to Don and Theo. "They'll need to send the driver here to take Earvin back to the hotel." By now, the three of us had positioned ourselves near the kitchen. Still in full view of the demonstration, but far enough away so we wouldn't be overheard. "Did either of you get a good look at that cut of his? It's deep. And wide. I don't think he ran into anything. More like a knife ran into him. That's a pretty long gash. Deep, too."

Theo nodded. "He really should have it checked out, but that's his business. Maybe once he gets back to Geneva on the Lake someone there will convince him to get to an urgent care center."

Don grinded his teeth and then bit his lower lip. "I doubt he'll go. They ask too many questions. And once they check out his injury, they may find it couldn't have been caused by bumping into something. If he was attacked, chances are it wasn't random. I mean, where on this wine trail is the guy going to get accosted? Inside another winery or a restaurant? Not likely. My guess is he got into an altercation with someone he knew and whoever it was doesn't play nice."

"The guy should at least get a tetanus shot," Theo said.

I laughed. "Tell him that. Listen, while Earvin was giving his demonstration at Two Witches, a classy-looking auburn-haired woman walked in. Fortyish. She didn't stay long. Only a minute or, two but Earvin froze for a second and the two of them shot each other looks."

"What kind of looks?" Theo asked.

"The kind where one person widens his or her eyes and the other person narrows theirs."

"And you could see those details?"

"Only on Earvin's face. I'm kind of assuming the rest."

"Well, don't assume, Norrie. It could have been anything."

"Or, it could have been the woman from Belgium. Hortensia Vermeulen. The one whose trash I ransacked. Oh and, by the way, Franz translated the note I found. It was written in Dutch. Dutch! That's what they speak in Belgium. Anyway, the note didn't say much, except the person who wrote it told the other person they have unfinished business that wouldn't go away in spite of the fact that the person went away. Something like that."

"And you think the woman who was in your winery was Hortensia and that she might have been responsible for what happened to Earvin?" Theo asked.

"All I'm saying is these little clues are adding up. Maybe the note was meant for Jules and she never gave it to him. Or maybe it was a rough draft and she did give him the real deal."

Don chucked. "Sorry. The only real deal Jules got was the one that put him six feet under."

Suddenly, the audience applauded.

"He must be finishing up," Theo said. "We've been so busy gabbing, we weren't paying attention. Oh hell, I'd better call that limo company."

I grabbed him by the wrist. "You might want to hold off and see if Earvin has other plans. Could be he made his own arrangements for when he leaves the Grey Egret."

"Good idea."

"Meanwhile, I'm not off the hook with Deputy Hickman. I need to make that call and I need to make it now. Give me a minute."

While Don and Theo moved closer to the presentation table where Earvin was still conducting his demonstration, I stood in the entryway of their kitchen and dialed the sheriff's office. Once again, Gladys Pipp picked up the phone.

Hmm, maybe I don't have to speak with Grizzly Gary. I can simply leave a message with Gladys. "Hi, Gladys. I need to leave a message for Deputy Hickman."

"That's good because he's not in his office. There was a ruckus at one of the wineries so he and another deputy went to check it out."

"Which winery? Can you tell me? Not mine, I hope. I was just there. I'm at the Grey Egret and I didn't hear any sirens going up our driveway."

"Your neighbor's winery. Gable Hill. Shh. Not a word you heard this from me."

"My lips are sealed. Thanks, Gladys. Have a good day."

"What about your message for Deputy Hickman?"

"Oh my. I must really be losing it. Please tell him Earvin Roels showed up at the Grey Egret after all."

"That's it?"

"For now."

"Trouble in River City," I announced as soon as I ended my call with Gladys and walked back to where Theo and Don were standing.

They both looked at me as if I had two heads.

"River City. *The Music Man.* Geez, I figured if anyone would get that reference, it would be one of you."

"Oh, we got it all right," Theo said. "Wouldn't want to let our team down. We were just surprised you knew the reference."

"Very funny. Anyway, that was Gladys Pipp on the phone. I was spared another lecture from my favorite deputy. He's over at Gable Hill because there was some sort of ruckus there. I'm calling Stephanie right now."

Before anyone had time to form a sentence, I had placed the call and the phone was ringing.

"Hi. This is Norrie Ellington from Two Witches. Is Stephanie available?"

The voice at the other end sounded hesitant. "Uh, this isn't the best time. We had a little problem with the chocolate demonstration, and it kind of escalated. Oh, hold on a second, Stephanie's stopped cryin—I mean, she's on her way over. I just motioned to her she had a call. Is everything all right at your winery?"

"Can you please put Stephanie on the line?"

I could hear lots of background noise, but it sounded pretty normal for a tasting room. I figured whatever happened, Deputy Hickman got things under control.

"I'm waiting for Stephanie to get to the phone," I told the guys.

"No worries," Don replied. "Let us know what you find out. We've got to wrap things up with Earvin."

The two of them shot off toward the demo table, and I leaned against their kitchen doorframe, waiting for Stephanie to pull herself together and talk to me. At first, I thought something went wrong with the cell phone connection, but what I thought was a weird static turned out to be Stephanie wheezing.

"Norrie? One of our tasting room employees said it was you on the phone. Is everything all right at your place because it's a catastrophe over here. Hold on a second, will you?"

I couldn't possibly imagine what had happened because the Chocolate and Wine Festival was usually a pretty calm event, unlike the fall tastings when the college fraternities rented out tour buses and the students drank themselves into oblivion.

"I'm here," Stephanie said. "Stanislav washed up and put on a clean apron. He's resuming his demonstration."

"What happened? I found out from Gladys Pipp at the public safety building that Deputy Hickman was called over to your place. Long story but I had to call him because Earvin disappeared but then he showed up. Bruised but tight-lipped. What's going on?"

"As you know, we had a huge crowd but everything was under control and our guests were all seated around the long oak table we use for special events. Stanislav was quiet and focused as he arranged the utensils and cookware to his liking. The tempering machine was running smoothly, and the chocolate smelled heavenly."

"Did he knock over the machine, spill chocolate, and have a meltdown?"

"Not exactly, but close enough."

"Oh my God. What?"

"Aspen and Ivy, our tasting room girls, were assisting him. Aspen's a family and consumer science major so she's pretty familiar with how things go in a kitchen."

"Family and consumer science? You mean Home Ec?"

"Yeah, Home Ec. Anyway, Stanislav was explaining to the crowd how to temper the chocolate so it's shiny and breaks off with one snap. His confection was a passion fruit and mango square. A thick creamy mixture that he started to dip when, when, oh, good grief, Norrie, it was horrible. Simply horrible."

"What? What was horrible? I've ruined lots of recipes."

"Not Stanislav."

"Oh no. Your tasting room girls? They messed up?"

"No. Out of the blue, this deranged man, although he didn't look really deranged, he was clean shaven, in his late forties or early fifties maybe, wearing a sharp black turtleneck, pressed trousers, and a black overcoat, stormed over to the demo table and, before anyone could stop him, he snatched the dipping fork from Stanislav and flicked the chocolaty mixture all over Stanislav's face and his pressed white chef's jacket."

I could hear Stephanie pausing to catch her breath, so I didn't say anything and waited.

"Norrie? Are you still listening?"

"Uh-huh. Then what?"

"*Then,* Stanislav had a meltdown. He began screaming in Russian and then another language. German maybe or Dutch. The man who flicked the chocolate grabbed Stanislav by the arm and said something in one of those languages as well. I was positive it was going to get ugly, which it did, so I called the sheriff's office and told them we needed assistance."

"Holy Mackerel! How much uglier did it get?"

"Ugly enough. Stanislav shoved the man back and pointed a finger into his chest, at which point the man snatched the dipping fork and all but poked out one of Stanislav's eyes."

Wow. So much for that age-old expression–poke your eyes out with a fork. "Please don't tell me you had an actual brawl on your hands."

"We would have, but fortunately, something weird happened. This woman, who was probably in the audience but who the heck noticed, stood up and ran to the front of the room. Yelling in Russian, German, Dutch, or Greek, for all I know. The man who accosted Stanislav stopped dead and, after giving our beautiful oak table a kick, stormed out of the winery. The woman was right behind him and none of us tried to stop them."

"Stephanie, was the woman an auburn-haired woman wearing a calf-length winter coat?"

"Who had time to look at her coat, but come to think of it, her hair was on the reddish-brown side. Why? Do you know her?"

"If it's who I think it is, we may all get to know her before this chocolate event is through."

I told Stephanie about my hunch regarding the two international guests who arrived at Geneva on the Lake around the same time as the chocolatiers.

"And those deputies aren't going to pursue it?" she asked.

"Nope. According to Deputy Hickman, they have their own leads and my imagination would be better suited to writing screenplays."

"Hmm. Doesn't mean we can't snoop around. Listen, I've got to get back to the tasting room before some other disaster strikes. Thank God we only have four more days with this hellish event. And to think, I used to love chocolate."

Chapter 15

Don and Theo were absolutely stunned when I told them about the near melee at Stephanie's winery. "Think we should call Rosalee and Catherine to see if anything went wrong at their wineries?"

"Nah," Theo said. "They're probably busting their butts as it is. Look, knowing what a drama queen Catherine is, I guarantee if someone dropped an olive and stepped on it, she'd be on the phone. But I will say this much, something fishy is going on for sure, and I think Jules's murder is in the center of it."

"We need a plan. Nancy Drew always had a plan." *Oh my God! I'm taking advice from a fictional character.*

Theo's jaw dropped, but Don had no problem responding. "Your last few plans, if I'm not mistaken, bordered on insanity, and that's putting it nicely. Before you go rushing off with some harebrained scheme, at least run it by Theo and me. Fair enough?"

"Sure."

When my sister and her husband left for the rainforests of Costa Rica, they told me I could rely on Theo and Don for any help I needed. What she didn't tell me was she probably gave them a "heads-up" and told them to watch out for me. Most likely she used words like *unpredictable* and *overly zealous.* It was that obvious.

I glanced at their tasting room, and the audience was mesmerized by Earvin's presentation. Emma didn't look quite as nervous and that was a relief.

"I'd better head back to my own neck of the woods," I said to the guys. *Because right now, I'm starving and there's a bistro sandwich with my name on it unless Fred sells it to someone else first.* "Call me tonight and let me know what happened with Earvin. Like if he went with the limo or if it was something else."

"You got it, Nancy," Don said. "We'll also let you know if we discover a secret staircase."

I laughed on my way out the door and headed back up the hill. At least the nasty wind wasn't in my face this time. I figured things hadn't slowed down in our tasting room or Cammy would have called my cell. Sure enough, the place was bustling when I got inside. I made a beeline for the bistro and, in a matter of seconds, had my hands wrapped around a ham and cheese sandwich.

"Emma doing okay?" Fred asked. "She looked like a scared rabbit."

"She's doing a fantastic job. I really owe her for stepping in."

"More like being tossed in."

"Yeah, that too. Hey, want to hear the kicker? Earvin, that rat scoundrel, showed up after all and took over. It was really freaky. He was all disheveled and had a gash over his eye. Said he crashed into something."

"No kidding. This is probably going to sound odd, but a couple of guys came in after the demonstration was over. They weren't ticketed customers for the event, just out and about grabbing lunch. Anyway, I overheard one of them say, 'Slow down on the booze or you'll wind up eating dirt like that other guy.' And then his friend answered with, 'He wasn't kissing the far end of the damn parking lot, he was trying to get away from that *Fatal Attraction* broad with the reddish hair.'"

Eating dirt? Fatal Attraction broad? I dropped the sandwich on my plate mid-bite and quickly covered my mouth. The timing made sense. After all, the woman would have had plenty of time to threaten Earvin, if that's what she did, and still make it over to Gable Hill Winery in time to break up the fracas between Stanislav and the mystery player from abroad. "Did they say anything else?"

Fred shook his head. "No, but when you said Earvin was disheveled, I wondered if it wasn't him those guys were talking about. Then again, it could have been anyone. These wine trails are packed with people during the events. And some of them hit the wine pretty hard."

"Well, I doubt Earvin got that cut from something he accidently ran into, or from a little tussle in the parking lot. Unless that tussle involved something sharp. Hmm, far end of the lot you said?"

"That's what the guy said."

"Our far end is toward the winery lab. Lots of bushes on the side of the lot and some big trees."

"You think you'll find something if you scope out the area?" Fred asked.

"Probably litter and maybe some paper cups, but it'll plague me if I don't. Besides, if I wait until tomorrow morning, the vineyard crew will have tidied up. They're up and at it before dawn. Geez, in Manhattan, some of us are just getting home from a night out. Anyway, the snow is hard and shiny by now, real easy to spot something."

"Maybe you should let Earvin deal with it. He can notify the sheriff's office."

"We couldn't even talk him into going to an urgent care center. I think he's hiding something or scared of something. For all we know, he could be the next victim. It's no secret Jules Leurant was murdered."

Fred pulled his long ponytail tighter. "True, but that didn't involve blood. Whoever killed Jules had to be crafty and deliberate. That doesn't fit with the description of the woman those guys gave."

"Maybe she's both—clever *and* unhinged. Then again, Theo and Don would tell me I'm jumping to conclusions. Anyway, the parking lot's only a few yards away, the wind has stopped howling, and I could use some fresh air after gobbling down that tasty sandwich."

"If you find anything, let me know."

I smiled, thanked him, and darted out the door before I got tied up chatting with Cammy, Lizzie, or, worse yet, Glenda. She'd probably want to cast a purifying spell on me or spray something noxious on my clothes to ward off evil doers. Yeesh.

Thankfully, no one saw me, and even if they did, it would have been impossible for them to drop what they were doing and chitchat. The chocolate event brought out lots of customers and, from what I could see in our tasting room, no one was shying away from the Cabernet Sauvignon.

Maybe I was going overboard with this little investigative jaunt of mine in the parking lot, but it wasn't as if I was in a rush to settle down at my laptop and work. It was hard to think of romance with bodies cropping up all around me. Even with a packed tasting room, the far end of the lot only had a few cars. The vineyard crew had seen to it that the snow was removed and piled up on the sides. Only a thin white surface of snow was visible on the gravel.

For years, my father debated whether to have the lot paved. Ultimately, he decided to leave the gravel because a paved lot in winter would mean slippery surfaces and would require sanding, or worse yet, salting. The gravel counteracted the snow so the surface didn't pose as much of a threat for walkers.

I ambled down to the far end, not really sure of what it was I was looking for. Sure enough, there were a few empty cups, a plastic bag that rolled around in the wind, and what looked like an empty candy wrapper. Too bad I wasn't trying to solve a mystery of who went off their diet.

It was easy to see where some of the cars had been parked because the ground underneath them wasn't as frozen as the rest of the lot. Pulling my scarf tighter, I decided to have a closer look at those spaces. If what Fred overheard was the case, it would stand to reason the altercation, or whatever the heck it was, took place in one of those spots.

Bending down, I studied the ground, hoping to find a file, a pair of scissors, or anything that would smack of a sharp object that nearly poked Earvin's eye out. No such luck. Nothing. Zilch. If indeed the *Fatal Attraction* woman was holding something of the kind, she wasn't careless enough to drop it. That kind of stuff only happened in the movies.

Fred was right. This was something Earvin needed to deal with, not me. But Earvin *wasn't* going to deal with it, and the last thing we needed was another dead chocolatier. That kind of thing didn't bode well in keeping with winery events. I kicked the gravel and watched the small pieces of rock go airborne before landing near my feet. That was the moment I saw it. Not a piece of gravel and not a sharp object, but something caught my eye because its pearly white color reflected in the late afternoon sun.

It was a button. And if I wasn't mistaken, it looked like the same kind of pearled button on the collar of Earvin's classy white chef's jacket. I was about to grab it when I remembered something, fingerprints. I immediately pulled out a nasty old tissue from my pocket and used that instead to retrieve the button.

"This can't be a coincidence," I said minutes later as I ran through the winery, waving the old tissue in the air.

Cammy looked up from her tasting table, as did Sam, Glenda, and Roger. Only Lizzie muttered something about needing larger trash receptacles. I went straight to the bistro, where Fred was chopping up some green peppers and held the tissue under his nose.

"Please tell me you didn't find a roach," he whispered.

"No, a clue. Thanks to what you overheard earlier, I think we can conclude it was Earvin and that auburn-haired woman who were duking it out in our parking lot, for lack of a better explanation." I opened the tissue and pointed to the button. "Look. It's a pearl button. It looks exactly like the ones on the chef's jacket Earvin wore today. Oh my gosh. Earvin! He's probably still at the Grey Egret. I've got to call them and ask Theo or Don if he's missing a button."

Fred didn't say a word as I grabbed my phone.

"Theo? Is that you? Is Earvin still there? Hurry! See if he's missing a button on his chef's jacket."

"He's over by the door on his cell phone. What's going on?"

"No time to talk. Just look."

"Aargh. Hold on."

I hated dead air space on the phone. I never knew if the call died or what. And as much as I detested canned music while I was on hold, it was better than nothing. Unless someone had no taste in music. Then I'd take dead air space.

"Holy crap, Norrie. I couldn't tell. He had his overcoat on."

"Is he still on the phone?"

"Yeah."

"Theo, you absolutely have to find a way to get that overcoat off him and check out his chef's jacket. If he's missing a button, I know what happened to him."

"You're going to owe me big time. Big time!"

Again, dead air space. This time longer.

"I got your answer but my God! We might be sued. The only thing I could think of was to accuse him of walking off with our apron. He immediately opened his overcoat and all I saw was the soiled chef's jacket. And yes! Yes! You'll be happy to know it's missing the third button down. Earvin told me he left the apron on the counter. I apologized profusely. Heaven help us. We've got two more days with this guy."

"If he lasts that long."

Chapter 16

"Chances are, it *is* Earvin's missing button," Theo said. "So, what's the big hoo-hah?"

"Okay, the courts would consider it hearsay but Fred heard customers talking about a scuffle in our parking lot. The far end of the lot. They saw that woman with the auburn hair and, thanks to my little discovery, we now know who she was scuffling with. It had to be our chocolatier. Face it, the woman probably had a small knife on her or maybe a sharp manicuring tool. Those things can be deadly. Trust me."

"Unless Earvin wants to press charges, there's nothing you can do. Drop it."

"I'll tell you what I need to do. What *we* need to do. We need to find out once and for all if Hortensia Vermeulen is the same woman."

Theo let out a groan that seemed to go on indefinitely. "And I suppose this little escapade of yours involves more snooping around the hotel?"

"We don't have to snoop. We can just sit in their ostentatious bar near the lobby tonight and see if she comes in. Chances are the bartender knows her by name. They always do when it comes to important guests. And she has to be important if she's staying in the high-priced-over-the-top Chapel."

"Norrie, we can't go because—"

"Theo, it's important. That woman's business with Earvin might have been the reason Jules Leurant was murdered."

"And if you find out it's the same woman? Then what?"

"Okay, here's where it gets a tad dicey."

"Oh no."

I switched the phone to my other ear and rolled my neck. "If it is her, we've got to find out if she's got a prescription for Ambien in her room. Right now, she's not a suspect as far as those deputies are concerned. From what little I could gather from Grizzly Gary, they're looking at the other chocolatiers as well as poor Stephanie."

"So, you plan on doing what? Getting into her room? Good thing you're dating a lawyer. You'll need him."

"Bradley's out of town and I won't need a lawyer. Not if I'm careful. The night cleaning crew is different than the daytime one. I won't pretend to be Hortensia. I'll tell whoever's working in that part of the hotel that I paid her a visit and left my bag in her bathroom."

"Like I said, good thing you're dating a lawyer."

"So, will you do it? Come over to Geneva on the Lake this evening?"

"You really don't read your emails, do you? There's one marked URGENT from Madeline Martinez. There's an emergency WOW meeting at Rosalee's tonight. Her house, not Terrace Wineries. Seven thirty. Madeline couldn't hold it at her place because one of her kids has a scout meeting there. Anyway, you can present your little plan to them and see their reaction."

"Oh crap. Really? An emergency WOW meeting? Why?"

"The email didn't say. Only that it was important."

"Ugh. At least Rosalee usually has good cookies." For the life of me, I couldn't imagine why we needed to hold an emergency WOW meeting right in the middle of an event that seemed to be stressing everyone out. It didn't matter. If Hortensia Vermeulen did have business with Earvin, she wouldn't be leaving the Finger Lakes until after the grand competition on Saturday.

By the time I got off the phone with Theo, the crowd had thinned in our tasting room. Cammy and Glenda were putting the opened bottles in their mini-fridges for tomorrow, while Sam and Roger were chatting it up with the customers at their stations.

Lizzie waved me over as soon as she spied me. "I hate it when our guests leave trash all over the place, too. Is that why you waved that tissue?"

"Huh?"

"The tissue. You came in here waving a tissue. I usually throw the trash out and not make a big deal of it."

"It wasn't trash. It was a clue."

As soon as I said the word "clue," I knew I should have kept my mouth shut. I had no choice but to tell Lizzie about my find.

"You need to be up front with that master chocolatier. Hold out that button and see what his reaction is. That's precisely what Nancy Drew would do."

That, and know how to spell out SOS backwards with lipstick...

I thanked Lizzie for her insights before returning to the tasting room to let Cammy know what I'd found.

"I'd stay and help you guys clean up," I said, "but I've got an emergency WOW meeting tonight. Don't ask because I don't know why either. I haven't had a moment to work on my own stuff and I'm petrified I'll miss a deadline."

Cammy raised her palm in the air and motioned for me to slow down. "It's okay. We're fine."

"I'm not so sure about everyone else. Listen, if you're going to be up late tonight, I'll call and explain."

"Late is any time after midnight. Remember, I get hauled into my family's bar at all hours if someone doesn't show up. They should rename the place Cammy's At All Hours instead of Rosinetti's."

I laughed. "Thanks. Catch you later."

Charlie was butting his food dish against the wall when I walked into the house. Yikes. Had I forgotten to feed him this morning? It seemed like days ago when I got up.

"Hang on, Charlie. Kibble's on the way." I poured him a giant helping and then, feeling bad that he might have gone hungry, I added a few mini pieces of Swiss cheese to the mix, along with some leftover ham. And while I wasn't exactly starving after consuming the sandwich Fred made me, I figured I should at least have a small bite to eat in case Rosalee hadn't gotten around to baking cookies.

Since I was more of a preparer than a cook, I made myself a grilled cheese sandwich and washed it down with a Coke. Francine would have cringed. At least the bread was organic.

The kitchen clock said five fifteen and that gave me a full hour to work on *Beguiled into Love.* Maybe that was what happened to Jules. Maybe that woman beguiled him because she wanted something and when he didn't come through, or *couldn't,* that was when she killed him. Of course, I'd need to find a spray bottle of Ambien in her room and even if I did, Deputy Hickman would tell me the evidence was obtained illegally and I was under arrest. Terrific.

The next hour and a half flew by and I had fifteen minutes to freshen up and get over to Rosalee's. At least she was right across the road and, in good weather, walking distance. Not tonight, though. Too dark, too cold, and way too creepy.

My Toyota started right up and I headed directly to Rosalee's house, after making sure I had closed the doggie door so Charlie wouldn't be tempted to follow me as he'd done on numerous other occasions when I went out after dark.

Three vehicles were already parked in front of Rosalee's farmhouse and I recognized all of them—Stephanie's SUV, Catherine's sedan, and Theo's well-worn winery truck. Seconds later, Madeline's white Land Rover appeared. She pulled up next to me, slammed the door of her car, and groaned. "Just what we need, a meeting tonight."

"Um, I thought you called the meeting," I said.

"I had no choice. Catherine was insistent. Insistent and somewhat over the edge. She wouldn't tell me what was going on over the phone, only that we needed to meet and it had to be done right away."

By now we were at Rosalee's front door and I rang the bell.

A voice from inside hollered, "It's open. We're in the kitchen. Come on in!"

I was familiar with the layout of Rosalee's house and walked directly into her kitchen with Madeline at my heels. Two of Rosalee's Corgis were sprawled out in the foyer, and I could see another one under the kitchen table. As for the fourth, it was anyone's guess.

The WOW crew was gathered around the huge oak table and everyone was talking at once. At least I was in luck. There was a huge platter of shortbread cookies smack dab in the middle. Usually only Theo attended the WOW meetings but apparently since the email said URGENT, Don was there as well.

"Help yourself to coffee," Rosalee said. "Cups are on the counter and I made a full pot."

I waited while Madeline poured herself a cup and then did the same. We took the last two seats at the table and muttered our hellos to everyone.

"Okay. The gang's all here," Don said. "Now can someone tell us what's going on?"

Catherine picked up the napkin in front of her and fidgeted with it until she tore off a small corner. "Allete thinks her life is in danger and refuses to return to our wineries tomorrow for her planned demonstration."

I all but jumped out of my seat. "Why? What happened? Did someone splash chocolate on her too?"

"Too?" Madeline asked. "Who got splattered with chocolate?"

Stephanie rolled her eyes, leaned into the table, and gave us a blow by blow description of what had happened to Stanislav at her winery. To hear her tell the tale, the Red Wedding from *Game of Thrones* paled in comparison.

"That's horrible," Rosalee said. "Adolescent behavior, if you ask me, but I'd hardly consider it a reason to be concerned. We get nutcases in our wineries all the time. Fortunately, it's winter because some of them aren't the least bit shy about removing their clothing."

Rosalee's comment set off a series of side conversations that finally ended when Theo said, "Let's get back to Allete. What's her issue?"

I looked at Catherine and noticed the napkin she had been holding was now reduced to a small pile of pieces. She took a deep breath and rubbed her hands together. "Something crawled down Allete's arm, underneath the chef's jacket she was wearing. It happened while she was showing the audience how to create multi-layered florets on top of chocolate ovals. It was disastrous. She shrieked and began to remove her jacket, only hers had the kind of buttons that were in two straight lines in front and the more she tried to unbutton them, the worse it got. She kept screaming in French before she was finally able to remove the jacket."

"Then what?" Don asked.

"The jacket landed on the prep table and, in full view of our customers, a nasty-looking spider made its way out of the sleeve. That's when one of our visitors shouted, 'Is that a brown recluse spider? They're poisonous as hell.'"

I bit my lower lip and grimaced. "I'm afraid to ask what happened next."

Catherine hugged her arms to her chest. "One of our tasting room employees grabbed a glass and quickly covered the spider. We trapped it and moved it into a jar. I brought the damn thing with me in case any of you know if it's dangerous. Oh, good Lord! We had the exterminator over just a few weeks ago."

"What about Allete?" Madeline asked. "Was she bitten? Is she all right?"

Catherine gathered the small scraps of her napkin into her hand, stood, and dropped them into Rosalee's kitchen garbage container. "No. She wasn't bitten, but she was convinced someone put that spider into her chef's jacket before she put it on. We tried to explain that this is a rural area and New York has lots of spiders, but she was inconsolable. Said she thought whoever murdered Jules Leurant was after her next."

"I can get this solved in thirty seconds," I said. "Well, not thirty seconds, but close enough. Godfrey Klein, my brother-in-law's entomology partner at Cornell's Experiment Station, will be able to identify that sucker in no time flat."

Rosalee flung her hands into the air. "What are you waiting for? Pull out that cell phone of yours and make the call!"

Chapter 17

"You sure it can't wait until tomorrow?" Godfrey asked when I got him on the line. Everyone in Rosalee's kitchen stopped talking and listened to my part of the conversation.

"No, it's a matter of—"

"Please don't tell me life or death because you just told me no one got bit."

"It's not that, it's worse." I then made a pleading sound and used the word "please" at least half a dozen times. "Listen, how about if I meet you at Dunkin' Donuts on Hamilton Street? They're open late and it's real bright inside. You'll be able to get a good look at the spider. I'll even buy you a donut."

"Can't you just snap a photo of it with your phone and email me?"

"I want to be absolutely certain. A photo won't do. Please?"

"One donut? You're going to make me drive out in the cold for one donut?"

"Fine. Two. What do you say?"

"Twenty-five minutes. And you'll need to buy me coffee, too."

"You're the best. See you in twenty-five minutes."

"Okay, everyone," I said when my call to Godfrey ended. "You all heard that. I'm on my way to get an official answer."

"Do you want any of us to go with you?" Stephanie asked. "It's not a problem for me. My husband can put the boys to bed instead of having a love affair with the remote."

"Nah. I'm fine. The roads are clear and it's not late. But how are we going to get Allete back in the game tomorrow?"

"We'll stay here and figure something out," Don said. "Is that okay, Rosalee?"

"Fine with me. I'm not going anywhere, and the Corgis don't look as if they're in a hurry to leave the house either."

I stood and put my coffee cup in the sink. "I'll call Theo's cell since it's on speed dial and let you know what I find out. Meanwhile, he and Don can fill you in about Earvin's disappearing act today and the tussle he had in our parking lot."

Madeline helped herself to another cookie and turned to face me. "You mean there were more shenanigans going on?"

I chuckled. "Interesting choice of words."

Although the usual cars were parked in front of Wegmans, Hamilton Street in Geneva was practically deserted when I got to Dunkin' Donuts. I figured the college kids were either studying or hanging out at the bars and the locals weren't about to leave their warm houses for a late-night java stop.

Godfrey was sitting by the window and he had a cup of coffee in his hand. There was also another one on the table. I watched as he brushed a few strands of his wispy light brown hair from his face. I had to admit, there was something endearing about his receding hairline and cherubic face.

"Hey," he said as I approached the table, "it's cold and I figured you could use a hot coffee right away."

I smiled and took a sip. "What will it be? Jelly? Frosted? Glazed?"

"Surprise me but don't make it glazed."

I came back to the table with two cream-filled donuts and one maple frosted. Godfrey grabbed the maple one and motioned for me to sit. "Okay. Where's this man-eating spider that made me leave the comforts of home?"

"It's in my bag. Hold on a second."

I sat down, looked around to make sure no one was watching us, and then placed the jar in front of him. Seconds later, he erupted in gales of laughter. So hard, in fact, that, at one point, I thought he'd choke.

"What? What's so funny?"

"You're looking at the Parasteatoda tepidariorum, better known as the American House Spider. Perfectly harmless. These poor guys have horrible vision and have been known to build new webs if they can't find their way back to their original one."

"That's it? A benign insect?"

Godfrey picked up the jar and took a closer look. "Spider. Not insect. I can't believe someone went into hysterics over this little guy. I suppose you'll want me to relocate him."

Or dump him and step on him. Either or. "That would be great. Oh my gosh. Give me thirty seconds to shoot off a text to Theo to tell him the spider wasn't poisonous."

"No problem."

Godfrey munched on his second donut while I gave the all-clear to Theo.

"Okay. I'm done," I said to Godfrey. "With that part of the mess anyway."

"What do you mean?"

"Ugh. It's a long story. Next cup of coffee is definitely on me."

"I'm not going anywhere and this place doesn't close for at least an hour."

I took a large swallow from my coffee cup and, beginning with that unpleasant visit from Deputy Hickman informing me that Jules Leurant's body was found dead in the snow, I went on to explain everything that had happened in the past week.

When I finished, Godfrey took my wrist and gave it a squeeze. "No wonder you were such a wreck over the spider incident. *That,* on top of the chocolate fiasco at Stephanie's place and your guy disappearing without a word only to come back looking as if he'd been in a street brawl."

"It's not these little incidents by themselves. It's what they all may have in common."

"What do you mean?"

"I think whoever killed Jules may be sending a not-so-subtle message to the others. Earvin Roels little 'street brawl' involved an auburn-haired lady. Probably the same one who broke up the altercation at Gable Hill Winery. If you must know, I did some snooping at Geneva on the Lake and well, um, I kind of went through the trash belonging to a female guest from Belgium."

"Totally lost but go on."

"Belgium. That's where Jules is, I mean *was,* from. How many international guests from Belgium are going to be staying at the same hotel as the chocolatiers? I thought it was too much of a coincidence, but the sheriff's office wouldn't listen."

"I really hate to ask this, but how did you know there was someone from Belgium staying at the hotel?"

"From a friend of Cammy's who works in reservations, but before you get all hot and bothered over it, Cammy's friend only told us the guest had a passport from Belgium. She wouldn't give us any more info or she'd lose her job."

"Good for her."

"So, like I said, I went through the trash by the woman's door and found a boarding pass. It was made out to Hortensia Vermeulen."

"Hortensia Vermeulen?"

"Dear God! Don't tell me you know who that is."

"Nooo, but I've seen that name before. At least I *think* I've come across that name before. Darn it. I get so much paper mail and email from Cornell that I sometimes glaze over stuff unless it pertains to me directly."

Godfrey tapped his fingers on the table for a second and shook his head. "It'll come to me. Probably at three in the morning. Well, it's getting late, what do you say we call it a night and you can rest easy that the chocolatier from France has nothing to worry about from the itsy-bitsy spider."

"She might not have anything to worry about, but we do. She refuses to give her demonstrations tomorrow. Listen, if we can convince her that the spider was harmless and most likely it was in the wrong place and not the result of someone trying to scare her, maybe we can get her to reconsider."

"We? What's with the 'we?'"

"She's not going to believe me. You're the renowned entomologist. She'll listen to you."

"Wonderful. I've just become renowned."

"You have a doctorate. That's renowned enough. Come on, Godfrey. Drive over to Geneva on the Lake and we can both convince her."

"Norrie, it's after nine."

"Trust me. These are international chocolatiers. They're not farm boys or girls who go to bed at dusk. They're probably just sitting down to dinner or hanging out at the bar, which, by the way, is quite classy."

"Classy bar or not, I have to be at work first thing in the morning."

"Then let's get a move on."

I yanked him by the arm and he groaned. "One hour. That's all I'm giving you. One hour. And believe me when I tell you, I can't wait for Jason to get back from Costa Rica."

Godfrey followed me to Geneva on the Lake, which was less than two miles from Dunkin' Donuts. Thanks to Bluetooth, I called Theo from the road and told him I had a plan. He promptly relayed that info to the others and all I could hear were groans and one gasp. I think it was Catherine.

"Relax, Theo. And tell the ladies to chill out, too. Godfrey's with me. We're going to show Allete the spider and Godfrey will explain that it's a common house spider that got lost from its web and not the result of someone trying to harm her."

Theo moaned. "What are you going to do? Knock on her door and show her the jar with the spider in it?"

"Um, er, I hope not. I'm banking on the fact she'll be hanging out in the bar or maybe finishing up dinner."

"If she's in the dining room, do not take out that spider. Do you hear me?"

"I hear you. You're practically screaming. This is the best option I can think of, given the timeframe. Unless, of course, you and the rest of WOW came up with something better."

Dead silence. "Rosalee thought we could threaten her with a lawsuit, but good luck with that."

"Guess spider-in-the-jar is the plan for now."

"Good. That means we can adjourn this WOW meeting," Theo said. "I'll set up a phone tree to let everyone know how you fared with Allete. Call me as soon as you can get her to agree to be at Terrace Wineries tomorrow morning."

"There's always plan B," I said.

"What's that?"

"We bribe her."

Chapter 18

Allete Barrineau was seated in one of two oversized armchairs near the marble fireplace that graced the bar. Her shoulder-length ash-brown hair cascaded around her neck. Dressed casually in jeans and a dark turtleneck sweater, she looked nothing like she did at the opening event, or in her magazine photos.

"See?" I whispered to Godfrey as we entered the room. "I told you she'd be here. People need to unwind. Darn it. That other armchair is facing hers, and I can't see the woman who's in it. Only that perfectly coiffed hairdo of hers. Let's move in closer. Act nonchalant."

"As opposed to what?"

"Very funny. Oh my gosh. Look at her hair. Look at her hair."

"Whose? And what am I looking at?"

"Not Allete. The woman. It's not the firelight that's casting a reddish hue on her hair, it *is* reddish. You don't suppose it's the same woman who gave Earvin a dueling scar and who broke up the chocolate fight at Stephanie's winery, do you?"

"No clue. Look to your left. There are two available chairs around that small bistro table. I say we sit down before someone else does."

"Fine."

Godfrey and I were only a few feet from Allete and the woman she was speaking with. I looked around the room but didn't see Stanislav, Earvin, or anyone else remotely involved with the chocolate festival. "I suppose we should get a drink from the bar so we don't look as if we're on a stakeout. What goes good after two cups of coffee and donuts?"

"A Tums." Godfrey stood and gave me a wink. "I'll get us club sodas with lime."

I watched Allete as Godfrey made his way to the bar. She didn't appear to be nervous, but she wasn't exactly caroling with laughter. When Godfrey returned, the women were still conversing.

"We can't stay here all night," I said. "We've got to make a move."

Before I could respond, the woman across from Allete stood and walked right past us. Unlike Allete, she wore dark slacks, a dark top, and what appeared to be a white silk pashmina. I didn't know why my eyes focused on her scarf first, but it was only a matter of seconds when I got a better look at her face.

I all but sunk my fingernails into Godfrey's wrist. "It's her. It's her. The auburn-haired woman. Take a good look."

Godfrey turned his head and stared as she blew past us. "Geez Marie. I've seen her before. Well, not her, but her likeness. Maybe in a photo."

"You're no help. Wait a sec. She's only going to the bar. We still have time to find out who she is. Meanwhile, we've got to speak with Allete. Now. While she's alone."

I grabbed my bag and charged over to the now-empty armchair directly across from Allete, sat down, and pulled the chair closer to her. Godfrey stood directly behind me, and I prayed I wouldn't louse things up.

"Allete? I'm not sure if you remember me, but I'm Norrie Ellington from Two Witches Winery. We met at the opening reception for the chocolatiers."

Allete extended her hand and said hello. "I hate to be rude, Miss Ellington, but I'm with someone at the moment and she'll be right back."

"This will only take a second. I heard about the unfortunate incident today at Gable Hill Winery, and that's why I'm here. I'm with Dr. Godfrey Klein, from the New York State Agricultural Experiment Station, Cornell University, to be precise. Dr. Klein is familiar with the species of spider you encountered and well…"

Okay, so maybe it wasn't exactly a smooth segue. I took out the jar from my bag and held it inches from her face. That was when she let out a deafening scream followed by at least three or four "Oh, *mon dieu*."

I tried again. "This spider is really a very—"

"Deadly and poisonous one? And you've brought a New York doctor to tell me that its poison got into my skin somehow? Oh, *mon dieu*! I thought I felt a bite. I felt something."

Allete started to hyperventilate and Godfrey stepped in front of my chair. "Calm down, Miss, Miss…"

"Barrineau. Allete Barrineau."

"The spider is harmless. Not dangerous. It's a common American house spider. Try to take a slow, deep breath."

By now, at least six or seven hotel guests crowded around us. One of them offered a large glass of water to Allete, and she took furious gulps. "I'm better. Thank you."

One by one, the guests who surrounded Allete returned to their seats and Godfrey stepped away from Allete.

"I didn't mean to scare you," I said. "We came here to tell you that you were never in danger. Those spiders sometimes get lost from their webs and that's probably what happened to the one that got into your chef's jacket."

Allete brushed some strands of hair from her face and looked around. "Are you certain?"

"Positive," Godfrey said. "I'm an entomologist, not a physician. Trust me when I tell you, the spider in that jar isn't a threat. As an entomologist, I work with the wine growers on this lake to ensure their grapevines are free from pests and will produce quality wine. This is a burgeoning region and its success also depends upon its ability to showcase its product. That's where you come in. We need you to continue with your chocolate demonstrations so our stellar reputation as a region will continue to grow. If you let us down, you're letting down hundreds of people who earn their livelihoods in the wine-making industry."

Holy Cow! This guy can lay it on thicker than peanut butter. Too bad he's not running for office.

Allete widened her eyes and remained silent for a moment. "I wish it were that simple, Dr. Klein, but if you must know, I think the chocolatier from Belgium is plotting to kill me. He already murdered his uncle and will stop at nothing to get what he wants."

"Murdered his uncle?" I all but choked getting the words out. "How do you know? How can you be sure?"

"Why do you suppose Jules Leurant's longtime assistant quit? Because he feared for his life. And who else would he fear it from, if not Earvin Roels? He didn't fool any of us with that meek and mousy behavior. Jules's body was hardly cold when Earvin revealed his true self. Yes, I'm basing my opinion on gossip, but gossip has its roots in the truth."

"Did you tell this to the deputy in charge of the investigation? Deputy Hickman?"

"More than once. On the day Jules's body was discovered and again a few hours ago when the deputy questioned me again. He and another deputy were here at the hotel."

"Really?"

"Yes. But it was useless. He asked the same questions over and over again. 'Did you notice anything out of the ordinary at the opening reception?'

'Did you hear anything out of the ordinary?' 'Did you see anyone acting strangely?' Finally, I threw my hands in the air and said, 'No, no, no!' The only one acting strangely was that deputy."

I stifled a laugh. "Allete, Earvin Roels won't be anywhere near you tomorrow. He'll be at my winery and at the Grey Egret. I promise you. I'll speak with Rosalee Marbleton and Catherine Trobert tonight to make sure they post someone around you at all times for your safety. Will you please reconsider? This isn't a competition for us, it's a matter of survival, including the reputations we must protect."

Try topping that one, Godfrey.

Allete swallowed and took a deep breath. "You can tell the hundreds of workers that Allete Barrineau also has a reputation to protect and I shall be at those wineries tomorrow."

Godfrey extended his hand and she shook it. I, on the other hand, put the spider jar back in my bag and gave her a quick wave. "Um, your friend...I don't see her. I hope she didn't feel as if we intruded on her evening and left."

"It doesn't matter. She's a guest at this hotel. I can converse with her another time."

"Oh, I thought she might have been involved with the chocolate festival. There are so many business people associated with it, not to mention news media."

"I wouldn't know," Allete said. "I only met her tonight. Sometimes it's nice to chat with someone who speaks your native language."

"She's French, too?"

"No, Belgian."

At that moment, Stanislav strode into the bar and walked directly to where Allete was seated. "Are you all right? I overheard someone by the elevator saying a French woman was screaming in the bar. Sorry I'm late. I had to take a phone call." Then he looked at Godfrey and me as if we were wallpaper. "My apologies. It has been a very trying day. Have we met?"

I introduced Godfrey and reintroduced myself. "Yes, it's been a very long day. Hopefully tomorrow will go smoother." I thanked Allete again and rose from the chair.

Stanislav immediately plunked himself down and leaned closer to Allete.

When Godfrey and I had reached the door to the lobby, I turned and glanced back. Allete and Stanislav were face-to-face and the auburn-haired woman had returned.

"Don't even think it," Godfrey said when we were a few feet out the door. "We got Allete to agree not to walk out on her demonstration tomorrow, and if you go back in there to try and find out that woman's name, you run the risk of undoing everything."

"Aargh. You're right. But it's really tempting."

"It's also really late, and didn't I hear you tell Allete you were going to call Rosalee and Catherine about having extra security tomorrow?"

"Yeesh. I'll call them as soon as I get home. Well, one thing's for sure, those deputies aren't making any headway with the investigation into Jules Leurant's death."

Godfrey held the door open for me. "What makes you say that?"

"Because if they were, they wouldn't be harping on Allete about what she saw or didn't see. I don't think they have anything except the report from the coroner and that was pretty sketchy, if you ask me. 'Contributing factors leading to suffocation' leaves the field wide open for interpretation."

"Or speculation in your case. The news media mentioned Ambien spray on the wineglass. That didn't get there by itself. I would imagine those deputies are looking into that, and if they have reason to believe it's one of the chocolatiers, they can get a search warrant."

"If Stanislav, Allete, or Earvin sprayed that Ambien on Jules's wineglass, they wouldn't be so careless as to keep the bottle in their possession. Unless one of them has a serious problem with insomnia. Godfrey, if I can find that out, it would be like staring at the smoking gun."

"Please tell me you don't plan on doing anything that involves sneaking into their rooms."

"No. Just their conversations."

Godfrey walked me to my car, which was right next to his, and made sure it started. Suddenly, I remembered something. I reached into my bag, pulled out the spider jar, rolled down my window and handed the jar to him. "Oops. Don't want to go home with this guy. Listen, I really can't thank you enough."

"It's okay. I have to admit my life was kind of on the boring side until you arrived at Two Witches. Keep me posted about the event and don't do anything rash. Got it?"

"Absolutely."

I pulled out of the parking lot first and he followed me to the road before turning right into Geneva as I headed left to Penn Yan. I wasn't sure if Godfrey was being protective of me the same way Theo and Don were, as a result of Francine and Jason's insistence, or if it was something else.

It was the something else I couldn't define. I had a hunky boyfriend, even though he was stuck somewhere in Yonkers for business, but for reasons I couldn't explain, or didn't want to, I found myself wondering how I really felt about Godfrey. Dammit. I never should have kissed him a few months ago, even though it was one of those thank-you-I'm-eternally-grateful-for-your-help kisses. So what if it was on the mouth. Rats! Kissing always complicated things.

Chapter 19

I called Theo the second I got in the door so he could do his phone tree thing.

"Don't bother putting Rosalee and Catherine on the tree," I said. "I have to call them myself." I went on to explain about what happened with Allete, and he couldn't believe we pulled it off.

"Yeah," I went on, "Godfrey was a regular Winston Churchill. You should have heard him."

"I heard enough from the WOW women to last me well into the next decade. Anyway, we better keep our fingers crossed nothing goes wrong with Earvin. I don't think Don's nerves could stand it."

Once off the phone with Theo, I called Rosalee and Catherine. Both assured me they'd have someone on "Allete duty" the next day. Then I rechecked the doggie door to be sure Charlie wouldn't be tempted to wander out at night and headed up the stairs to my bedroom. The combination of donuts, coffee, and club soda made my stomach feel as if it was on overdrive. Way too uncomfortable to get into bed right away so I did what every self-respecting millennial would do—I pulled out my iPhone and checked my emails.

Drat! Renee emailed to ask if I could possibly submit my screenplay a week sooner because "the production company was checking out a location in Guadalupe for a new series." She went on to say she'd be staying at the Trade Winds Resort and would have full access to her email. Full access to the beach and spa was what she should have said. Terrific. Renee would be getting hot stone massages at a five-star resort while I got to deal with demanding chocolatiers, frigid temperatures, and now a new and closer deadline.

I scrolled past my other emails, since none of them required my attention. Sales notices from department stores, offers for computer and phone upgrades, and a reminder from Walden's Garage that my car was due for an oil change. I was about to power off the phone when another email caught my eye. It was from GPipp@ycpsb.org.

Why Gladys Pipp would be sending me an email from the Yates County Public Safety Building was anyone's guess. I tapped the screen and took a breath. Her message was brief but unsettling.

"Norrie, make sure no one tampers with the ingredients for those chocolate demonstrations. Call me in the morning. Gladys."

Call her in the morning? I bloody-well wanted to wake her up that very instant. Instead, I forwarded the message to everyone in WOW, as well as Cammy, and I marked it URGENT. I also added "Just got this. Gladys must know something so take it seriously."

Yep, try going to sleep after something like that. I didn't know what annoyed me more, Renee's exciting trek to Guadalupe or some impending disaster at the winery tomorrow. I was so wired I felt as if I'd need an Ambien spray bottle the size of an industrial pesticide fumigator just to get the job done.

The way I saw it, I had two choices—read one of Jason's boring entomology journals or take out my screenplay and do a bit of writing. *Beguiled into Love* won out and I was able to turn out the lights and finally close my eyes at two fifty-three. Charlie never budged from his spot at the foot of the bed, so I wound up sleeping in a tight little curl with my knees up to my waist. By the next morning, I had a serious kink in my neck.

Gladys wouldn't be at the public safety building until eight, but I was positive Theo and Don would be up and about. It was a little past six and every self-respecting winery owner was probably on his or her second cup of coffee. I dialed their home phone while I waited for my K-cup to finish brewing.

Don picked up on the second ring. "I told Theo you'd be up but he insisted I wait." Then I heard him yell, "It's Norrie!" Then back to me. "Hell of an email from Gladys. What do you suppose she found out?"

"It can't be good. I'm calling her the minute that building opens for business. Boy am I glad I've got someone on my side in that place. She probably came across some tidbit of information on Grizzly Gary's desk. Something he can't leak to the public just yet, but something she felt we should be aware of."

"Okay, fine. Whatever it is, call us back when you know. By the way, kudos for pulling off that bit of business with Allete last night."

"Yeah, well, I hope she doesn't change her mind. We're not off the hook yet. And Earvin better arrive at Two Witches with bells on. Catch you later." Granted, the tasting room staff wouldn't arrive at work until nine, but Fred and Emma were bound to be in the bistro cooking up the food they'd need for today's meals. It was another frigid morning and the snow in our vineyards glistened from the crust of ice that had formed on top of it. Another picture-perfect postcard for the Finger Lakes, unless you actually had to be outdoors.

I made myself a slice of toast, fed Charlie, and took a hot shower before throwing on some clothes and trekking to the tasting room. Sure enough, Fred was frying up bacon and sausage while Emma was in the process of baking what looked like cornbread muffins.

"Norrie!" Fred exclaimed. "Is everything all right? It's barely seven."

"Yeah. I'm still convincing my brain I'm not sleepwalking. Listen, I got an unofficial message from someone at the public safety building. She said to make sure no one tampers with our chocolate. The chocolate for the demonstrations. Everything's safe, isn't it?"

"Gladys, huh? Wonder what she knows."

Or who she knows since everyone seems to be familiar with her.

"Uh-huh. Gladys."

"All of the ingredients were delivered yesterday from Geneva Restaurant Supply. Everything was packaged, and we stored the block chocolate at room temperature in our pantry. I'll make sure the pantry door stays locked until we need to get in there. We should be fine."

"Do me a favor and have Emma double-check the pantry. Everything should look exactly as it did when she stored the stuff yesterday."

"Norrie, Emma didn't store it. Remember? You sent her to the Grey Egret."

"Oh gee, yeah. I forgot."

"Glenda from your tasting room gave me a hand and we stored it. The open ingredients, like corn syrup, were put in the large kitchen fridge."

The muscles in my neck began to tighten up. "Oh my gosh. Anyone could have gotten in there while we were working. Sometimes customers mistake it for the restrooms, even though the sign says, 'KITCHEN STAFF ONLY.'"

"I'll give it a look-see as soon as I can take these meats out of the frying pan. Give me a second."

Fred placed the thick cut Applewood bacon and sage sausage on paper towels while I made a mental note to have lunch at the bistro today.

"All set," he said. "Let's go."

Fred opened the door and let out a gasp. "What the heck! There's a red ribbon dangling from one of the wire shelves and it's got some sort of charm on it. Looks like an eyeball."

I groaned. "Glenda. Glenda must have returned to the fridge with one of her amulets or charms for warding off evil. And don't get me started on those red ribbons she uses for the same purpose. She must buy them wholesale. How does everything else look?"

"Exactly the way I remember it from yesterday. The corn syrup on the second shelf to the right and the small jars of jam lined up by size."

"Don't be surprised if you see more red ribbons in the pantry. Glenda's been pretty spooked about Jules's death. Okay, I guess we can relax for a few minutes until I find out what's going on with Gladys."

Fred made me a Grande caramel cappuccino and I carted it off to my office. I figured I'd catch up on some winery correspondence while I counted down the minutes until eight. For some reason, I scrolled back to a few of the emails Henry Speltmore had sent us regarding the chocolate event. Henry's emails tended to be real snoozers, so it wasn't exactly my fault I'd overlooked them. Who wrote long diatribes in an email?

The first one dealt with etiquette on the wine trail. No wonder I skipped to the next. That one, at least, was partially interesting. Henry gave us the background on the chocolate manufacturing company that supplied the product for the chocolatiers. Come to think of it, that was probably where Don got his info.

Then I remembered something. Around Christmastime, I saw something on CNN about merger talks between two prominent chocolate manufacturers. One of them was Puccini Zinest and the anchor mentioned something about Puccini Zinest springing back from the loss of its CEO a year ago. Something about an untimely death. The anchor also mentioned the major chocolate competition in the states. The TV was on in the living room and I was in the kitchen. I heard the word, "Puccini," and thought maybe the Smith Opera House in Geneva was going to showcase one of the great Puccini operas. I'd gotten hooked on Italian opera when my freshman class got to see a performance of *Madame Butterfly* from a visiting opera company in Sydney, Australia. I rushed into the living room. Even given my penchant for M & M's and Milky Ways, I was disappointed as hell to hear it was some chocolate company.

Now, all of sudden, I wondered about those merger talks. It was no secret our chocolatiers got paid beaucoup bucks for endorsements. Like Olympic athletes touting Adidas and Nikes, these chocolate aficionados were praising the daylights out of their sponsors. I really needed to get my hands on some of those fancy-dancy culinary magazines to find out who was paying whom and whose account would be dropped after the winner of the Chocolate Extravaganza competition was announced.

If that wasn't a motive for murder, I didn't know what was. Then there was the matter of Jules Leurant. Despite his hubris, Jules was a master chocolatier and, with him out of the way, not only would Allete and Stanislav reap the rewards, but they'd use it to become the CEOs of their own chocolate manufacturing company. Unless that was the merger Puccini Zinest had in mind. Remove the competition, stack the deck, and wait a year or so until the new company was established. I thought about that for a moment and dismissed it. People who were greedy for money didn't want to wait that long.

Of course, there was Earvin. No doubt he'd reap some benefits, too. Endorsements paid big time. I wondered which company Puccini Zinest wanted to share a bed with. Would they keep it European with someone like Teuscher or go U.S.A. with Scharffen Berger or maybe even Hershey? As much as I wanted to do a little digging on all of them, I had more pressing things to deal with, namely Gladys Pipp.

It was one minute past eight and one minute later than I originally planned to call her. I picked up the winery phone and punched in the numbers.

Gladys answered on the first ring. "If this is an emergency, hang up and dial nine-one-one. Good Morning. Yates County Public Safety Building. Non-Emergency Line. Gladys Pipp speaking. How may I be of assistance?"

"Gladys! This is Norrie. I didn't sleep a wink last night after I read your email. What's going on?"

Gladys lowered her voice. "I have to keep this brief. Deputy Hickman is out on a call, but he can walk in at any second. He got a memo from the coroner's office yesterday regarding the contents of the piece of food found in Jules Leurant's throat. It was chocolate."

"Yes. I know. Everyone knows. That's what got Stephanie Ipswich into so much hot water. She made an off-hand comment about him choking on a bonbon."

Gladys cleared her throat. "He may have choked, but the poison in it would have killed him anyway."

"Poison? A different poison? I thought he died from getting spacy with that Ambien spray on the wineglass and then passing out and suffocating in the snow with some help from his assailant."

"That's on the *pending* report. Now things have changed. I thought you needed to be aware of this because who knows where that piece of chocolate came from."

"Um, Geneva on the Lake. Little chocolate bites were served at the opening event and no one else died from ingesting them."

"Of course not, dear. Whoever served Jules Leurant that piece of chocolate must have been the very person who infused it with—Oh, good morning Deputy Hickman. I'll be right with you."

"Guess that's my cue to get off the line, huh?"

"That's right. We're open until five."

"Thanks Gladys. I'll catch you later."

Chapter 20

"It was a double homicide," I said to Theo when I got him on the phone a few seconds after I hung up with Gladys.

"What? Another body? Where? When?"

"No, not a person, a method. I spoke with Gladys and she told me she saw a recent addendum to the coroner's report. They tested that bonbon Jules had in his throat and the chocolate had been poisoned. Poisoned! She wanted us to know so we'd be really careful about who's serving our confections."

"What kind of poison?"

"She didn't say. Deputy Hickman walked in on her and she had to hang up. He doesn't know it was me on the other end of the line."

"Holy Cow. Either someone wanted to be doubly sure Jules Leurant got knocked off or we've got two killers on our hands. Did she say how the investigation was going?"

"No. It was a short call. Anyway, I'm going to head back to the house to get some work done on my screenplay. The producer moved the deadline up a week."

"Yeesh. When you get back to your tasting room, let us know how it's going with Earvin and if there's anything we should be concerned about."

"Anything? Try everything."

As it turned out, I got mired under with the screenplay and didn't make it back to our tasting room until after "the incident."

The minute I set foot in the door of our winery, Cammy rushed over and grabbed me by the arm. "I was about to call you. Glenda, believe it or not, got Earvin to calm down."

"Calm down? From what? What did she do to him? Please don't tell me she doused him with essential oils. We're not even supposed to have that stuff near the wine or it will mess with the aromas."

"Not Glenda. Your goat! Alvin."

"Alvin? First of all, he's not my goat. He's Francine and Jason's goat. It was their idea to have a goat at the winery for family enjoyment. I would have opted for swings or a teeter-totter. What happened? Did Alvin break loose again? Oh God. Do NOT tell me he broke loose and chased Earvin."

"Er, well, he didn't exactly break loose, but he did get out for a few minutes. One of the vineyard workers, Travis, I think…was adding hay to the pen and left the gate open slightly. Yeah, come to think of it, it was Travis. He's the cute one with the dark hair. Anyhow, with the cold weather and all, Alvin's been a bit high-spirited. You know, racing and stomping around. He got out of his pen and charged down the path to the parking lot the second Earvin got out of the limousine. According to the driver, who had just opened the door for Earvin, Alvin stopped dead in his tracks in front of the limo and spit right in Earvin's face. Then, the goat made a beeline for the winery lab, but fortunately, one of our guests, who happened to be in the parking lot at the time, slowed him down by offering him a bagel. By that time, Travis came running with a rope, snagged the goat, and got him back in the pen."

Under ordinary circumstances, I would have burst out laughing, but given yesterday's escapade with Earvin, not to mention Stephanie's fiasco with Stanislav, and the most recent Allete spider catastrophe, I was in no mood for humor.

"I take it Earvin did *not* handle the situation well," I said.

"Understatement of the year. He flew into the tasting room sputtering in tongues. Most likely German or Dutch, but who the hell knows. And here I thought it was his uncle Jules who was the germophobe. Anyway, it was Glenda, of all people, who got Earvin to take a breath and compose himself. Good thing, too, because the place has been packed. The regular tourists, who aren't part of the chocolate event, have been coming and going all morning."

I rolled my eyes and waited while Cammy continued. By now, we were standing near the kitchen door, with a full view of the demonstration table.

"Glenda happened to be holding a clean towel for wiping off the tasting room tables. She immediately handed it to Earvin and ushered him to the restroom. Then she made him a cup of that crazy herbal tea of hers and gave it to him the second he exited the restroom. Talk about poised and ready at the scene."

I thought back to the first and last time I'd tasted one of Glenda's herbal tea concoctions. "That crazy herbal tea of hers is some sort of blend of chamomile and some other stuff that can knock out an elephant."

"Apparently, it worked. Not the knock-out part, but it certainly got him to calm down. Look, he's at the demo table with Emma. I wouldn't approach him if I were you. Best to leave things as is, if you know what I mean."

"Oh, I do. I sure do. It's like walking on eggshells around these prima donnas."

Cammy laughed. "With all this tumult with Earvin, I forgot to ask. What's with Gladys's message about food tampering? Did you call her?"

I gave Cammy the rundown about Jules succumbing to either a poisonous bonbon or an overly zealous murderer with a penchant for Ambien spray. "There might be two killers. The bonbon and the spray bottle."

"Or three. Bonbon, spray bottle, and shove-him-in-the-snow."

"Good grief. If this were a book, it would be Agatha Christie's *Murder on the Orient Express.*"

"Did Gladys mention if the deputies have any leads?"

"No. We didn't have much time on the phone. Come to think of it, the news media has been pretty quiet about it, too."

"Not once that bonbon news gets released. So, what was it? Arsenic? Cyanide?"

"Gladys never got a chance to tell me. I don't think it's anything like that. I don't even think you can get those poisons anywhere."

"Oh, before I forget, you got a fax from the entomology department at the Experiment Station."

"Put it in John Grishner's box. They're always faxing him about vineyard pests. Mealy bugs, leafhoppers, and what was that other one? Oh yeah, the glassy-winged sharpshooter. Godfrey went into a longwinded explanation about that thing. Called it a vineyard cancer."

"Okay. Will do."

"Uh, take a look at the demo table. Is it my imagination or is Earvin acting kind of woozy?"

"Oh no. Oh God no. It's that tea of Glenda's. I think it's making him a bit spacy. You'd better get over there, Norrie."

I edged my way to the side of the large semicircle we set up in front of the presentation area. All the seats were taken and the event attendees seemed intent on the demonstration. I tapped my teeth and watched, hoping Earvin's skill as a chocolatier would compensate for any lightheadedness that might be an effect of the tea. I was wrong.

116   *J.C. Eaton*

Earvin swayed as he demonstrated how candied centers were added to chocolate molds. Then he started to explain how to infuse additional flavors into the chocolate centers by using what looked like a metal syringe.

Cammy snuck up next to me and whispered, "Is that a hypodermic needle?"

"Um, I don't think so. It looks more like a small turkey marinade injector. Francine's got one in her cutlery drawer. Yeah, it's a marinade injector. Hypodermic needles don't have three separate injector tips."

"Good to know."

Just then, Earvin leaned over the tray of small chocolate molds and all but fell on top of it, had it not been for Emma, who caught him as his head was about to land on top of the tray.

"I've been poisoned!" he announced. "The room is spinning. That royal SOB Stanislav is responsible. He murdered my uncle and now I shall suffer the same fate."

With that, Earvin stumbled toward the kitchen, but not before managing to topple over the fifty or so wineglasses we had stacked on a nearby table. The crash was deafening and what followed was worse.

"Call nine-one-one!" someone screamed.

"Already did," someone else in the crowd replied.

A middle-aged woman wearing a teal cloche shouted, "Have we been poisoned, too?"

"No!" I shouted back from the other side of the room. "No one's been poisoned. It's a reaction to some herbal tea. I'm certain of it." *Well, fairly certain.* "Mr. Roels will be fine."

I knew from past experience, when they received a nine-one-one call, they didn't turn around. Maybe it was just as well. At least the attendees would realize Earvin had an unfortunate reaction and not a near encounter with death. *I hoped.*

Fortunately, Sam had gone into the kitchen to get some napkins and wound up with Earvin instead. With Sam's stocky build and muscular arms, he caught Earvin before the poor chocolatier hit the ground. Literally. Then Roger rushed over from his table and the two of them got a chair underneath Earvin. That was probably the best way to describe it because Earvin wouldn't have recognized a chair if it landed on his head. Meanwhile, Lizzie grabbed a broom and was frantically sweeping up the broken glass.

"Poi…Poi…soned…" Earvin kept muttering. Finally, he closed his eyes and leaned back.

Glenda, who had made him the tea in the first place, looked as if someone had drained the blood from her face. "It was only herbal tea. A lovely blend of chamomile, valerian root, passionfruit, lemongrass, and rosehips."

Sam winced. "Sounds like witch's brew if you ask me." Then he looked my way. "Uh, sorry, Norrie."

Meanwhile, a shell-shocked Emma stood motionless behind the demonstration table. It seemed everyone in the crowd was talking at once, and a few people took out their phones and started snapping pictures. I cringed. *These better not wind up on Facebook or Instagram.* "It's all right." I gave Emma a nudge. "Our presentation can continue."

Emma leaned into my ear and whispered, "How? I don't know what I'm doing."

I looked at the chocolate molds and bit my lower lip. Earvin had filled all of them with a strawberry ganache that he had made earlier, and he had just finished demonstrating how the additional chocolate was poured over the mold to seal in the flavor center. Then what the hell was that marinade injector for?

"Um, it seems we need a minute or two to re-organize," I announced to our guests. "We'll be right back."

I hustled Emma to my office and shut the door. "The EMTs are going to be here any second. It will be pandemonium. Are you sure you don't know what to do? We've got to keep our audience's attention or the only thing notable about the chocolate fest at Two Witches will be the chocolatier who might have been poisoned."

Emma widened her eyes and shook her head. "I watched him pour the chocolate into the molds and helped with the ganache, but I have no idea what he planned to infuse with that marinade injector."

"Hang on."

I charged to the computer and Googled, "infusing flavorings into chocolate molds." In seconds, a zillion YouTube videos cropped up. Working as a screenwriter, I knew how to speedread my way through text, so I skipped the videos and went directly to the blogs.

"According to this article, chocolate is sensitive to temperature. The damn flavoring must be the same temperature as the chocolate or the chocolate will seize. Go into shock or something. Can you believe it?"

Emma nodded. "Mr. Roels...Earvin...filled that marinade injector from a pan in the kitchen. He must have heated up the oil."

"Wait a minute! Wait a gosh-darned minute. Our guests aren't going to be tasting the stuff we demonstrate on the table. They'll be sampling Earvin's pre-made chocolates. Heck. So what if we shock and seize the stupid chocolate. Come on, Emma. We can wing it!"

And just as Emma and I raced back to the demonstration table, the sound of sirens blasted through the winery. The kitchen door was wide open and, within seconds, four EMTs were hovering over Earvin.

Chapter 21

"Everything is fine," I announced to our guests. "The paramedics are in the kitchen with Mr. Roels. No need to worry." *Unless you happen to be Mr. Roels...*

I pointed to the molds that Earvin created and, dredging up the information I had perused on the internet a few seconds ago, I gave what best could be called a haphazard explanation of filling chocolate molds and infusing additional flavorings.

Emma was quick to point out the facts about temperature variations and the need to heat up the flavored oils. I wasn't exactly sure of the precise timing for injecting the molds. Was it while the chocolate was still warm or when it cooled slightly? It didn't matter. Before I could get into that part of my fly-by-the-seat-of-my-pants explanation, one of the EMTs walked over to where I was standing.

"Are you the winery owner?" Her dark brown hair was pulled into a tight ponytail and given the crow's-feet around her eyes, I guessed her age to be fortyish.

"Uh, yeah. I'm Norrie Ellington. Will Mr. Roels be okay?"

"We should speak privately."

Oh no. Not the "we should speak privately." Anytime anyone uses an expression like that, you know it means trouble. I immediately turned to Emma. "And now, our chocolatier's assistant will explain how to enjoy your samples with our Cabernet Sauvignon."

Like the tasting room staff, Emma was conversant with the process for pairing wine with chocolate and, without missing a beat, she began to explain how to maximize the experience.

I looked around the room and, except for Glenda, everyone was at their tasting table. When he thought no one was looking, Sam ran his finger across his neck and pointed to the kitchen, as if I wasn't worried enough about the "speak privately" comment. Like a puppy running after its master, I followed the EMT into the kitchen and took a deep breath.

One of the EMTs, another woman, slightly younger with brown chin-length hair, was on the phone. Another bad sign. The remaining EMTs, both men about my age, were taking Earvin's vital signs.

The EMT, who told me we needed to talk, walked over to the double stainless sink, picked up the cup of tea Earvin had been drinking, and waved it under my nose. "It doesn't appear as if your friend has been poisoned, but if he drank from this cup, he most likely ingested marijuana. Here, you can smell it yourself."

"Marijuana! Let me smell that!"

Sure enough, it was an aroma I recognized. Not because I used the stuff, but who on earth hadn't smelled it wafting through a dormitory or, better yet, at a concert. Still…marijuana? At our winery? Glenda was into all sorts of herbal remedies, but I seriously doubted she'd add that particular herb or weed, or whatever it was, to her teas.

Just then, I heard Earvin's voice. "Is there anything to eat around here? I'm starving."

The EMT who took Earvin's vitals joined his colleague and me. "Mr. Roels appears to be recovering from his episode. Of course, without a lab analysis of the substance he ingested, we won't really know for sure what caused his reaction."

I can tell you what caused his reaction. The guy got stoned.

"Does Mr. Roels carry a medical marijuana card?" the EMT asked.

I shook my head. "I doubt it. He's a visiting chocolatier from Belgium, not a New York State resident."

The second EMT who'd taken Earvin's signs walked over to us. "Mr. Roels has refused further medical assistance and doesn't wish to be taken to the hospital. That is, of course, his prerogative."

I looked past the EMTs to where Earvin was seated, and our merry chocolatier appeared to be more alert and responsive than he was a short while ago.

The EMT continued. "Since we cannot say for certain what Mr. Roels drank, only that it altered his ability to function temporarily, we have no choice but to notify the Yates County Sheriff's Department."

Oh Goody! Where's my lawyer/boyfriend when I need him… "Um, are you really sure you need to do that?"

The EMT gave a nod. "It's protocol."

Throughout the entire question and answer process with the EMTs, I thought I heard someone sniveling. Short bursts of sobs or nasal congestion. I glanced around the kitchen and, sure enough, there was Glenda, wedged between the two stainless steel refrigerator/freezers. She gave me a wave and then proceeded to dab her eyes with a bright fuchsia handkerchief before approaching us.

"I made that tea," she said, "and there was absolutely no marijuana in it. I swear on my life! Only chamomile, valerian root, passionfruit, lemongrass, and rosehips. It's my soothing, calming tea. I drink it all the time when I'm stressed."

Then Glenda walked to the sink, picked up the cup, and took a whiff. "This is NOT the tea I made. I can't even smell the lovely rosehips."

"Is the cup the same?" I asked.

Glenda held up the cup and grimaced. "Definitely. It's the only Vincent Van Gogh cup we have. We've got a few Monets but only one Vincent. Some stinker must have added marijuana leaves to the tea or maybe even the oil after I handed it to Mr. Roels. No wonder I couldn't smell my own ingredients. And that oil is potent. A friend of my mother's uses it when her arthritis acts up. The oil is real easy to come by if you have a dispensary card."

The EMTs looked at each other and the woman with the ponytail spoke. "I'm sure that's something the sheriff's deputies will address." Then one of the EMTs asked Earvin how he was feeling and Earvin responded in one word—hungry. With that, the EMTs packed their equipment and exited the winery.

"I'll have Fred make you a sandwich," I said to Earvin. "You might as well wait here in the kitchen and unwind." *Unwind? The only one wound up is me. I need to unwind. I need to drink some of that tea. With or without the new ingredient.*

Glenda somehow pulled herself together and went out to the tasting room. Cammy, Sam, and Roger had taken the customers Glenda would have had, so Glenda wound up going from table to table assisting whoever needed her the most. From what I saw at the tasting tables, our guests weren't too fazed about having Emma replace Earvin. They seemed to be enjoying their strawberry-filled chocolates and the wine that went with it. I only prayed my explanation of filling and infusing chocolates wouldn't show up on anyone's Facebook videos.

Lizzie swept up the broken glass and informed me that a case of forty-eight wineglasses cost us between sixty and eighty dollars.

"We can order from one of the discount glassware companies," she said. "Since we don't have our logo on the glasses, they're not that expensive. About fifteen to nineteen dollars for a case of twelve."

"Might as well order four cases," I said. "Maybe we can send the bill to Henry Speltmore at the wine association so they can pick up the tab."

Cammy must have overheard my comment because she called out, "That'll be the day."

I hurried over to the bistro and returned to the kitchen with a turkey and cheese wrap for Earvin. He took it with barely a thank you and devoured it as if he'd been with the Donner party for the past few months, instead of at our winery for the last hour or so.

"Everything's settled down here," I said to him. "Do you think you'll be all right to conduct your demonstration at the Grey Egret this afternoon?"

Earvin dabbed the side of his lip with a napkin. "As long as the Grey Egret doesn't obtain a goat or make herbal teas in the next few hours, I should be perfectly fine."

"Um, it wasn't Glenda's tea that rendered you, well, off-kilter. Someone tampered with it and added marijuana. Weren't you listening to what those EMTs said?"

"All they told me was my head would clear up and I'd be fine. They said if I felt worse, I should seek medical attention."

I thought about it for a moment and then realized the EMTs had been talking with me and not Earvin. Probably just as well.

"Yeah, well, that makes sense. And you do seem to be doing much better." *Although, most people who smoke or ingest pot seem to be euphoric, not miserable. Then again, everyone reacts differently to recreational drugs.*

"Unfortunately, incidents like this get reported to the sheriff's department, and they're going to send a deputy over here to speak with you." *And grill me as if it was the Spanish Inquisition.*

"What can I tell them? A miserable goat spat on me and an eccentric employee of the winery gave me a calming tea that had been laced with marijuana?"

At least I hope it was marijuana. Sure, smelled like it. Heaven help us if it was something really horrible. "Yes, that will suffice. Miserable goat and wacky tea."

"Can I get another one of these wraps?" Earvin asked.

"Sure."

I headed for the bistro when I recognized a voice that I wish I hadn't— Deputy Hickman. He had just come inside the winery and asked Lizzie, who was at the cash register, if she knew where I was.

"Right here." I walked up to the deputy.

"Ah, Miss Ellington. No doubt you're aware of the reason for my impromptu visit."

I did a mental eye roll. "No doubt. But let me begin by saying the presumed marijuana in Mr. Roels's tea didn't come from our winery. Honestly. We sell wine. That can make people high if they consume too much. Why on earth would we introduce an illegal substance?"

Deputy Hickman put his hands on his hips and groaned. "Miss Ellington, if you'd let me get a word in edgewise I would appreciate it."

Edgewise...sidewise...whatever.

I closed my mouth and widened my eyes as Deputy Hickman spoke. "This is the third winery this morning that reported a similar incident. Not with tea, mind you, but in the coffee Mr. Vetrov was drinking while at Billsburrow Winery, and in some sort of a horchata drink Miss Barrineau had set down next to her demonstration table at Terrace Wineries."

"Holy cow!"

"Indeed. Holy cow. It would appear, Miss Ellington, we have a prankster in our midst who seems to be deriving some sort of sick pleasure from monkeying with people's drinks."

"Not people. Chocolatiers. Esteemed world-famous chocolatiers." *Except maybe for Earvin, but by the time he's done, who knows.*

"We are aware of that. I'll need to pour the remains of Mr. Roels' tea into a sterilized plastic bottle from our lab, and, along with the cup, bring it in for testing. I've already done the same with Miss Barrineau's sample. Unfortunately, Mr. Vetrov dumped his coffee down the sink and rinsed the glass so we only have his word about the matter."

"No problem. Did you, uh, want to speak with Mr. Roels? He's in the kitchen."

"I'll take a statement from him, yes. I'm afraid that's all I can do at this point."

I escorted Deputy Hickman to the kitchen and showed him where we had set the cup of tampered tea. Then I left him alone with Earvin and returned to the tasting room.

The wine and chocolate pairing was still going strong, so I left things as they were and darted back to my office to call Theo and Don at their winery.

Don picked up on the third ring. "Hey, Norrie. Thanks for calling. Is everything going okay with Earvin?"

"Not exactly. Alvin spat on him, he freaked out, Glenda gave him some calming tea, someone laced it with marijuana, I think, and anyway, the EMTs arrived. Then Deputy Hickman."

"Oh …the siren. Theo was convinced it was on the road and not our shared driveway. We were too busy to look out the windows. Is Earvin going to be all right?"

"Yeah. He's fine. Hungry as hell but fine. Funky mood, too. I thought people were supposed to be happy on that stuff."

"Usually. Do you think he'll make it to our winery or do we need to call in another favor from Emma?"

"He should be fine. He doesn't have to give his demo until two thirty. But that's only part of why I called. Two Witches was the third winery where someone spiked the chocolatiers' drinks. Deputy Hickman told me Rosalee's place and Madeline's had similar experiences. Except for the goat."

Don chuckled. "I shouldn't be laughing but picturing Alvin was too much. What was Hickman's take on the marijuana?"

"A prankster. But I don't think so. I think someone is trying to unnerve those chocolatiers. But why?"

"I could see it if it was only one. That would make sense. To get him or her out of the game. But all of them? Maybe Hickman's right. Maybe we've got a kook and nutcase floating around the lake. Wouldn't be the first time. Anyway, I'll let Theo and our employees know. We'll keep a good eye on anything that goes near Earvin's mouth."

"Good idea. Catch you later."

When I stepped back into the tasting room, Lizzie informed me that Mr. Roels' driver had arrived and was taking him back to the hotel for a short respite.

"Someone better tell the hotel's front desk to make sure Earvin gets a wake-up call or he may not make it to his afternoon demonstration."

"Someone?" Lizzie asked.

"Okay, fine. Me. I'll call Geneva on the Lake."

Chapter 22

This time there was a man at the front desk who took my call. I explained it was paramount Mr. Roels be given a wake-up call. The receptionist told me only the guest could request such a thing. I then told him if he didn't notify Mr. Roels of the time and he missed his demonstration at the Grey Egret, the fault would rest with Geneva on the Lake. So much for tourism promotion from the Seneca Lake Wine Association.

The receptionist agreed to make an exception in my case. I thanked him and went on to my next call. Given what Deputy Hickman had told me, I had to find out from Rosalee exactly what transpired with Allete.

"I have no idea," Rosalee said when I got her on the phone. "All I knew was that Miss Barrineau held the glass out and told my tasting room staff it 'didn't taste right.' Once a few of my employees took a whiff, they were convinced someone added marijuana to the mixture."

"Um, who mixed it? Is it something your winery serves?"

"No. It's that bottled stuff we sell along with sodas and juices. Still, I doubt it came that way from the company. Miss Barrineau placed the glass on one of our counters while she prepped at her demonstration table."

"Hmm. Plenty of time for someone to add a secret ingredient."

Rosalee made a grumbling sound and cleared her throat. "That's what we thought, too. To be on the safe side, I called the sheriff's department. Deputy Hickman arrived and took it for testing."

"I know. He was probably at your winery right before coming to ours."

I then went on to tell her about Earvin's bout with marijuana and the fact that there was a similar incident at Madeline's winery.

"You think someone's trying to sabotage this damn event?" she asked.

"That or get one of those chocolatiers so anxious he or she won't be able to compete."

"Oh brother. By the way, was that siren headed to your place? We couldn't be sure."

"Yeah. When Earvin got dizzy, one of our guests immediately dialed nine-one-one."

"Just what we need. More drama at our wineries. At least the news crews didn't show up."

"Bite your tongue. We still have one more day. And an afternoon."

As it turned out, we were on the news after all. Well, Stephanie was and she wasn't any too happy about it. It was the early evening news and it followed an afternoon of nail biting on my part, wondering what other "fresh horror" awaited us with this chocolate festival.

As things turned out, a rather groggy, according to Theo, Earvin showed up on time for his presentation at the Grey Egret and somehow pulled off an extraordinary demonstration of fillings and infusions. I put in a quick call to Madeline between my call with Rosalee and eating my lunch. I gave her the rundown on Earvin, as well as what Rosalee told me about Allete's latest incident.

Madeline's explanation of the tainted coffee in Stanislav's cup was similar to the other incidents. "One of our employees handed Mr. Vetrov a cup of dark roast she had made. Black. He said he preferred it that way. Anyhow, Mr. Vetrov took it with him to the demonstration table in our tasting room. He set it down on the small counter adjacent to the table as he set-up for the presentation. When he finally took a sip of coffee, he shouted something about someone trying to drug him with marijuana and stormed into our kitchen and dumped the cup in the sink before any of us could smell it. Then he rinsed the cup and put it in the strainer."

"What about the rest of the coffee? Was anyone else's coffee tampered with?"

"No. Only his. I called the sheriff's department to report the incident, seeing as how these were high-profile celebrities and what with one of them turning up dead, I didn't want to take any chances."

"Good idea."

"Deputy Hickman wasn't too pleased about the lack of evidence but said it was probably a prank and not to worry about it."

"Yeah. He told me the same thing. But I'm worried. True, a bit of marijuana in someone's drink isn't going to render them unconscious, but what if it's more than that?"

"What do you mean, Norrie?"

"Maybe today's little episodes were just that. Little episodes meant to throw the chocolatiers off course. What if whoever is behind this tries something worse tomorrow?"

Madeline gasped. "My God! I never thought of a possible repeat. I'll have to assign at least two employees to keep an eye on anything Stanislav Vetrov goes near. I'm also going to email Henry Speltmore about this. I doubt he'll be much help. He'll probably send all of us another one of his longwinded emails about tourism and professionalism. Still, he *is* the president of the wine association."

We agreed to keep each other, and everyone else in WOW, up-to-date with anything out of the ordinary. I just didn't expect it to be about the nightly news at seven, featuring Wade Gallagher on 8 WROC.

It was Catherine who called me, insisting I stop whatever it was I was doing and turn on the TV. "I've got to call poor Stephanie. You and I can chat later."

Why she called me prior to dialing Stephanie was anyone's guess, but Catherine was known to be a bit flighty at times. I closed my laptop, got up from the couch, and hunted around for the remote. It was wedged between the cushions and, by the time I located it, I had missed most of the story. Most, but not all. I did manage to catch a rerun of that dreadful video from the opening reception when Stephanie said she wished Jules would choke on a bonbon. My God. The bonbon. The poisoned bonbon. Was that what this was about?

Without wasting a second, I phoned Don and Theo.

"Guess you saw it, too," Theo said. "Antifreeze. The lab released the results from the substance found in Jules's throat. Said it was chocolate with antifreeze in it, but it wasn't the cause of death. Not enough time. They're still going with the Ambien spray on the wineglass causing the guy to get woozy and pass out in the snow. Then, of course, someone made sure he was face down."

"Why run that awful footage of Stephanie?"

"Ratings."

"Ugh. I better give Stephanie a call. That is, if Catherine finally got off the phone with her. Catherine was the one who told me about the news story in the first place. At least she didn't mention her son, Steven, but give it time."

"Stephanie has nothing to worry about," Theo said. "It was a flip remark. Over and done. Tell her to let it slide when you talk to her."

"Theo, do you think there's really one murderer out there and he or she used multiple methods to get the job done? Or do you think we've got a regular murder club going on?"

"I think more than one person wanted Jules Leurant dead, but only one killer got lucky."

"Did the news anchors explain how the antifreeze got into the chocolate? I missed that whole part of the broadcast."

"They sure did. Even held up a sample piece of chocolate and zeroed in on a tiny pinprick on the bottom of the chocolate. Once the internal mixture has cooled and the chocolate is hardened, the chocolatiers can use a flavor marinator to inject whatever they want. In this case, it was poison."

"I saw one of those things today. Earvin had it for the demo. Doesn't take a rocket scientist to figure out how to inject something toxic. And antifreeze is real easy to come by. Heck, every convenience store and gas station from here to Buffalo sells it. Walmart, too, for that matter. Especially in the dead of winter."

"It's a clever killer, all right," Theo said. "The stuff tastes sweet, that's why there are warnings to keep it away from pets."

"I wish this miserable event would be over with already. I can't help but feel as if whoever's behind it may be planning something worse."

"What's worse than murdering someone?"

"Murdering more people."

"Look, make sure your staff is extra vigilant tomorrow. We'll get through this, Norrie."

"If you say so."

I tried to get back to my screenplay, but I was way too antsy to concentrate. Unlike my sister, who would use an opportunity like this to bake a quiche or maybe even a loaf of lemon-zucchini bread, I decided to see if Godfrey might be in the mood to grab a pizza or something. After all, it was only a few minutes before eight and, in a college town like Geneva, the restaurants and pizzerias wouldn't be filling up until well after nine.

Godfrey answered on the second ring and didn't sound at all surprised to hear from me. "I had a mental bet with myself as to whether you'd call me tonight or wait until I was at the Experiment Station tomorrow. I figured you'd be too busy during the day with those chocolate pairings."

"Huh? I called to see if you wanted to grab a pizza. What are you talking about?"

"Didn't you read the fax I sent this morning?"

"Come to think of it, Cammy mentioned a fax, but I was pretty sure it was meant for our vineyard manager, so I told her to put it in his box. The staff mailboxes are in an alcove adjacent to our entrance. Usually John Grishner sends over one of his crew to get the mail. The fax is probably sitting on John's desk. He's been inundated with the winter trimming. Once he leaves his office, he's outdoors most of day. He'll probably read it tomorrow morning first thing. Why? Is there some horrible godforsaken winery pest that's about to wreak havoc on us?"

"Not as yet, but John will be shaking his head when he reads that fax."

"Why?"

"Because it has to do with that auburn-haired woman we saw when we went to talk with Allete about the spider incident."

"You found out something? You know something? What? What? Who is she?"

"Whoa. Hold your horses. First of all, I'm not saying it was her, but there sure is a likeness."

"To what? Come on, tell me."

"You know how I gloss over all the department emails unless something is really directed my way?"

"Uh-huh."

"Well, for some reason, I clicked on to a recent email about a noted horticulturalist from Belgium, who's here to deliver a lecture at Barton Hall in Ithaca the Monday following the chocolate extravaganza. The woman we spotted chatting with Allete sure resembles the one in the photo from my email. And get this, her name is Hortensia Vermeulen. Wasn't that the name you found on that boarding pass when you routed through hotel trash? That *is* what you told me a few days ago, right?"

I all but choked. "Horticulturalist? What on earth would she be doing with Allete? And Stanislav. Remember, they were all having a little tête-à-tête when we left the bar at Geneva on the Lake."

"Maybe it's what Allete told us. Just that. Guests having a conversation."

"If she's delivering a lecture in Ithaca, why is she staying in Geneva?"

"Oops. Forgot to mention, she's also conducting a lecture at Hobart and William Smith Colleges on Friday for the department of environmental studies."

"Hortensia sure gets around, huh?"

"Sometimes neighboring universities work together when visiting academic dignitaries are in the area. They share the travel costs and other expenditures. Look, pizza sounds really good. How about we continue this conversation at Uncle Joe's in say, a half hour?"

"You got it!"

One heaping order of wings and a large sausage and olive pizza later, Godfrey and I were still ruminating about Hortensia Vermeulen and whether she had any connection with the chocolatiers. We were tucked in a small corner at Uncle Joe's restaurant on Genesee Street. A street that featured more than one family-friendly Italian restaurant. What I liked about Uncle Joe's was its ambience, in addition to the ethnic food. An eclectic collection of memorabilia and framed photos filled the plaid wallpapered walls and offset the colorful checkered tablecloths.

"You mean to tell me that all this time I've been chasing after some horticulturalist from Belgium?" I whined. "This doesn't make sense. And what about that note? It was written on Puccini Zinest stationery. Why would Hortensia write a note like that to someone?"

"Norrie, are you sure she's the one who wrote it? Maybe she's the recipient."

"Holy Crap! I never thought of that. It kind of changes things, doesn't it?"

Chapter 23

When we left Uncle Joe's Restaurant, I had more questions than answers. If Hortensia was a world-famous horticulturalist, then how was she connected to the chocolate industry? That was, *if* she even had a connection. Maybe it was what Godfrey said. Coincidental. That note could have meant anything. Still, I wasn't buying it. The note was written on Puccini Zinest stationery and that stuff wasn't readily available for purchase like the chocolate they made.

And what about that altercation with Earvin? Didn't that involve an auburn-haired woman? In fact, so did the unfortunate chocolate smearing incident with Stanislav that Stephanie told me about. The one that sent Deputy Hickman to Gable Hill Winery. Nope, this was no coincidence. Horticulturist or not, I was positive Hortensia was the auburn-haired woman.

Charlie was pushing around his dog dish when I got into the house, and I immediately filled it with kibble before I even bothered to take off my jacket. Too tired to hang it in the closet, I rationalized I'd be wearing it in the morning so it might as well stay put over the back of a kitchen chair. *That's right, Francine. I neglected to hang up my coat. And I may have neglected to feed the dog, but I can't remember. It doesn't matter. He shoves that food dish at me whether he's eaten or not.*

I was about to head upstairs when I noticed the light blinking on the landline. Uh-oh. Whoever left me a message probably tried my cell phone but it was on mute at the bottom of my bag. I walked to the phone and tapped the "play button."

"Hey, Norrie! I left you a voice mail on your cell. I've missed you like crazy. Marvin's driving me nuts with this latest legal matter of his. No sooner do I finish one thing with the client and he decides something else needs to be added, deleted, or changed altogether. If I never set foot in Yonkers again, it will be too soon. And the attorney on the other side of this settlement case is just as bad, if not worse. She keeps changing the wording around so we practically have to start from the beginning. Ugh. Oh, I'm sorry. Here I am rambling when I should be asking about you. How's the chocolate festival going? Bet you're having the time of your life with this one. Call me."

"Time of my life?" Is he insane? Don't they get the news in Yonkers? Then I remembered that upstate New York and the city area were two different entities entirely. I plopped myself on the couch, took my cell phone from my bag, and pushed speed dial for Bradley.

His voice was immediate. "Whew. Glad you're okay. I know we haven't had any storms in our area recently, but those roads get awfully slick with the slightest temperature change."

"Bradley Jamison, are you telling me you were worried about me?"

"Yeah, well, um…"

"The roads are the least of my concerns. Have you followed any of the news up here?"

"I haven't even followed the news down here. Why? Please don't tell me another body cropped up at your winery."

"No, at Geneva on the Lake. But holding a wineglass with our Cabernet Sauvignon in it."

"Poisoned?"

"Not the wine, a bonbon. But it was the Ambien spray that did him in."

"What Ambien spray? And who? Who are we talking about?"

For the next fifteen minutes, all Bradley could utter were words like "wow," "uh-oh," and "no way," as I gave him the complete epic poetry version of the events preceding, encompassing, and following the discovery of master chocolatier Jules Leurant face down in the snow. By the time I finished, Bradley was left with one word—"damn."

"So, you're telling me there might be three killers out there?" he asked.

"That's kind of the worst-case scenario Cammy, Theo, and I kicked around, but it could be one very clever, very diabolical murderer."

"Then let the sheriffs' department deal with it. Heck, let both county sheriff's departments deal with it. Please? I'm hoping to finish things up by Friday and get back there. That grand competition's Saturday night, right?"

Oh no. Godfrey's my "plus one." Now what? "Uh, um, that would be swell. Absolutely swell."

Who the heck uses the word "swell?" That's something a ten-year-old says when he gets tickets to a ball game.

"Sounds good," he said. "We'll talk soon. And remember, let the sheriff's department handle the investigation. Miss you!"

"Miss you, too."

When I got off the phone, I felt worse than I did back in ninth grade when I told two boys I'd go bowling with them. Keeping dates straight wasn't exactly my forte. When they both showed up at the house at the same time, it was a disaster. Especially the yelling. Not the boys. My mother. She offered them cookies and hot chocolate while I was forced to apologize for my "inconsiderate behavior." I glanced at the cupboard and wondered how much hot chocolate Francine had purchased.

"Saturday night is two days away," Theo said when I called him the next morning. "Anything can happen between now and then. Maybe Bradley's case will take longer, maybe a Nor'easter will pull up on the coast or—"

"Maybe I'll be super humiliated. Bradley is, after all, my boyfriend. More or less. Well, sort of. I should have just invited Godfrey to the opening reception and not the big hoop-de-dah."

"Bradley knows Godfrey's your brother-in-law's coworker and a friend of yours. I'm sure he'll understand."

"Trouble is, I don't understand. Hanging out with Godfrey comes easy to me. When I'm with Bradley, I'm always on my best behavior."

"Hey, as much as I'd like to play Dr. Phil with you, I really need to get over to the winery. Don's already there. Thank God this is the last day of those demonstrations."

"My sentiments exactly. Last thing we need is another Earvin Roels disaster. Travis felt awful about the incident with Alvin, but that could have happened to anyone. I have the tasting room staff on high alert so we don't run into another fiasco. The marijuana was bad enough."

"Yeah, speaking of that, did anyone on your staff notice anything strange with the guests who were in attendance for the wine and chocolate pairing?"

"Nothing that anyone brought up, but I'll check. It was a large crowd. Anyone could have spiked Earvin's herbal tea."

"Yeah, the wine trail certainly draws in its fair share of loonies. Catch you later."

It was only a little past eight, so I decided to make the most of my morning and pick up where I left off with my screenplay. Too bad I kept rethinking the Bradley-Godfrey dilemma because I wound up inadvertently inserting their names instead of the ones I'd assigned to my male protagonists. By nine thirty-eight, I gave up and closed the stupid laptop.

Earvin was slated to arrive at Two Witches by ten, so I changed out of my sweats, washed up quickly, and slipped into a decent outfit—turtleneck and fairly new black jeans.

With ample kibble in Charlie's bowl and fresh water, I locked the front door and took a brisk walk to the tasting room. That was when it hit me. Hortensia Vermeulen was supposed to give a lecture on Friday at Hobart and William Smith Colleges. What better way to find out if she was indeed the auburn-haired mystery woman than to attend that event. So what if the study of growing fruits, vegetables, and plants was about as interesting to me as one of Godfrey's mind-numbing seminars on insects. I absolutely *had* to be in that audience if I was ever going to get anywhere with my hunches.

Without wasting a second, my fingers were frantically dialing Godfrey's office. Thankfully, I'd mastered walking and talking a long time ago.

"Godfrey! Thank God it's you and not your voice mail. Tell me, can just anyone pop into that lecture Hortensia is giving on Friday or do they need tickets or something?"

"Whoa. Not even a hello? This must be important, so here goes. According to the email our department received, she's speaking on special techniques and methods for soil conditioning. You can't possibly be interested in—duh! I should have known. You want to find out if she's the auburn-haired woman."

"Bingo! So, do I need to get on a list? Get a ticket? What?"

"Actually, tickets were sent to the vineyard managers on Seneca Lake. Cornell and the colleges in Geneva always do that when one of their speakers can offer the community an opportunity to hear firsthand from a noted academic expert."

"John! I've got to find John Grishner. Thanks, Godfrey. Good talking to you."

I pressed the "end call" button before he could say a word. Then I pulled up John's cell phone number and dialed.

He answered right away. "Norrie? Is everything all right?"

"Fine. Wonderful. Well, sort of. Listen, did you get tickets to attend Hortensia Vermeulen's soil lecture at Hobart and William Smith this Friday? She's a horticulturalist from Belgium."

"Saw 'em. Tossed 'em. None of us have time. We've got to get the winter pruning done and, with the weather being so unpredictable, we've got to make use of every decent day we have. Why? Was there something pressing about soil maximization you wanted us to be aware of?"

"Heck no. I need to find out if Hortensia is somehow involved with the chocolatiers. Long story. Where did you toss the tickets? And please don't tell me they're in the landfill by now."

"Nope. Still in my overflowing trash basket next to the overflowing stuff on my desk. How about if I dig them up and drop them off at the tasting room before I leave today? They sent two tickets."

"That would be wonderful. Thanks a million, John."

I was in the tasting room and only a few feet away from Lizzie and the cash register when I ended the call. Earvin was at the demonstration table with Emma, and things appeared to be going smoothly. We had a moderate number of tasters at the different tables, and I presumed they were mostly event ticket holders who arrived early.

"Keep your fingers crossed we don't have another fracas in here today. I don't think my nerves can stand it," Lizzie said. "Tell me, have you gotten any further tracking down Jules's killer? Nancy Drew would have this solved by now."

Only if her publisher pushed up the manuscript due date. "Um, I'm working on it. Handbook and all."

"Good. Good."

"Say, Lizzie, did you happen to notice anyone going near the demo table where Earvin had his tea yesterday?"

"The demonstration table, no. But a woman with an ugly woolen hat went into the kitchen by mistake. Said she was looking for the restroom."

"Red or auburn hair?"

"The hat covered every last strand. She must have been having a very bad hair day to wear that thing. Why? You think she might have been the one who put the—" Then Lizzie lowered her voice to barely a whisper. "The marijuana in his tea?"

"You can say it out loud. The word's not illegal. And I'm not sure. I have some hunches, but I'm not sure."

"Nancy Drew always went with her hunches. You'd be wise to follow her example."

I stifled a scream and forced myself to smile. "Right."

Before I let Lizzie launch into one of her spiels about Nancy Drew, I walked over to Earvin and Emma and asked them how things were going.

Earvin glared at me as if I'd asked him to taste-test a toad. "The milk chocolate with caramelized centers and bittersweet drizzle will be magnificent, pending any unforeseen circumstances at your winery."

"Terrific." *You obnoxious little snob.* "Let me know if there's anything you need."

Earvin turned his attention to the tempering machine and, in that instant, Emma stuck her tongue out in his direction. I tried not to burst out laughing.

By now, the tasting room was filling up and Cammy directed the ticket holders to the circular seating we arranged in front of the demonstration area. Within minutes, our patrons filled the area. With Sam, Glenda, Roger, and Cammy all standing in the rear of the room, I figured it would be a good time to ask if any of them noticed anything unusual prior to Earvin drinking the loco tea.

They shook their heads in unison. Apparently only Lizzie's observation was notable. Then again, maybe the woman with the bad hair day simply made a mistake. It wouldn't be the first time someone went into the wrong restroom. Only this wasn't a restroom. It was our kitchen.

All eyes were on Earvin as he pontificated about tempering machines and chocolate consistency. A little water added gloss, too much water turned the stuff into unappetizing blobs. My God, it was like listening to our winemaker Franz or worse yet, his assistants Alan and Herbert, drone on and on about fermentation. I had one word for the whole shooting match—fussy! To wind up with a quality product, whether it was gourmet chocolate or award-winning wine, the mastermind behind the creation had to have far more patience than I could ever imagine.

I scanned the room and there were no obvious signs of impending doom, so I headed for my office. That was when Lizzie flagged me down and pointed to the phone.

Now what?

"Norrie, it's Rosalee. She said you didn't answer your cell phone. Here. Take the phone."

She handed me the receiver to our ancient wall phone—which had, quite possibly, the longest cord in creation. I moved out of earshot and lowered my voice. "Rosalee? Is everything all right?"

"Hell no. Why do you think I called you? You're better at dealing with these things than the sheriff's department."

"Things? What things?"

Rosalee groaned into the phone. "A death threat in the chocolate."

"Come again?"

"Oh, you heard me, all right. A damn death threat. Allete unwrapped one of those blocks of chocolate from the manufacturer and it was doing whatever it was supposed to do in that machine. Then she unwrapped the other block and that's when she saw it—someone had carved 'You Die, Allete' in the chocolate. Hard to miss."

"Um, probably a ridiculous question, but is Allete a basket case by now?"

"I wouldn't know. She locked herself in one of the bathroom stalls and refuses to come out. I've got a room full of people expecting to see a demonstration, not listen to someone wailing in the john."

I glanced at Earvin and he seemed calm and composed. "Hold on a sec. I'll call you right back."

There was no subtle way for me to sneak up and whisper in Earvin's ear, so I did the next best thing. I stepped in front of his demonstration table and announced, "I must pull Mr. Roels aside for a second. Don't worry, his competent assistant has everything under control."

Emma muttered, "Like hell I do," under her breath and I prayed no one heard her.

Without giving Earvin a moment to protest, I grabbed him by the wrist and pulled him to the doorway by the kitchen.

"We have an emergency," I said. "Well, not us. Terrace Wineries. Allete got a death threat. Well, a message that could be taken as a death threat in her chocolate and now she's in the restroom and won't come out. I have to send Emma over there to pinch-hit."

"Pinch what? I do not understand."

"Baseball. Never mind. I'll assign one of our tasting room employees to assist you."

"They must understand the basics of chocolate preparation."

"Earvin, I'm lucky if they understand the basics of pouring a drink at this point. Come on, back to the demonstration. You'll love working with Glenda."

Five minutes later, a dazzled Emma was on her way to Rosalee's winery and Glenda was trying desperately to assist Earvin as he drizzled a dark chocolate design on top of the coated caramel-infused candies.

It was a temporary fix because, as far as I knew, Allete was still sequestered in the ladies' room and Rosalee hadn't notified the sheriff's department. Maybe things had changed in the six or seven minutes since I'd spoken with her. I took the cell phone from my pocket, walked to the foyer, and called her back.

"I'm sending Emma from our bistro to take over. She knows what to do. Plus, the chocolates for the wine pairing were pre-made. You should be all set. Catherine, on the other hand, is going to have a conniption if Allete isn't at Lake View this afternoon. Rosalee, you have to call Deputy Hickman and tell him what happened."

"I'll tell you what happened. Someone's toying with that girl so she becomes a bundle of nerves. I don't think it's a real death threat."

"Um, that's not up to you to decide. Call Grizzly Gary, for crying out loud, because if something bad really does happen to Allete, we'll have hell to pay."

"Oh, I suppose you're right. I'll make the call. Oh, Emma just walked in. Good. The audience is getting restless."

"Once our demo is over, I'll head to your place."

"What on earth for?"

"Maybe I can talk Allete into leaving the restroom."

"Won't the sheriff's deputies do that?"

"From what I've seen, they may convince her to stay longer. Talk to you later."

Chapter 24

I was so flustered about the so-called death threat Allete received that I forgot, momentarily, about Hortensia Vermeulen's lectures at the colleges. Only one person would be able to identify her absolutely as the auburn-haired woman—and that was Stephanie. A woman fitting that description, according to Stephanie, was responsible for breaking up the chocolate-flinging melee that involved Stanislav and a man in a black overcoat. A man who knew how to hurl insults in German, Dutch, and Russian, according to Stephanie. When I asked her how she knew they were insults, she told me, "He wouldn't very well be complimenting Stanislav's chocolate-making skills while flinging chocolate sauce at him." Point well taken.

Without stopping to catch my breath, I called Gable Hill Winery's tasting room and asked for Stephanie.

"Oh my gosh, Norrie. Did anything horrific happen? When my worker said it was you on the phone, I panicked."

Terrific. Now I'm getting a reputation of being the disaster queen. "Not anything that would involve Stanislav directly. Madeline would have called you if there was a problem with his demo at her place. She'd want to give you fair warning before Stanislav shows up at your place this afternoon."

I could hear Stephanie exhaling. "Oh, that's good."

"Um, yeah. For now. Wish I could say the same about Allete."

"Why? What happened with Allete?"

"She got a death threat in her chocolate. It was carved into one of those large blocks from the manufacturer that the chocolatiers use for tempering. Rosalee thinks it's a bunch of hooey, but I told her to call the sheriff."

"It just happened? Right now?"

"Uh-huh. But that's not why I called. Do you have any pressing plans for tomorrow? The chocolatiers will be back at Geneva on the Lake prepping for the shindig on Saturday, so the foot traffic shouldn't be too bad in our tasting rooms."

"I can't think about tomorrow if some maniac is out there sending death threats to our wineries."

"Not our wineries. The chocolatiers. And not the chocolatiers. Only Allete, as far as I know. And I'll know more once I head over there, but right now, I need you to do me a favor."

"What favor?"

"Go to Hortensia Vermeulen's lecture on soil utilization or something along those lines. She'll be speaking tomorrow at Hobart and William Smith Colleges."

"Hortensia Vermeulen? Never heard of her. And soil management? That's why we have vineyard managers. That's the stuff they study in college."

"Not soil. Aargh. I should have made myself clearer. Sorry. I'm so wacked-out with all of this craziness going on. Hortensia Vermeulen is a guest at Geneva on the Lake. She's also a world-renowned horticulturalist from Belgium. But here's the thing. I think she might be the auburn-haired woman you saw breaking up the fracas between Stanislav and the foreign guy. And the same woman who was responsible for the injury above Earvin's eye. You've got to see her up close and personal. I only caught a quick look at her the day she unnerved Earvin in our winery. So, I need you to tell me if Hortensia Vermeulen is the same woman. I need to be absolutely sure. The only way we'll know is by going to that lecture. Don't worry. I've got tickets."

"Next time you get tickets, make it for a Bon Jovi concert."

"So you'll go with me?"

"Oh, I suppose. Are you really sure she could be the woman in question? I mean, what would a world-famous horticulturalist have to do with chocolatiers? Other than the fact they're famous, too."

"I keep asking myself the same question. Hortensia's lecture starts at ten at Albright Auditorium. I'll pick you up at nine fifteen so we'll have enough time to find parking."

The second I ended my call with Stephanie, I returned to the tasting room. Our guests were standing around the tasting tables, sampling chocolate confections with our Cabernet Sauvignon. And this time no one seemed to be worried about the wineglasses. Oddly enough, Earvin was milling around, too. From table to table. Talking with our patrons. If I didn't know any better, I would have sworn he was running for office and trying to solicit votes. Too bad he couldn't do the same thing at the competition. Given his demeanor and the way in which our guests were ogling him, it was as if he was an entirely different person than the one I'd gotten to know.

"Earvin seems to be in high spirits," Cammy whispered when I approached her table.

I glanced his way and narrowed my eyes to get a better look. "As long as those high spirits don't involve any questionable substances, we'll be fine."

To be on the safe side, I moseyed over to Glenda's table and pulled her aside. "You didn't give Earvin anything to eat or drink, did you?"

Glenda brushed a strand of her now blueish-mauve hair from her forehead. "Noo... but I did substitute that generic soap we have in our kitchen with my special calming cream soap. Aromatherapy works wonders. Earvin washed up in the sink before putting on food prep gloves."

"What's in the calming cream?"

"Lavender and oatmeal. Very safe. Very soothing."

I doubted the hand soap Earvin used was somehow responsible for his change in mood, but thankfully, his behavior didn't set off any alarms. Unlike Allete's. By now, the sheriff's department had sent someone to Rosalee's winery, and I hoped it wasn't Deputy Hickman because Allete would be camping out in Rosalee's restroom for sure.

"Good to know."

Next, I headed for the front door, where Lizzie was guarding the cash register. "Hey, Lizzie, please call the Grey Egret and let them know everything went well with Earvin. Don and Theo are probably wondering how it went, especially since Earvin's going to be at their winery this afternoon."

"Of course."

"Oh, and tell Cammy I'm going over to Terrace Wineries."

"Uh-oh. I knew it was trouble when Rosalee called. Anything I can do?"

"Follow the Nancy Drew Handbook and we'll be fine."

With that, I trounced out the door and headed up the hill to get my car. Minutes later, I pulled into the Terrace Wineries' parking lot. Sure enough, an official Yates County Sheriff's vehicle was parked directly in front of the building. Yep, nothing said "Come sample our wines" like an official sheriff's car.

Walking into Terrace Wineries, the set-up for the chocolate demonstration looked like ours, with circular seating and a large table. The utensils, machinery, and bowls seemed to compete with each other for space. Bits of chocolate flakes dotted the white tablecloth and a partially opened block of chocolate, with its unfolded white wrapper, stood off to the side by the tempering machine. I imagined it was "the death threat chocolate."

The customers who were seated in the demonstration area, and who most likely witnessed Allete's impromptu exit, were busy tapping on their cell phones or chatting with each other.

Rosalee was nowhere in sight. When I asked her employee at their cash register where I could find her, she pointed to the kitchen on my left. "She's talking with a deputy in there. That's why the door's closed. Say, you look familiar."

"I'm Norrie Ellington from Two Witches across the road."

"Oh, I should have recognized you from the last time you were here. You found a clue to Roy Wilkes's murder, didn't you? Rosalee was really impressed."

"Actually, one of your customers found it and gave it to me but—"

I never got to finish my sentence because in that instant, Deputy Hickman came barreling out of the kitchen and brushed past me to the corridor where the restrooms were located. He pounded on both the ladies' and the men's room doors. Then he shouted, "Miss Barrineau, you must vacate the restroom immediately. Do not force me to come inside and drag you out."

Then, it dawned on him it was me that he had all but collided with, and he turned. "I should have known I'd find you here, Miss Ellington. Do you have some sort of radar that points you in the direction of these kinds of disturbances?"

I shook my head and shrugged. "I have the same news apps as everyone else."

He then pounded on the ladies' room door and repeated his warning to Allete.

Rosalee, who was standing a few feet away, took a step or two closer and gave him a nudge with her elbow. "It won't get her out, Gary. Try another tactic and don't you dare go in there and break down one of my stalls."

Emma stood by the demonstration table but didn't make a move. So much for offering her services to Rosalee. I should have realized, that with a key piece of evidence on the table, it would be impossible to conduct a demonstration. I walked over to Emma and spun her around so we weren't facing the audience.

"Sorry. Looks like we're stuck until Deputy Hickman decides what to do with the chocolate."

Emma bit her lip. "I don't think he knows what to do with Allete. Everyone in this room can hear him. It's awful."

Sure enough, Deputy Hickman's voice got louder by the minute. Not wanting to have Rosalee's wine and chocolate pairing turn into a total bust, I asked one of her workers where I could find the tasting room manager. "You're looking at her. Letty Grebbins. I've been the tasting room manager here for over nine years and this is a first." Letty was about a foot shorter than me and at least fifteen or twenty years older. She was heavyset, with short brown hair and gray roots that needed to be touched up.

I extended my hand. "Norrie Ellington. Two Witches. Nice to meet you. Listen, I sent our bistro worker, Emma, over here to do the demo because Rosalee called and well, we've been through this kind of disaster before with our chocolatier. Not locked up in the restroom, but splitsville, if you know what I mean. Anyway, Emma can't do the demo because the threatening evidence is on the table."

Letty rubbed her temples. "Any suggestions?"

"Sure. Send the ticket holders to the sampling tables for the wine pairings. Once those deputies remove the evidence and give you an 'all clear,' Emma can do the demo instead of Allete."

Letty grabbed my wrist and gave it a squeeze. "I can't thank you enough." She fluffed her hair, puffed out her chest, and addressed the ticket holders. "Please move to the tasting room tables. I know it's a backwards version of the usual program, but we've had some unforeseen circumstances."

As far as the winery guests knew, Allete had some sort of breakdown or meltdown. They had no idea about the death threat in the chocolate, according to Rosalee. No wonder there was no hysteria, only the sound of chairs moving on wooden floors coupled with people grumbling.

The room noise made it impossible for me to hear any conversations between Deputy Hickman and Rosalee in the corridor by the restrooms. Any second now, Deputy Hickman would be in that ladies' room and Allete would be screaming her lungs out. I did the only thing that popped into my head. I charged for the ladies' room, elbowing both Deputy Hickman and Rosalee as I yelled, "Can't hold it! Sorry!"

Once inside, I locked the door and bent down to locate Allete's feet so I'd know which stall she was in. No time to admire her fancy leather ankle boots. I rapped on the stall and said, "It's Norrie Ellington from Two Witches. If you don't want our county's lead deputy to storm in here and kick your door down, you need to pull yourself together and get out of there."

Her response was a series of sobs, so I repeated myself. This time louder. My Spanish teacher once told the class that getting louder while trying to explain something to someone who didn't speak your language fluently was the worst possible thing to do. Then again, Allete seemed pretty conversant with English, so I yelled again. This time she listened.

She opened the door and peered out. "Whoever carved that message knew how to work the chocolate. It was no amateur."

Chapter 25

"Work the chocolate?" I asked. "I don't understand."

Allete exited from the stall and walked to the sink, where she splashed water on her face. She then took a paper towel and dabbed her cheeks. "Whoever wrote that message knew how to use sculpting tools to carve the letters so they were not only precise but aesthetically pleasing."

How thoughtful. An aesthetically pleasing death threat.

"Are you saying it was one of your competitors?"

"*Oui.*" She paused for a moment. "Earvin Roels must have found a way to do that heinous thing. I'm positive he murdered his uncle and now wishes to do away with the rest of his competition."

"And Stanislav?" I ventured.

"Absolutely inconceivable."

"Okay, fine. Let's consider Earvin for a moment. How could he possibly get over here to write the message in the chocolate without being seen, and then show up on time for his presentation at Two Witches?"

Allete squeezed the paper towel she was holding and then tossed it in the small trash basket by the sink. "Don't you understand? He could have done it any time. Those chocolate blocks are kept in Geneva on the Lake's kitchen and brought to the wineries on the morning of the presentation. Each block is marked for a specific winery. He could have snuck into their kitchen last night."

A strange thought crossed my mind. Could handwriting experts recognize carved letters in chocolate? Everyone had a certain style. A certain "give away."

"If that's true," I said, "the forensics team will know. They'll discover who's behind the threat and you won't have to worry." *What the heck am I saying?*

"I'm not worried about the threat. I am worried the killer will make good of it."

Suddenly, there was a loud pounding on the door. "Miss Ellington! Miss Barrineau! I must insist you vacate the restroom at once."

"Look, Allete," I said. "You're perfectly safe. Don't call more attention to the problem. All those deputies want to do is take a statement from you. Then you can continue your demonstration. It's your reputation, you know."

Allete shook her head. "Isn't it too late for my presentation?"

"No. The patrons are doing the wine and chocolate pairing first. Plenty of time."

I unlocked the restroom door and we stepped out. I introduced Allete to Deputy Hickman and he, along with Rosalee, escorted her to the kitchen, but not before the deputy motioned to the latest arrival from the Yates County Sheriff's Department. It was a guy from their forensics team and I swore his official jacket, with the letters FORENSIC spelled out on the back, looked at least two sizes too large.

"You'll see the evidence, Hal," Deputy Hickman said. "Just don't eat it."

"I'm on my way back to the tasting room," I said. "I can show Hal where the chocolate death threat is."

"Thanks, Norrie," Rosalee replied, but I swore I heard Grizzly Gary groan.

Hal followed me to the demonstration table, where Emma stood guard like a sentinel. The winery guests were still sampling the chocolates that Terrace Wineries paired with their Pinot Noir. Everything seemed to be going well, considering the main feature was on hold for a few more minutes.

"There's the block chocolate with the message on it," I whispered to the forensics deputy.

He, in turn, responded in a louder voice. "Thanks. Once I'm done taking photos of the scene, I'll process it for the lab and tell them to put a priority on it. That chocolate could very well have been poisoned."

Oh no. Not the word "poison."

The word "poison" carried through the room faster than a seventh-grade rumor.

Within seconds, someone shouted, "The chocolate's been poisoned."

It was no surprise that the demo table was besieged by guests demanding to know what was going on. Rosalee heard the commotion from the kitchen and raced to the room, with Deputy Hickman at her heels.

There was a flurry of cell phone snapshots that would most likely go viral.

"No one's been poisoned," Deputy Hickman shouted. "Repeat. No one has been poisoned. Remain calm."

I don't know about anyone else, but when I heard the words, "Remain calm," I got the opposite effect. Apparently, I wasn't the only one. More cell phone snapshots, only this time accompanied by threats of lawsuits and demands by at least four people to be taken to the hospital.

It took a full ten minutes for Deputy Hickman and forensic deputy, Hal, with the big mouth, to get the crowd under control.

"We're investigating a threat," Hickman bellowed. "Nothing more. A written threat on a block of chocolate. No different than someone scrawling a message on a bathroom door. Checking for poison is simply a protocol."

Then, for some inexplicable reason, I added my two cents. "No one ate that chocolate. The wrapper is still underneath it."

"What about the chocolates we've eaten?" a woman wearing a long-sleeved top and faux fur jacket asked.

"Those chocolates were prepared early this morning at Geneva on the Lake," I said. "The different varieties were delivered to the other wineries, but they all used the same ingredients. There have been no problems."

To make my point clear, I walked over to one of Rosalee's tasting tables, snatched a thumb-sized chocolate from the table, and popped it into my mouth. "Yum. Puts those store-bought ones to shame."

A few guests chuckled, and it seemed as if the tension-filled atmosphere dissipated.

Then Rosalee spoke in a slow, commanding voice. "Thank you for your patience and understanding. Like live theater performances, we cannot anticipate what may happen. We can only react. Please enjoy your wine pairings. The esteemed Allete Barrineau will conduct her demonstration in five minutes."

As Rosalee worked the crowd, Emma approached me. "Do I need to hang around here? I think Allete's got it under control. Look, she's already organizing the demo table."

"You're right. Let's sneak out of here before Deputy Hickman decides he wants a statement from me."

I tapped Rosalee on the shoulder and told her I was heading out.

"I owe you, Norrie. Thanks for coming to our rescue."

"About coming to the rescue, I was going to ask if you could come to mine. Our wineries all received two tickets for Saturday's competition and I told Godfrey Klein he could be my plus one. That was before Bradley Jamison called to tell me he'd be back from Yonkers and was looking forward to attending. So, um, if you're not planning on taking your sister, Marilyn, do you mind if I use your extra ticket for Bradley?"

"Take Marilyn? She'd give all of us indigestion. You can give my extra ticket to that young whippersnapper, but don't expect me to entertain him."

I tried not to laugh. When Rosalee was accused of murder last year and her attorney couldn't meet with her right away, he sent his associate, Bradley. One look at him and Rosalee told everyone she wasn't about to have "someone who just fell off the turnip truck" representing her.

"Thanks, Rosalee. I'll do my best to keep him out of your hair."

"It won't be my hair you need to worry about. Better keep those two beaus at arm's distance."

Aargh. Was it really becoming obvious about Godfrey? "Honestly, I'll be glad when the chocolate event is over."

Then Rosalee whispered, "The next time the wine association comes up with an idea like this, I'm going to ask for a vote of no confidence."

* * * *

Two Witches was a scene of tranquility when Emma and I returned to the tasting room. Fred made me a grilled cheese and bacon sandwich and, once I'd devoured it, I headed back to the house to finish that screenplay. *If* I could concentrate. The way things were going, it wouldn't surprise me if Renee pushed the deadline up by another few days so she could make the most of Guadalupe's beaches. I cringed. What was I going to hand her? A hodgepodge of clichéd dialogue? She'd be begging Conrad Blyth to return.

Conrad wrote wonderful Amish mystery screenplays but got kicked to the curb six months ago. I kept a poster on the wall reminding me not to wind up in his shoes.

The last three days had been nightmarish, not to mention the day before that when Jules Leurant was found dead in the snow. Now Allete was convinced Earvin was the killer, Earvin was convinced it was Stanislav, and I was bringing new players into the game with the auburn-haired woman whom I believed to be Belgium's noted horticulturalist, Hortensia Vermeulen. I really needed to slow down and digest the events that were clogging my mind and preventing me from focusing on my screenplay.

There was only one solution. Spill my guts to Don and Theo. I called the Grey Egret and invited the guys for dinner.

"You actually cooked something?" Theo asked when I got him on the phone.

"Not exactly. The Beef and Brew in Geneva will be doing the cooking. Doesn't slow roasted beef and cheddar soup sound good? I hate ordering out for myself. Besides, I really need to unload, and you and Don are the best listeners."

"Does your takeout order include their apple pie?"

"It will now."

"Then unload away."

"Great. Come up around seven. I don't think you need to worry about Earvin this afternoon. He seemed fine."

"Actually, he's here now. And not scowling."

"It's the calming soap."

"Huh?"

"I'll tell you later."

Just knowing that relief, in the form of Don and Theo, would be here this evening, I was able to make decent progress with my screenplay. And not once did I substitute Bradley or Godfrey's name for my characters'. I called my order in to the Beef and Brew and told them to have it ready by six. That gave me plenty of time for the drive.

I set the table in advance and took out a bottle of Cabernet Sauvignon from the wine rack in the basement. We were lucky our basement had the right humidity for storing wine—fifty to eighty percent, according to my father, who made it a point to impress upon us the proper way to store red wines. Unlike white wines, that should be enjoyed within a year or so, red wines could afford to hang around and age. Not indefinitely, but certainly for a few years. It was a no-brainer to store the wine on its side so the liquid would touch the cork and prevent it from drying out. As for the temperature in the basement, it had to be reasonable. Not arctic cold so it would freeze, but not warm either. My father hung a wall thermometer near the stairs and eyeballed the thing to make sure we were always in the forty-five to sixty range.

When Theo and Don arrived at a little past seven, I had everything ready for us, starting with giant bowls of cheddar soup and the Beef and Brew's mouthwatering biscuits. The steam from the soup hung in the air as the three of us spooned the creamy liquid into our mouths.

"I could live on this stuff," Don said. "Especially in the winter. It's damn cold out there and getting worse."

Theo tore off a piece of a buttery biscuit and took a bite. "Yeah, but at least there's no precipitation forecasted for the next two days."

"Hallelujah for small favors," I said. "I suppose all the national reporters and magazine bigwigs will be arriving tomorrow, huh?"

Don nodded and swallowed another spoonful of soup. "I understand the judges are going to be so closely guarded—it will be impossible to get near them."

"Okay, you can both beat me over the head for not reading every single email Henry Speltmore sent our way. Guess I missed that one. Who are the judges?"

Theo and Don looked at me as if I'd asked who the president of the United States was. Then they looked at each other.

"It's not funny, guys," I said. "I have lots of stuff on my mind. Deadlines, if you must know."

Theo laughed. "We'll cut you a break. There are three judges. The editor-in-chief of *Wine Spectator,* the editor-in-chief of *Food and Wine,* and the president of the Culinary Institute of America in Hyde Park, New York. Big enough bigwigs for you?"

"Oh yeah. Are they all staying at Geneva on the Lake?"

"Actually, no. Two of them are staying at Cornell's Statler Hotel in Ithaca and only the editor-in-chief from *Food and Wine* will be in Geneva. You really should read your emails, Norrie."

Don took another biscuit and bit into it. "Oh my gosh. I'm filling up on bread and I won't have any room for the beef."

Theo shot him a look. "Then stop eating the biscuits."

Suddenly, Don looked around the room and bent under the table. "Where's Charlie? He's usually begging for food by now."

"Oh, he's curled up in my bedroom," I said. "That rotten Plott Hound has been passing gas all afternoon and last thing I need him to do is ruin our meal."

"The only thing that could ruin my meal," Don replied, "is another incident with one of those chocolatiers. I'm surprised all of us aren't on anxiety medicine by now."

I stood up, collected the soup bowls, and put them in the sink. "Allete should be, the way she falls apart over everything. It's a wonder she can even get a night's—oh good God. The Ambien. How much do you want to bet that spray bottle was hers?"

Don handed the soup spoons to Theo, who, in turn, passed them to me. "Any chance you can get Gladys Pipp to spill the beans on that one? She seems awfully chummy with you."

"She just likes Francine's jellies and jams. But maybe I can prod a bit to see what she knows. She was very forthcoming about the bonbon Jules ingested. Meanwhile, Stephanie and I are going to attend a very important lecture on soil maximization at Hobart and William Smith Colleges tomorrow."

I placed a huge sauterne on the table with the most mouth-watering roast beef I'd ever seen. "And before you ask why, I'll tell you. I found out from Godfrey Klein that Hortensia Vermeulen, a Belgian horticulturalist, is the speaker. That's right. The very Hortensia Vermeulen whose boarding pass I found in the trash at Geneva on the Lake. I'm totally convinced she's the auburn-haired woman and Stephanie can ID her for sure. Stephanie was up front and personal when a woman fitting that description broke up the little chocolate-throwing incident between Stanislav and some foreign guy."

"Next thing you know, you're going to tell us the foreign guy is the other guest at the hotel. The one you mentioned earlier," Don said.

"He might be. He might very well be, but no one has seen hide-nor-hare of him since that incident. At least no one that I know of. But until I can nail down Hortensia, I can't get anywhere. Look, I hate to say this, but I think something awful is going to happen at that grand competition on Saturday. It's a feeling I have that I can't shake."

"We get it," Theo said. "But don't be impulsive. Especially if you do uncover a key piece of information. There's a murderer out there, maybe even more than one, and if they can do it once, doing it a second time comes easy. At least according to the TV shows I watch."

"Stephanie and I will be careful. As far as I'm concerned, every one of those chocolatiers is a suspect. Along with the two international guests from the hotel. Geez, why do those sheriff's departments have to take so darn long with the investigation?"

"Because they do it systematically and methodically, not emotionally and randomly."

"Sure, because it's not their winery's name that was bantered around. Aargh. Come on, dig in. There is an onion and potato pie, as well as green beans with almonds. I always think better on a full stomach."

We spent the rest of the evening tossing theories around and, by the time we got to the apple pie, we had enough plots to take over the mystery section at the library.

"It all comes back to motive," Theo said as he and Don put on their coats and walked to the door. "Everyone wants that grand prize. Greed and ambition know no bounds."

"Unless it's jealousy and revenge," Don added. "Of course, if that were the case, it would have been Stanislav face down in the snow and not Jules."

I handed Theo his scarf that had fallen on the floor. "It's what we don't know about those three that may really hold the answers. Maybe Stephanie and I will get lucky tomorrow and find out that Hortensia holds a large chunk of the puzzle."

"Either that or a large slab of soil that's up for analysis. Have fun."

The guys thanked me for the terrific meal and I, in turn, thanked them for being there whenever I needed them. I locked the door, finished tidying up the kitchen, and went upstairs to see if Charlie wanted one last turn out the doggie door. He looked up from my bed and went back to sleep. The room smelled like a cheese factory that had lost its central air-conditioning. I opened a window to air it out. Somewhere around the lake, I thought I heard a siren, but it could have been anything.

Chapter 26

The next time I decided to take someone with me on a reconnaissance mission, it wouldn't be Stephanie. She always reminded me of Christy Brinkley in her super model days—with the long blond hair and a smile that invited every male in a twenty-mile vicinity to drop everything and ogle her. Yep, I'd seen Chevy Chase's *Vacation* and believe me, Stephanie would have brought the guy to his knees the same way Christy did. Unfortunately, that was exactly what happened when we got to Albright Auditorium the following morning. Nine thirty-seven, to be precise, with the program starting at ten.

Usually visitors were smitten with Hobart and William Smith's neoclassical buildings, but not one single guy took a second look at Albright Auditorium once Stephanie made her way to the entrance. One would think a winter coat and jeans would cover that figure of hers, but apparently, the men on campus took one look at those long locks of hers and knew instinctively that underneath layers of winter clothing was a figure worth pursuing. And pursue it they did. It started the minute we got to the door.

Two guys who'd barely made it through puberty shoved me aside to hold the door open for her. I nearly tripped over myself and had to lean against the doorframe so I wouldn't fall. Then, if that wasn't bad enough, a sandy-haired man in a sports jacket and tie, who was chatting with a few coeds near the lecture hall door, walked over to us. Only, it wasn't us. It was Stephanie. He walked over to where Stephanie stood. I had become totally invisible. Invisible and sulking.

I'd always been told I was cute. Guys liked my soft freckles and one dimple. Same with my shoulder-length auburn hair. However, next to

Stephanie, I resembled Shrek's wife. I took a breath and waited for him to hit on her.

"Welcome to our program," he said to Stephanie. "I'm professor Mallory. Jacob Mallory. I teach environmental studies. You must be new to our lecture series because I haven't seen you here before. And please don't tell me you're a vineyard manager."

Stephanie used the back of her palm to flip her hair. I mentally rolled my eyes. *Didn't we give that maneuver a rest after tenth grade?*

"Actually," she said, "I'm Stephanie Ipswich and I own Gable Hill Winery in Penn Yan. I'm here with another winery owner, Norrie Ellington, from Two Witches."

Jacob turned his head slightly and gave me a nod. Then he returned his gaze to Stephanie. "Hmm, I must make it a point to do a bit of wine tasting. Needless to say, we've been trying to get Hortensia Vermeulen to speak at the college for years, but her schedule wouldn't permit it. Then, out of the blue, someone on her staff contacted our board and, next thing we knew, she was available to speak. It's not every day a world-renowned horticulturalist flies all the way from Belgium to deliver a lecture. Of course, she'll be at Cornell as well, but still, it's quite something."

"Interesting timing," I said. "This is the weekend for the Finger Lakes' Chocolate and Wine Extravaganza. You wouldn't happen to know if Ms. Vermeulen has anything to do with that industry, do you? I mean, maybe her expertise extends to cocoa beans as well."

Professor Mallory shook his head. "I doubt it. Her focus is on global integration in order to combat hunger. That's why soil maximization is paramount."

Terrific. This lecture is going to be as boring as hell. Stephanie better identify the woman right away.

Before I could respond, Professor Mallory continued. "I suppose that's why both of you are here. Anyway, I'm not sure if you've had a chance to read the email from our department. I know it was sent to the local vineyard managers. Unlike our other lecturers, Hortensia Vermeulen won't be fielding questions at the end of her PowerPoint. She'll make copies of the presentation available for anyone, but attendees are asked to submit their questions to her website. She will note the question and provide her response once she returns home."

"That's rather odd, isn't it?" Stephanie asked.

Professor Mallory adjusted his tie and shrugged. "Some of our speakers are more comfortable handling a crowd than others. I don't know Ms.

Vermeulen, so I can't answer for her. Anyway, we're pleased as punch she's at our college today, but I'm equally pleased to have met your acquaintance." *I may actually vomit. Right here. Right now, in Albright Auditorium.* "Um, it looks like this place is filling up quick. We really need to get inside and grab some decent seats. Up front. We need to sit up front. Much better acoustics." *And a better look at the speaker.*

"You don't have to worry about the acoustics. Everything in the lecture hall is state-of-the-art," he replied. "Besides, no one wants to sit up front. I know for a fact that my students will have commandeered the last row so they can sneak out unobtrusively."

We started for the door to the lecture hall when another man, presumably a colleague of Professor Mallory, tapped him on the elbow. "Jake, I need a moment of your time. Got a quick question about Thursday's student teacher visits."

Professor Mallory gave the guy a quick nod and then said to Stephanie, "I'll definitely make it a point to do some wine tasting. Enjoy the lecture."

I grabbed Stephanie by the arm and hustled her into the lecture hall. "Hurry up. We're here on a murder investigation not a flirt-a-thon."

Stephanie laughed. "When you're stuck with first-grade twins and the only conversation you have revolves around *SpongeBob SquarePants*, a bit of innocent flirting is fun."

"Oh brother. Come on. I see some seats in the first row."

The curtain was open and a huge screen was directly in front of us. Off to our left, only a few yards from where we found our seats, was the podium.

"If they don't mess with the lighting," I said, "you should get a really good look at her."

"Didn't you see her, too, Norrie?"

"I only caught a glimpse of her that day in the winery when she came in and spooked Earvin. I got a better look at her calf's-length coat than her face."

"One thing for sure. She won't be wearing a coat for this lecture."

Professor Mallory was right about the seating. Other than two students at the far end of the row, Stephanie and I had the whole area to ourselves. Even the row behind us was scantily filled. Beyond that, it was a packed house. Who would've thought soil maximization was such a hot topic.

I made sure my cell phone was on mute and leaned back. A few seconds later, the chairperson of the environmental studies department approached the podium and read what seemed to be Hortensia's vitae. Then he introduced her. The woman seemed to be the same height and weight of the woman I had observed a few days ago. And, she had the same auburn-colored hair. With her gray tailored suit and white top, she reminded me of Lana Lang.

"Is that her?" I poked Stephanie in the elbow.

"Shh. I can't tell. She's too far away. Looks like her."

"Damn. Francine owns a pair of opera glasses and I should have brought them. Take another look. Can't you tell?"

"Shh. No. I don't think I'm going to be able to make a positive ID unless I'm up close and personal."

"Crap. We're going to have to sit through this entire thing?"

And sit through it, we did. I never wanted to hear the terms "geogrids," "stabilization," and "residue retention" in the same sentence again. And if hearing them wasn't enough, I could see them on the gigantic screen in front of me.

When the presentation was over, Hortensia received an enthusiastic applause. I think that was because everyone was glad it was over. She told the audience to visit her website and submit all questions to an address she provided—exactly what Professor Mallory said she'd do.

"Now what?" Stephanie whispered.

"Now we charge up those steps to the right of the stage and thank her for the tremendous presentation before she bolts. I'll talk. You take a good, hard look. Follow me."

With that, I jumped out of my seat and raced to the stage. Stephanie was a few feet behind me and moving as fast as she could in heels. Yep, heels. Who wore heels in the Finger Lakes in winter? What we didn't count on was that the fastidious cleaning crew from the college had polished the stage floor. One step onto that slippery surface and Stephanie slid past me and into the podium.

The narrow stand, complete with a built-in light, toppled over and literally trapped Hortensia Vermeulen in place. At least for a second, and that was all we needed.

"Oh my God! I'm so sorry," Stephanie said. "All I wanted to do was thank you for the marvelous presentation. And invite you to visit our winery during your stay. Gable Hill Winery on Route 14 in Penn Yan."

Stephanie offered Hortensia her hand so the famed horticulturalist could step over the obstruction we had managed to create. As Hortensia looked down to see where she was stepping, Stephanie inched in closer for a better look. And I caught a look at the ring Hortensia was wearing. If the stunning chocolate-colored gemstone was real, she could swap it for a piece of Dubai. Even one of those sharp gold prongs on the thing would be worth a fortune.

"I'm afraid that's not possible," Hortensia said. "I have a full schedule and a flight back to Belgium on Tuesday. Everyone has been so gracious. Including the management at my hotel, Geneva on the Lake. They insisted I attend a most coveted event Saturday night and secured a ticket for me. For once, it will be nice to be on the other side of the podium, if you know what I mean."

I took a step forward and nudged Stephanie a few inches to my left. Then I looked directly at Hortensia. "You must be referring to the Chocolate and Wine Competition. It's the culminating event for the Seneca Lake Wine Trail's Chocolate and Wine Extravaganza. Our winery, Two Witches, is also hosting."

Hortensia didn't as much as bat an eyelash. "Yes. I've had the pleasure of making the acquaintance with one of the chocolatiers who is also staying at my hotel. Fascinating profession, I must say."

At that moment, the department chair who'd introduced Hortensia to the audience rushed onto the stage. "Ms. Vermeulen cannot be kept much longer. Please visit her website with your questions and comments."

He took Hortensia by the elbow and ushered her off stage. I waited until they were out of sight and then mouthed the question, "Was it her?" to Stephanie.

"Look around, Norrie. Everyone's left the lecture hall. They probably set a world's record for fastest exit in history. And yes, it was her. It was absolutely her!"

"How can you be sure?"

"You can't fake the shape of your ears and that's something I noticed when I watched her break up the scuffle between Stanislav and that man. But there's more."

"What? What more?"

"Hortensia Vermeulen was wearing a wig."

I gasped. "A wig? How do you know?"

"Oh, believe me, I know wigs. Sometimes there's no cure for bad hair days. Anyway, Hortensia Vermeulen was most definitely wearing one. A decent synthetic one. When she bent down, I got a good look at it. The part was perfect. No one's hair is parted that perfectly. And, there was no static. Absolutely no static in her hair. I noticed that when she was onstage."

I instinctively lifted a palm and flattened my hair. "You notice static?"

"Uh-huh. I'm constantly battling static in the winter. The lack of moisture in the air makes it impossible for anyone's style to look good. No wonder she traveled with a wig."

"Forget the wig," I said. "You should have seen the killer ring on her finger. The big question is, what the heck is Hortensia Vermeulen, horticulturalist extraordinaire, doing in our wineries and why wouldn't she admit she'd already been to yours?"

"Same way people don't want to admit to murder."

Chapter 27

At least Stephanie and I cleared up one mystery. Hortensia Vermeulen knew, or at least was acquainted with, all three of the chocolatiers, not just the one she claimed to have met at Geneva on the Lake. And I certainly knew who that was—Allete. Godfrey and I interrupted their conversation in the bar. But Hortensia also had a little chitchat when Stanislav returned to the bar that same evening, and she didn't admit to that. And if she didn't own up to a cozy conversation, she certainly wasn't about to confess her little scuffle with Earvin in my parking lot.

I kept mulling over her strange behavior when it came to the chocolatiers, but as far as pointing a finger at her for Jules's demise and the bizarre events at the wine pairings, I really couldn't. Stephanie told me she thought there was something suspicious about the woman, but until we could delve further, we were virtually stuck.

"Guess I'll try to Google Hortensia this afternoon in between bouts of writing," I said as Stephanie and I exited Albright Auditorium. "I'm kind of on a tight deadline."

"I'll see what I can do. The school bus doesn't drop the boys off until three forty, so that gives me a bit of time as well."

We agreed to call each other before the day was out. Then I literally grabbed her by the arm and raced her to the parking lot before another one of the campus Lotharios caught a glimpse of her. I dropped her off at Gable Hill Winery a few minutes later and then made a quick stop at home to change out of my nice slacks and sweater into some old jeans and a sweatshirt before making a beeline for our tasting room. My stomach was rumbling, and I desperately needed something to eat. I didn't plan on hanging around the winery.

When I stepped inside the building, Glenda was at the cash register.

"Hey, Glenda! Where's Lizzie?" I asked.

"She had to make a deposit at the bank. She'll be back soon. Do you need her?"

"No. That's the last thing I need. Not Lizzie or her constant nagging about how I'm tracking down information about Jules's murder. If I hear the name Nancy Drew one more time, I'll heave."

Glenda adjusted the purple flower she'd placed behind her ear with a bobby pin. "I understand. Lizzie is from another generation, and she relies heavily on the wit and wisdom of their icons. Not that it's necessarily a bad thing, but there are much more efficient ways and means to find out who's responsible."

Oh no. Did I just unleash the Kraken? "Glenda, I—"

"Before you say another word, let me tell you I'm here at your disposal. A simple séance set near the site where Jules's body was discovered would, most assuredly, be your best bet. Provided, of course, that Jules hasn't moved on. And I seriously doubt he has because, well, he was murdered and souls don't move on when there's unfinished business."

"Um, uh, interesting thought. I'll keep that in mind. But *I* have to move on. I have lots of unfinished business, including lunch." *And a screenplay.* "Catch you later."

I blew through the tasting room with only a wave of my hand. Cammy waved back but everyone else was otherwise occupied with customers. The demonstration table had been taken down, and I imagined Seneca Restaurant Supply had picked up their tempering machine, along with any of the other utensils they'd provided.

Emma confirmed my observation when I spotted her behind the Panini maker a few seconds later. I couldn't order a chicken salad sandwich fast enough.

"Thank God that chocolate fiasco is over!" she said. "I would have carried the machinery to Seneca Restaurant Supply's van myself, if it wasn't so heavy."

"Honestly, Emma. I really don't know how to thank you. You've been amazing."

A faint blush appeared on Emma's cheeks and she grinned. "It really wasn't all that bad. I mean, I learned a lot about making chocolate confections. But I could have lived without the drama. You have no idea what it was like working with Earvin. If everyone thought Jules was an egotistical lout, Earvin had him beat. I've never met anyone so demanding."

"Well, the chocolate demonstrations may be over as far as our wineries are concerned, but tomorrow night's the competition, and I think all three chocolatiers will be out for blood. Oops. Wrong choice of words, huh?" Emma chuckled as she handed me the sandwich. "Fred's trying a new recipe. This one has grapes and dill in it. Strange combination, but it tastes really good. By the way, have you heard anything about the official investigation into Jules's death? All I hear and read are the words, *'continuing* or *on-going* investigation.'"

"That's all I hear as well."

I let Emma get back to work and wolfed down my sandwich. She was right. It *was* good. Then, as fast as I blew into the winery, I made my exit out. My to-do list had grown with the new task looming over my head—digging up dirt on Hortensia. I rationalized I could spend maybe an hour on that endeavor and then plunge back into my screenplay for the remainder of the afternoon.

Unfortunately, I didn't count on a phone message from Franz. I saw the red light blinking the minute I set foot in the kitchen. Ignoring Charlie's whining for more food, I walked to the machine and pushed the button.

"Norrie, it's Franz. The gentleman from the Netherlands who's staying at Geneva on the Lake is Daan Langbroek. He's a well-known businessman, but you may be more interested in something else. He's Allete's ex-husband. I have this on the best authority. The sommelier at Geneva on the Lake is a friend of mine. I trust you'll be discreet about my source. If I don't see you later today or tomorrow, I'll definitely see you at the chocolate competition. Have a nice day."

Oh my God! Allete's ex-husband. *That* would certainly explain the chocolate spewing incident at Stephanie's winery. But it wouldn't explain Jules's murder. It wasn't as if Allete was cavorting with Jules. I picked up the receiver and dialed Gable Hill Winery. Stephanie's boys were still at school, so I knew she'd be at work.

"Hold on a minute, please," the voice at the other end of the line said, "she just went back to her office. I'll buzz her."

Two seconds later, I shared Franz's newfound information without so much as pausing to take a breath.

"Holy cow! This is like a soap opera. What else did you find out about Daan Langbroek?"

"Uh, nothing yet. That's all Franz's message said."

"Give me two seconds. I'm at my computer."

Before I could answer, she said, "Crap. The whole thing is written in Dutch. Including his tweets. Give me another second."

"I, um, er—"

"Ah-hah. LinkedIn's got it in English, too. Holy moly! Daan Langbroek's no slouch."

"What do you mean? What are you looking at?"

"Well, it's most definitely the well-built, light-haired man I saw getting into it with Stanislav, but I had no idea Allete's ex-husband owned a digital transformation company."

"A what?"

"Think paperless. My husband talks about this stuff all the time. Hmm. Allete must have gotten a raw deal on their divorce settlement because, according to what I'm seeing, Daan's company has to be pulling in megabucks."

"That must really be eating away at her. No wonder she and Stanislav are so driven about winning the competition."

"Talk about driven," Stephanie said, "Allete's ex must still be pining for her. Otherwise, why fly overseas just to give her new beau a hard time?"

"Don't ask me. I'm no expert on matters of the heart. I only write the stuff."

"Well, you'll have a lot to write about if you take notes. Tomorrow night's competition could be uglier than we imagined if Daan and Stanislav get into it again."

"Aargh. Hadn't even considered that. I don't suppose you've had a chance to Google Hortensia yet, have you?"

"Typing in her name as we speak. Let's compare notes later, okay?"

"Absolutely!"

No sooner did I get off the phone with Stephanie when Cammy called.

"Oh no!" I mumbled. "What now? What's happened?"

"Sorry. I should have known you'd be on edge but guess who just walked into our winery?"

"Don't tell me. Steven Trobert? Catherine finally got under his skin to the point of no return so he took a flight from Portland to Rochester? I don't know why she insists on fixing us up. It's not as if—"

"Norrie, quit babbling about Steven. I'm sure he's safe and sound in Maine. Meanwhile, Robin Roberts, Hoda Kotb, and Rachael Ray tasted our Cabernet Sauvignon and loved it but left a few seconds ago in their limo. Get your butt down here! Zyra Baroody from CNN is here with Ilene Shannon, the Irish food maven. The place is teaming with cameras and the two of them are asking a zillion questions. Oh, and there are magazine editors here as well."

I didn't remember what I said to Cammy, but I charged to the nearest mirror and stared. I definitely looked like one of the two witches. The makeup I had carefully applied in the morning was now caked around my eyelids. In addition, my hair seemed to have flattened in the last hour. There wasn't enough mousse in the world to save me.

At least the slacks and sweater I wore this morning were still hanging over a chair in my room. It took me all of ten seconds to swap out my comfy clothes for that more polished look. As for my hair, it was long enough for me to pull into a neat little bun-like ponytail. A swipe of a damp cotton ball across my eyes and I re-applied the liner.

To make the look complete, I grabbed one of Francine's scarves, wrapped it around my neck, and shot out the door, not even bothering to zip up my jacket. My car started right up, and I made it to our tasting room in record time.

Sure enough, the New York entourage had arrived. I took a deep breath, walked over to the tasting room table where Jordaine Waverly from *Food & Wine* was seated, and introduced myself.

"This event has turned the culinary world upside down," she said. "The murder, the trysts, and a nail-bitter of a competition. This is something none of us want to miss."

I thought I might have misunderstood. "The trysts? Plural? I thought there was only one."

Jordaine moistened her deep mauve lips and adjusted the thin gold chain around her neck. "Now that wouldn't be much fun, would it? Allete and Stanislav are getting as hackneyed as Angelina and Brad were. But things are about to heat up now that Anika Schou has graced the Finger Lakes with her presence. She and the late Jules Leurant—"

"Jordaine, is that you?" The woman's voice was distinctly British. I turned my head and recognized her at once. It was England's most notable food writer and TV personality, Mary Berry. Francine adored her baking shows.

Mary rushed to where Jordaine stood and gave her a hug. "I'm so jet lagged from the flight across the pond I doubt I'll ever recoup. I figured the best way around it was to hop in a limo and visit a few of the wineries. Are you staying at Geneva on the Lake as well?"

Dammit! Who the heck was Anika Schou and why did she matter? Now I'd never find out. Well, maybe later, when it was too late. I felt like I was intruding on a personal conversation, so I took a few steps back and collided with Cammy, who was setting out more wineglasses.

"It's like we stepped into another world," she said.

"Yeah. One that Henry Speltmore didn't bother to put into his emails."

Chapter 28

"Oh God no!" Cammy said. "Roger's got Zyra Baroody and Ilene Shannon at his table. Any second now, one of them will make an offhand comment and that will give him all the excuse he needs to launch into one of his never-ending lectures about the French and Indian War."

It was true. Roger, now retired from education, completed his dissertation on the French and Indian War. It wasn't as much of an academic endeavor for him as a passion. I imagined the worst—gruesome descriptions of battle scenes, long-winded explanations about military strategies, and, gulp, geographical references that could put a seasoned insomniac to sleep in seconds.

I had to do something.

Without wasting a minute, I took off and all but skidded into his tasting room table. "Roger, I'm so sorry to interrupt, but Cammy needs you. Something about wineglasses. I'll take over."

"Excuse me, ladies," he said to Zyra, Ilene, and the other few women who were at this table, "Duty calls. Much as it did for General Edward Braddock when King George II ordered him to go to Virginia and remove—"

Oh Lord! I actually know this. It's the French. General Braddock had to get the French out of Fort Duquesne. This is one of Roger's favorite stories.

"The French!" I shouted. "Now we can all relax and enjoy our wine." I gave Roger a little nudge with my elbow and he got the message.

"Wineglasses. I'm on my way."

Zyra and Ilene looked at each other and then at me.

"Sounds like all of you are really into American history," Zyra said.

"History, art, wine…we're kind of eclectic around here. I'm Norrie Ellington and I co-own this winery with my sister. She's in Costa Rica, researching insects with her husband. Uh, not a hobby. He's an entomologist with Cornell. Boy will they be sorry they missed meeting celebrities at our winery."

I was babbling on and if I kept it up, they'd be wishing Roger would return. Unfortunately, I couldn't seem to shut up. "You must be looking forward to the chocolate competition tomorrow night. I hope the three remaining chocolatiers can make it through the event unscathed. They never did find Jules's killer. Oh, don't get me wrong, I'm not insinuating the other chocolatiers are in any danger, but it does put everyone on edge a bit, don't you think?"

What the heck am I doing? Scaring the daylights out of TV personalities and chefs who could make or break our region? If Henry Speltmore gets wind of this, he'll be writing a ten-page manifesto about proper winery conversation.

"Oh, I think we'll be fine," Ilene said. "It's not as if any of us are in this competition and out for each other's throats. I wonder what the competition organizers have decided regarding the latest fly in the ointment, so to speak. It's been radio silence from their end, and, believe me, we've tried to get the skinny on what's going on."

Zyra nodded and took a sip of her wine. "If I knew, I could let my network know. You'd be surprised at how fast they can put a documentary together."

Fly? Ointment? Documentary? This was worse than tuning into the middle of *NCIS*.

Rather than asking outright what they were referring to, I took another approach. One that worked well for me in the past when I had no clue about something one of my professors explained in class.

"Um, could you expound on that for a minute?"

Ilene laughed. "A minute? We'd need an hour and as much as we're enjoying your hospitality at Two Witches, we wanted to check out a few of the other wineries. But here it is in a nutshell—the fourth chocolatier is on scene to claim her rightful place in the competition. Rumor has it she's been in the area for over a week but no one can confirm it."

"Fourth chocolatier?" I was dumbfounded.

Then a lady sitting next to Ilene turned toward me. "I write a blog on culinary arts and I've been following this competition as well. Anika Schou from Denmark was fourth on the list. She's the one who should be competing against Allete and Stanislav, not Earvin. Up until this past week, Earvin was tucked away in his late uncle's shadow. Now, all of sudden, he's in the limelight with Allete and Stanislav. That's not going over too well in the culinary world. You should see the tweets. Not to mention the diatribes on Facebook."

"That's right," Ilene said. "The organizational committee had better make a decision and make it quickly."

"Does Earvin know?" I asked. "He's supposed to be at Geneva on the Lake preparing for tomorrow night's event. He'll be devastated." *Either that or he'll go on some wild rampage in the kitchen. I hope they've locked up the knives.*

Then I remembered…What was it Jordaine said about Anika and Jules? It was right after she used the word "trysts." Rats. If only Mary Berry had caught a later flight, I could have gotten Jordaine to tell me. I can't very well march over there and reintroduce the subject.

I was so engrossed in my latest rumination that it took me a moment to process Ilene's answer. "He's been living under a shell if he doesn't. I'm glad I'm not part of that committee. It's hard enough judging the contests my publisher and sponsors arrange, let alone interpreting the rules."

I hadn't really thought about the fact that there could be more competitors higher up on the list than Earvin, but it certainly made sense. Too much sense. What if Earvin knocked off his uncle to get the position of third competitor? He'd guard that position like a junkyard dog, even if it meant doing to Anika what he'd done to Jules. That was, *if* he had done it at all. True, he had a prime motive, but he wasn't the only one.

At that moment, Zyra gave Shannon a pat on the wrist. "We'd better get a move on if we expect to hit a few more wineries." Then she turned to me. "Your Cabernet Sauvignon is marvelous. I wish I were pairing it with a steak right now. Love that bold flavor. I can almost taste hints of bell peppers."

"She's right," the lady with the blog added. "Sometimes red wines are overaged in the oak and lose the intense fruity flavors they were meant to have. This one is perfect. Too bad the last taste on Jules's lips was marred by a sleep-inducing drug. Did the authorities ever find out where it came from?"

"Not that I'm aware of," I said. "We rely on the media like everyone else."

The lady took another sip of her wine and narrowed her eyes. "It's the social media you should be following. And I'm not referring to the internet. In my experience, sometimes the most reliable sources come from the local scuttlebutt, to be blunt."

Oh my gosh. The local scuttlebutt. By now, Gladys Pipp must have some idea what Deputy Hickman is up to.

Zyra and Ilene stood and buttoned their coats.

Faux fur must be popular this season. "I look forward to seeing you at the competition. And thanks for visiting our winery."

The two celebs left the tasting room, along with the blog lady. I managed to catch Roger's eye near Cammy's table and gave him a wave with my wrist. He waved back and marched right over.

"It's all yours," I said. "Thanks for switching gears."

Roger shrugged. "No big deal. Hey, I think Cammy's getting really overworked. At first, she seemed to forget she needed my help but when I reminded her about the wineglasses, she immediately had me scrutinize them. No harm in being extra cautious. Can you believe it? A few customers mentioned Ambien and our Cab-Sav in the same breath."

"Ouch."

I stepped aside and let Roger take over the table. Then I went into my office and called the Grey Egret. One of the employees put Theo on the phone.

"Norrie, I can't talk now. Hoda Kotb and Rachael Ray are here. Don is bumbling all over the place. Next thing I know he'll be yammering about old family recipes."

"Um, not with what I'm about to tell you. D'Artagnan just joined *The Three Musketeers.*"

"What are you taking about?"

"There's a fourth chocolatier—Anika Schou from Denmark. She's demanding to replace Earvin. And that's not all. Something about a tryst involving Jules, but Mary Berry showed up and ruined it."

"The tryst? My God, you're sounding as bad as Don when he gets anywhere near a celebrity. And what's with Anika Schou?"

"I don't know. All I can tell you is listen to the gossip today. That prep kitchen at Geneva on the Lake must be a real hotbed by now with that crew. I wouldn't be surprised if they tried to sabotage each other."

"All they're doing is working on their recipes for tomorrow. Like studying for an exam. And they're not all in the kitchen at once. There's a separate timeframe for each of them. It was in Henry's email marked, 'Practice Schedule.'"

"Who sends an email marked 'Practice Schedule?' I thought it was some boring article he forwarded. Three or four slots?"

"Three."

"Then there will a bloodbath."

"Meet us tonight at Port of Call for drinks," Theo said. "Around eight. We can commiserate."

"Won't the place be packed?"

"That'll be half the fun. Besides, Don always finds a way to snag a table."

Chapter 29

Port of Call, a fantastic lakeside restaurant with an enormous deck, was situated five miles from Geneva. Theo and Don introduced me to it when I first got here, and it fast became one of my favorite places to eat. In winter, with its enormous stone fireplace and cozy atmosphere, it made me forget about the dreariness that took over the area after the holidays. The food was exceptional, too, and the main reason, according to Theo, that Don insisted on eating there whenever they could.

When I arrived at a little past eight and met up with Theo and Don in the foyer, the place was teeming with guests. We had no choice but to elbow our way to the bar, along with the sea of humanity that engulfed the place.

"An hour and forty-five minutes for a table," Don whined. "We might as well grab the first seats that become available."

I glanced around the restaurant and gave Theo a poke in the arm. "Looks like every foodie from Manhattan is here, not to mention all the culinary writers. Isn't that—"

"Yes. Yes. It's Christina Tosi, baker extraordinaire. I can't tell who she's conversing with."

Don turned away from the bar and stretched his neck. "Rachael Ray. Are you satisfied?"

"I'd be more satisfied if I could get another minute with Jordaine Waverly. She was about to dish the dirt on Jules when Mary Berry showed up."

Theo looked around. "Sorry, Norrie. I don't see either of them here, but there's always tomorrow at the competition."

Two seats at the bar opened up and Don motioned for Theo and me to take them. Seconds later, another chair was freed up and Don convinced three people to "skootch over by one seat so he could join us."

No sooner did I order a glass of chardonnay from another local winery than I spied Deputy Hickman walking in.

"This can't be good," I whispered. "Port of Call doesn't seem like the kind of place he'd frequent."

The three of us watched as he strode past the bar into the huge dining area.

"I can't see where he's headed," I said.

Theo wasted no time standing and scanning the area. "Holy Crap. If I'm not mistaken, that's Stanislav. And he's with Allete. They're seated by that greenery to the side of the fireplace. Don't tell me that's where Grizzly Gary's going. Hold on. Hold on. That's exactly where our boy's headed."

I jumped from my seat and took a few steps forward. It was hard to get a good look because the bar area was so densely packed. "I need to get in closer. I'll try to be inconspicuous."

Don blew enough air out of his mouth to resuscitate a rhino. "That'll be the day."

Rather than making a beeline into the dining area, I skirted the perimeter of the restaurant, making sure I kept a wide enough berth between me and the packed tables, but not so wide that I couldn't overhear a key tidbit of information.

"That's what I've been saying, Jeff. The man was found dead in his hotel bathtub and the issue of foul play was never resolved. Ironic, too, huh? And during the holidays, no less. According to the hotel staff, he had just returned from attending an international chocolate exposition in their ballroom. You'd think the Dutch authorities would've put a rush on such a high-profile case. Too bad it's turned cold."

"Yeah. That's the question that's been cropping up all over. Why would the CEO of Puccini Zinest have overdosed on a sleeping medication if he wasn't being treated for a sleeping condition?"

"You think the Ambassador Holland Hotel might have put a kibosh on the investigation to avoid bad press?"

"Wouldn't surprise me. Money's been known to pay for silence."

Puccini Zinest. Ambassador Holland Hotel. Chocolate exposition. That was around the time of Puccini Zinest's merger talks. Only no one mentioned the other party. I looked closely at the table and recognized one of the men—Jeff Glor from CBS's nightly news. Holy Cannoli! Who the heck wasn't here?

I pretended to read something on my cell phone so I could overhear more of the conversation, but they moved to another topic. Rats. It didn't matter. I was on a mission to see what Deputy Hickman was up to and couldn't afford to get waylaid with yet another "shiny thing," even if that thing had something to do with the chocolate festival.

All of a sudden, I got my answer. One second I was looking at the screen on my phone and the next I was staring at Stanislav being escorted out of Port of Call by Deputy Hickman. Not a major scene with handcuffs or anything like that, but a scene nonetheless.

Allete was a few feet away from Stanislav and, even with the noisy chatter in the restaurant, I could hear her voice. "I'm calling your embassy at once. *Mon dieu.*"

As tempting as it was for me to approach Deputy Hickman, I knew I'd be the one to wind up in handcuffs. Instead, I zeroed in on Allete and ushered her back to their table.

"What's going on?" I asked.

I would have had better luck coaxing the information out of Alvin. Spit or no spit. Allete pulled a handkerchief from her bag and began to sob in it. "They think, they believe, *mon dieu,* he would never…"

Never what? Never what?

Allete reached for the water glass on her table and took a gulp. "A spray bottle of Ambien was found in Stanislav's room. I think that dreadful deputy is about to arrest my beloved for the murder of Jules."

Okay, I might not be an investigator and maybe I never finished reading Nancy Drew's handbook, but I knew one thing—no one could enter your premises without your permission or a search warrant.

"I don't understand, Allete. The authorities can't simply walk into someone's room, even if that someone is staying at a hotel."

"The deputy said their office received an anonymous phone call telling them they would find a spray bottle of Ambien with Stanislav's fingerprints on it in his room. They had other information, too, but I don't know what. It doesn't matter. It was sufficient for them to secure that permit."

"The search warrant?"

"Yes. That."

"Allete, does Stanislav have trouble sleeping?"

"Not in the least. He sleeps like a bear in winter. *Mon dieu.* I must call the hotel to arrange for an earlier limousine back. I need to make some phone calls. This is an outrage. An outrage!"

"The hotel isn't very far from here. I could drive you. It's no bother."

"Thank you, but I prefer to use the limousine service, if you don't mind."

"I'm sure it was a misunderstanding. Everything will be sorted out."

"I wish that would be the case."

Allete tossed her rich ivory pashmina over her shoulders, picked up her bag, and walked to the reception area. I followed her movements before returning to the bar. That was when I caught sight of someone else. It was none other than Hortensia, and she made a beeline for Allete like nobody's business.

"Ten to one Hortensia was Allete's limo service," I said to Theo and Don when I got back to the bar and gave them the lowdown on everything I'd seen and heard in the past fifteen minutes.

Theo rubbed his chin and sighed. "The Ambien bottle, huh? Those spray bottles are really small. In fact, if it had a green label on it, it would look like my generic Flonase. I Googled the Ambien image when we first found out that stuff was sprayed on the wineglass. If Stanislav did have it in his possession, it wouldn't be something that was easily visible in his room."

"Are you saying you think he was set up?" I asked.

"Big time. Maybe Allete was right with all her wailing. Maybe Earvin did kill his uncle and now he wants to remove the rest of the competition. Too bad he has another chocolatier to contend with."

I bit my lower lip and shook my head. "Unless *she* was responsible for the set-up. And for spooking the other chocolatiers. Ilene Shannon did mention something about Anika Schou being in the area for the past week. Of course, it was unconfirmed."

Don reached for a skewer of garlic shrimp the bartender had placed in front of him. Apparently, while I traipsed across the restaurant on my fact-finding mission, he and Theo ordered the appetizer medley. Two portions, no less. "Unconfirmed," Don said. "Guess that's the new term for rumor mill. Huh? So, what do you think Allete's up to?"

"Easy. Finding out who set up her boyfriend. But what Hortensia has to do with it is beyond me. Allete claimed they simply met as guests at the hotel, but I don't believe it. Oh no. I was supposed to do some internet searching on Hortensia and compare notes with Stephanie. Then Cammy called about all the celebs in our winery and I kind of got sidetracked."

"Most likely Stephanie got sidetracked too, or she would have called you," Theo said. "Look, if my eyelids are still open when we get home, I'll see what I can dig up on Hortensia as well. How does that sound?"

Before I could answer, Don cut in. "Much better than the two of you snooping around in places you shouldn't. Just limit your internet searches to safe sites and you'll be okay."

"Oh my God. Did my mother contact you all the way from Myrtle Beach? That's something she would say."

Don gave me one of those self-satisfied grins and smiled. "Good."

"I don't know about you guys, but I feel as if the proverbial you-know-what is going to hit the fan, the likes of which we've never seen. First thing tomorrow, I'm calling Gladys Pipp. If they've got Stanislav in lock-up, it's going to be a disaster."

"Not for Anika Schou," Don replied.

I turned to Theo. "Anika Schou. We should add her name to our internet search, too."

The three of us filled up on the appetizer medley and topped it off with blueberry cheesecake crumble and flavored coffees. I had just put my spoon on the napkin when the bartender informed us there was an available table.

"Maybe another time," Don told him. "We need to brace ourselves for one more day of craziness at our wineries before the chocolate event is over."

The bartender nodded. "It's been wild here, too. I haven't seen so many celebrities since that big women's rights convention in Seneca Falls, and they were mainly politicians who didn't tip well."

We were still laughing about the guy's comment when we exited the restaurant and walked to our cars. A light snow began to fall and dissipated by the time I made it home. Typical of the fickle Finger Lakes weather. I secretly prayed for a blizzard to engulf Yonkers so I would be spared the humiliation of having invited two men as my plus ones for tomorrow's grand chocolate festival finale. But that was the least of my concerns. When I got in the door of my house, there was a priority mail envelope waiting for me.

Oh hell no! Not an official letter from the production company cancelling my movies the same way they did to poor Conrad Blyth. I tore into that thing before I even pulled the key out from the door. My heart was pounding and it took me at least ten or fifteen seconds to realize what I was staring at. It was an advance copy of tomorrow night's chocolate festival program. Henry Speltmore sent it, complete with a photocopied note that read, "Thank you, participating wineries. I rushed these out as soon as they arrived in my office from the printer. Unfortunately, it was too late to redo the program. Hence, you will note an addendum on Earvin Roels. Looking forward to a delectable experience Saturday night. Henry."

Delectable? Nerve wracking maybe, but not delectable.

Chapter 30

Charlie bolted out the kitchen door and thirty seconds later pawed at it to be let back in. I forgot I'd closed his doggie door when I left earlier for Port of Call. A quick refill of his kibble and the Plott Hound was set for the night. I changed into sweats, turned on the TV, and booted up my laptop.

It was only ten fifty-five, and, like Theo, I was chomping at the bit to do some serious internet searches. Anika Schou's was easy. She was Denmark's golden girl as far as chocolatiers were concerned. There wasn't a single Danish culinary magazine within the past year that didn't have her photo in it. Tall, lithe, and fair skinned, with hair that looked almost platinum, Anika was the poster child for chocolatey confections. Nothing in any of the articles I perused sent up a red flag, so I got down to the real business that was gnawing at me—Hortensia Vermeulen.

My God! I had no idea how absolutely boring her scholarly articles on indigenous and urban horticulture were. Except, of course, for the one on organic horticulture. That one was so dull it made the others seem riveting. It was useless. I was mired under and getting nowhere. Then it dawned on me. Images! Why on earth didn't I simply click the images line right below the Google search box? Duh.

Granted, photos from lots of other women named Hortensia got into the mix, but I was certainly able to zero in on the lady in question. Same auburn hair with a slightly reddish hue. Wig or no wig.

I was getting tired and everything seemed to blur. Still, I kept going and even forced myself to watch a video clip of her delivering a speech on acrid soil and its ramifications on small gardening plots. She sounded just like she did at Albright Auditorium. Same accent. Then I noticed something peculiar. In seconds, I was on the phone with Theo.

"See for yourself," I said. "Watch the clip. Hortensia's left-handed. Watch how she turns the pages of her speech in that binder she's got on the podium. She's using her left hand, but when Stephanie and I saw her at the college, she was clearly right-handed."

"Maybe she had carpal tunnel surgery or something. Or maybe she's ambidextrous. Doesn't mean anything. Look, Norrie, I've been scanning the internet, too, and if ever there was a dead end, this is it. Now, Anika Schou…that's a different story. Turns out she was at the chocolate festival in Munich last year when Jules and Stanislav had their verbal altercation."

"How do you know?"

"Because I Googled her competition schedule and scoped out the candid shots taken at the festival. There's actually a photo of someone stepping in between Jules and Stanislav, but off to the right is Anika. I'm positive it's her. And she's got a smirk on her face that makes the Cheshire Cat look like an amateur."

"You think she tried to get one of those men knocked out of the competition so she could move up a notch? The Munich festival was the qualifier for this one. Catherine told me the day she went over all those ridiculous demands from the chocolatiers."

Theo let out a sigh. "Well, it didn't work because Jules, Stanislav, and Allete were the final three."

"All the more reason to add Anika to our suspect list."

"Speaking of suspects," Theo said, "let me know what you find out from Gladys. If Anika winds up securing Stanislav's place in the competition, there won't be enough facial tissues in the world for Allete."

"I'll keep you posted. I'm going to poke around the internet for another half hour or so and then call it a night."

"Yeah, it's lights out here, too. Don's already snoring."

I took my own advice and went to sleep twenty or so minutes later. Unfortunately, I didn't stay asleep. I bolted awake shortly after three and, for the life of me, couldn't get back to a decent night's sleep. I was plagued by a series of dreams, complete with would-be assassins.

First, Earvin, in a scenario that involved lacing someone's tempered chocolate with antifreeze. Then Stanislav with a food marinator and whatever lethal concoction he'd come up with. Hortensia kept reappearing too, only, in her case, she was holding a silvery weapon of sorts and aiming it at someone's face. Allete appeared in my hazy visions, too, only she was screaming her lungs out over a spider crawling on the table.

The only suspect who didn't appear in my foggy dreams was Anika. By four thirty-nine, I'd had it. I got up, made myself a cup of mint tea, and decided to peruse the program booklet Henry Speltmore had delivered to all of us in WOW. I hoped it would be a snoozer and I could get back to sleep. It wasn't.

I had to admit, the Seneca Lake Wine Association went all out on this one. The program booklet was spectacular. Full color photos of delectable chocolates in various stages of production coupled with panoramic vistas of the Finger Lakes. And that was only the introduction.

Each chocolatier had a section devoted to his or her biography, including professional photos, family snapshots, and all sorts of candid pictures taken at the various events and competitions. Yep. Someone sure did their homework. With the exception of Allete, who grew up in the countryside of Le Blanc, France, all the contenders were born and raised in metropolitan cities—Moscow for Stanislav and Antwerp for Jules. Of the three, only Jules was born with the proverbial silver spoon in his mouth, but in his case, it was Flanders Royal, the premier chocolate company of Belgium. Jules was the great grandson of Maurice Flanders, a chocolatier who established the business in Antwerp after World War II.

I think it was Don who told me Flanders' stock plummeted in the past year and they were looking to re-brand. Maybe that was why Jules was in the competition. A little seed money never hurt.

There was a separate stapled pamphlet on Earvin Roels that included some staged photos and a brief biography. Like his uncle Jules, he, too, was born and raised in Antwerp.

Leaning my head against a pillow on the couch, I decided to read the program cover to cover. A half hour later, having digested everyone's family background and absorbing the glossy photos, it was as if someone lifted a veil from my face. I knew with absolute certainty who Jules's murderer was, but I had no way to prove it. Not yet. Then an idea popped into my head and I couldn't get it out. It was a plan, in a vague sense of the word, but I wasn't sure how I'd pull it off.

Worst of all, it was the type of plan Theo and Don would never agree to. Not in a million years. That was why I didn't clue them in. Same deal for Cammy. But it didn't matter. The one person I really needed to convince was Godfrey Klein. Without his help, I'd never be able to catch a killer.

By now, it was five thirty and every self-respecting winery owner was up and about. I figured it was time to join that club, at least for one morning. I washed out my mug of mint tea and filled it with a K-cup of my latest favorite—McCafe Medium Roast. Then I made myself some toast and refilled Charlie's food dish.

The sound of kibble being poured must have awakened him because he shook himself from where he was standing at the top of the stairs, ambled down, ate a few mouthfuls, and headed to his doggie door. I lifted the plastic screen and a cold gust of air blasted my legs before he went out.

I turned on the Weather Channel and, with no impending disasters facing the Finger Lakes, I took a piping hot shower, got dressed, and rehearsed what I'd say to Godfrey when I got him on the phone. I knew he'd be in his office, even though it was Saturday because, like my brother-in-law Jason, Godfrey couldn't seem to stay away from the Global Species Database for too long.

Still, it was only seven ten and even Godfrey wasn't that fanatical. That left Gladys at the public safety building. If my plan was going to work, I had to find out what happened with Stanislav—and who better than Gladys to let me know. With forty minutes to spare before she clocked in, I pulled up my screenplay and tried to focus on *Beguiled into Love.*

That lasted all of twenty minutes when I slammed the lid on the laptop and made myself another cup of coffee. My recent epiphany about Jules's murder, coupled with a shaky but hopeful plan, made it impossible for me to concentrate on anything else. So, I took a chance and dialed Godfrey at the Experiment Station. I figured my call to Gladys could wait a few more minutes.

Godfrey answered on the first ring, and I was actually speechless for a second. "Norrie? Is that you?"

"Uh, yeah. I really didn't think I'd catch you this early but I took a chance."

"I was asked to assist the department with the new arthropod museum project and, believe it or not, this was a good time for me. What's up?"

"Cornell is planning on building a museum about bugs and spiders?"

"More of a community outreach program."

"Good. Because that's exactly what I wanted to talk with you about."

Godfrey laughed. "This I've got to hear. Usually the only words out of your mouth when it comes to arthropods are 'kill it, kill it now.'"

"Very funny. Well, this may sound a bit odd, but do you happen to have any harmless yet scary-looking species you could sort of loan out for the day? I have a hunch, well, actually more than a hunch about who murdered Jules and the only way I can prove it is by establishing a little scenario that involves an insect or two."

The line went quiet and I wasn't sure if it was the phone company or Godfrey.

"Are you still there?" I asked.

"Oh, I'm here all right. Astonished, maybe, but still on the line. Listen, Norrie, as much as I'd like to help you out, I can't loan out or gift anyone with any of our species. First of all, we're audited. Everything is accountable. Species arrive from other labs as well as their natural habitat. And while we certainly cannot count every single ant, let's say, in a colony, we cannot take a risk and allow one of them to intermingle within another environment."

"One ant? Seriously? And I need something more substantial."

"I'm afraid to ask what you have in mind. Don't tell me. I don't want to be implicated in anything if your scenario or plan, or whatever it is you have in mind, goes haywire. Look, let those deputies do their jobs. Last thing you need is to put yourself in danger. Don't do anything impulsive. Please?"

"You have nothing to worry about. No danger involved. Honestly. Anyway, I'll meet you tonight at Geneva on the Lake."

"Got my suit and tie all picked out. Remember, don't do anything impulsive. Okay?"

"Okay."

Technically, it wasn't impulsive. It was planned. A bit sketchy, but planned.

With Godfrey unwilling to secure the specimen I needed, I had no choice but to do it on my own. I had plenty of experience this past fall with overwintering pests, but thanks to the precautions I took around the house, we didn't have any. However, I was positive we'd have an abundance of creepy looking spiders in our basement.

Granted, I hadn't noticed any when I went down there the other evening to grab a bottle of Cabernet Sauvignon for the beef dinner with Theo and Don, but I wasn't on spider patrol at the time. Without wasting a second, I took an empty bell jar from our pantry, and, even though our basement had at least four light bulbs overhead, grabbed the flashlight like I always did after watching too many horror movies. I walked down the wooden stairs and paused for a second to let my eyes adjust to the dim lighting. I glanced at the wine rack and looked above it at the wall. Our house was one of those old farmhouses, originally built in the late 1800s but modernized at least three or four times since. However, no one bothered to update the basement. The walls were the original stone walls and the perfect hiding spots for all sorts of arthropods. Godfrey would have a field day.

It took me all of thirty seconds and God knows what kind of spiders I managed to wrangle from the wall with an old paint stirrer, but there were at least two that seemed to be alive. I flashed the light into the corner behind the wine rack and made a mental note to either call an exterminator or see if John Grishner could do something about the disgusting earwigs. Dead or alive, they looked the same. For good measure, I took an old wadded up tissue from the pocket in my sweatpants and used it to pick up three of those.

With my mission accomplished, I went back upstairs and put the bell jar on the counter, making sure the lid was firmly in place. I wondered if there would be enough air for the spiders to survive. Not willing to take a chance, I found a metal meat skewer and poked a few teeny weeny holes in the lid.

It was at that precise moment when Theo called my cell phone with a stunning revelation.

Chapter 31

"Turn on Channel 8 WROC if you haven't done so already," Theo said. "They're doing a feature on tonight's chocolate competition, and they're running the footage from the opening reception."

"Oh no. Please don't tell me they're reliving that bonbon comment of Stephanie's."

"Not yet. Hurry. Turn it on and stay on the line with me."

I clicked on the remote and plopped myself into the nearest chair. Sure enough, the anchors were babbling away about the chocolate competition as footage of the reception continued to unroll.

"Oh look," Theo said. "There's Catherine grabbing you by the wrist."

"Aargh. To talk about Steven. Wait a sec. The camera just moved to Allete."

"If her neckline plunged by so much as a fraction of an inch more, the network would've been censored."

"No kidding."

I watched intently as bits and pieces of the reception I hadn't noticed before were plastered in front of me. And then I homed in on something that made me gasp.

"What happened Norrie? Did you spill your coffee or something?" Theo asked.

"My God. That woman. The tall one with an oval tray of canapes. Take a good look. It's Anika. She looks just like the photos I saw of her. I'd bet my life on it. Her hair's pulled back and she's wearing glasses, but it's her all right. Those rumors are true. Anika's been in the area. Been in the area and probably plotting to remove one of the chocolatiers from the competition so she can get in. Why else would she be pretending to be one of the wait staff?"

I gulped. My original assumption about Jules's murderer was pretty solid, but what if Cammy had been right all along about there being three separate killers? What was it she said? Something about the poisoned bonbon, the Ambien knock-out spray, and the person who rolled Jules over in the snow so he'd be face down. If my theory was correct, and this new revelation about Anika was also correct, then all I needed to do was find the third killer. Unless, of course, none of it was right.

"I'm calling Deputy Hickman," Theo said. "He needs to contact Channel 8 WROC and track down Anika and question her."

"Um, she might not be the only killer."

"What do you mean?"

"I may have found some evidence pointing to another suspect."

"Who?"

A loud crash and I was literally off the hook. "Damn it," Theo said. "Isolde just knocked over a lamp. She goes nuts when a fly gets into the house. We'll talk later."

Anika and my suspect were the top contenders in the scenarios I had pieced together, but that still left Stanislav out there. Or, *in* there if he was still being held in the public safety building. Wasting no time, I called Gladys.

After her usual introduction about hanging up and dialing nine-one-one if it was an emergency, Gladys finally said hello on behalf of the Yates County Public Safety Building.

"Good morning, Gladys. It's Norrie Ellington. Sorry to bother you so early in the morning but I absolutely need to know if Deputy Hickman released Stanislav Vetro last night or if he kept him in lock-up. Can you talk or is my favorite deputy breathing down your neck as we speak?"

"He's out on a call. Minor disturbance at a gas station. And yes, according to the information on my computer, Stanislav is still being held for questioning. They can keep him for twenty-four hours, but unless they charge him with something, he has to be released."

"Oh my gosh. That means that if he's released, it can be as late as this evening."

"Or, I'm sorry to say, it might not be at all. He may be charged with the murder of that other chocolatier. The one from Belgium."

"Jules. Jules Leurant."

"Yes. Him."

"Gladys, I swear this conversation won't go anywhere except between the two of us, but can you tell me if the evidence against Stanislav is really strong? I already know about some tip the deputies got and the fact that an

Ambien spray bottle was found in Stanislav's room, but that's not enough to charge him. There's got to be something else."

"I could lose my job, Norrie, if this leaks out."

"It won't. I swear."

"The anonymous caller pointed out something else in Stanislav's room. A flavor marinator. The caller insisted we'd find remnants of antifreeze in it. Deputy Hickman rushed it off to the lab and we're waiting for the results."

The bonbon. Holy Crap!

"Gladys, between you and me, this whole thing reeks of a set-up. It's way too easy."

"I agree. Nevertheless, it's up to Deputy Hickman to make that call. Is this going to ruin that big competition tonight? It's been all over the news. In fact, you'll never guess who my sister-in-law saw at that new indoor Mennonite Market a few minutes ago. She called me right before you did. It was Hoda Kotb! There are TV and magazine celebrities all over the village."

"Um, yeah. They were at the wineries yesterday. I'm not sure about that competition, but there may be a replacement in the wings." *Or a murderess.*

"That's good to know. I'll have to catch it on TV. Way out of my price range to attend."

"Me, too, but it's paid for by the wine association. Tell me, did anyone visit Stanislav late last night or at the crack of dawn?"

"No. Even if they wanted to, he's not allowed visitors. He hasn't been charged yet."

The way in which Gladys said the word "yet" made me think Stanislav would be charged. I thanked Gladys and rushed off to check my email. I figured news about Stanislav's detainment had to have reached Henry Speltmore by now and even if it hadn't, Anika's bid for that third spot certainly would have. The wine association had to make a decision about replacing Earvin with Anika by now.

Sure enough, there was an email from Henry under the file name, "Chocolate Competition Update." He began by thanking everyone for their commitment to the wine trail, their appreciation of tourism, and their willingness to spread goodwill throughout the region. If I didn't know better, I would have thought it was a belated holiday greeting card. Then he finally got to the gist of his message—the fourth chocolatier.

"After careful consideration," the email read, "Earvin Roels will be replaced by the rightful contender to the competition, Anika Schou from Denmark." It went on to say how appreciative the Seneca Lake Wine Association was for Mr. Roels' willingness to step in and replace his uncle by giving demonstrations at the local wineries and that they "would certainly welcome him back should he ever decide to visit the region again."

I all but choked. "Should he ever decide to visit the region again?" We'd be lucky if he didn't get his hands on a small nuclear device and make toast out of all of us.

The real bummer was I'd been counting on Earvin to be taking part in the competition, but that wouldn't prevent me from going through with my little plan to expose Jules's killer. Henry's email did state that Earvin would have a seat of honor next to the other wine trail bigwigs at tonight's event and, knowing Earvin, he'd be there.

The entire extravaganza had disaster written all over it, but it was too late to do anything about it.

I was about to phone Theo when the phone rang and I grabbed it.

"Norrie, it's Stephanie. Sorry I didn't get back to you the other night about Hortensia but the truth is, I got nowhere. If she's hiding anything, it would take a team of archeologists to uncover it. On the other hand, I did find some rather interesting information about Puccini Zinest."

"What?"

"Well, you probably know their CEO's death is still under investigation in the Netherlands, but are you aware it was only after he was dead and buried that talks of a merger with another company were all over the news?"

"That doesn't seem so unusual."

"Unless it was the only way to get a merger on the table."

"Gosh, Stephanie, you're beginning to think the way I do. That's pretty scary. Anyway, we've got our own murder to contend with. And Deputy Hickman's placed Stanislav in the county lock up. It happened last night. Right in front of me at Port of Call."

"Does Henry know?"

"He should by now, but his latest email was about replacing Earvin with Anika. I'm not even sure the judges are aware of the situation with Stanislav. When I left Port of Call, Hortensia, who just so happened to be there, made a mad dash for Allete."

"Yeesh. Looks like old Henry is going to eat crow and welcome Earvin back to the competition after all. Guess we can all look forward to some surprises tonight, huh?"

"Um, you might say that."

"Okay. See you tonight. Oh, and Norrie, I wouldn't be too worried about having people think your Cabernet Sauvignon had anything to do with Jules's death. The media made it pretty clear it was the wineglass."

"True, but people don't remember wineglasses. They remember wine."

When I got off the phone, I checked the bell jar to make sure those spiders were still crawling around. They only had to last another ten hours or so. Then it would be too late for me to prove anything.

I spent the rest of the morning opening and closing my laptop, deciding which of Francine's winter cocktail dresses to wear, and revisiting my loosely plotted plan for tonight's gala competition event. At least I didn't have to spring for a fancy dress I'd never wear again. Unlike Francine, who was forced to attend numerous formal events that involved the entomology department, I could live on urban chic in Manhattan.

In addition to my ticket to the event and my "plus one," the wine association had also given us a ticket for our winemaker and one for our tasting room manager. Cammy spent the past month clothes shopping for "the occasion of the century," and as for Franz, I didn't think he'd have to look any farther than his closet for appropriate formalwear.

If I was really serious about pulling off my plan tonight, I needed to sneak a peek at the set-up for the competition. I knew where the side entrance to Geneva on the Lake's kitchen was located and the last time I was there, the door wasn't locked. I crossed my fingers I'd find the same deal today.

With my stomach grumbling, I made myself a peanut butter and jelly sandwich before jumping into my car and making the quick drive up the lake. The soft snow that had fallen earlier gave the hotel grounds a fairy tale look. I parked out back, took a deep breath, and walked to the side door that led to the kitchen. Sure enough, the door opened without any trouble and I stepped inside the building. The kitchen was straight ahead and the aroma of seared beef and garlic made me wish I'd never eaten that peanut butter sandwich.

At least five chefs were bustling around the place, and I was mesmerized as I watched them season all sorts of meats. It had to be the preparation for tonight's event. I figured we'd be dining in one of the ballrooms, but I wasn't sure where the competition would take place. Surely, it wouldn't be in such close proximity as to compromise the flavors from our meal.

I studied the movement from the chefs and a thought hit me. Whenever I was in a hurry with work and someone asked me a question, I answered quickly to get it over with so as not to waste time. I hoped the chef I was about to disturb held the same philosophy.

"Excuse me," I said to a burly-looking gentleman. "I'm with the wine trail and I need to check out the room where the chocolate competition will be held. I seem to have made a wrong turn somewhere."

Without even bothering to look up, the man replied, "Second floor reserve ballroom. Across from the main elevator. It should still be open, but I'd put a move on if I were you or you'll need to have someone at the concierge desk secure the key."

"Thanks. The food smells amazing. What are you serving tonight?"

"Everything. It's a Brazilian steakhouse event."

No wonder Gladys said she couldn't afford it.

Thankfully I remembered my way around the building from the last time I was here. And, like the last time, I took the stairwell. Sure enough, the reserve ballroom was open and set up for the competition.

Four long tables, complete with every accoutrement of the trade, were positioned horizontally so the audience would be able to watch the chocolatiers as they worked. I eyeballed the scenario because it looked so familiar. Then I realized why. It virtually paralleled the set-up from *MasterChef*, a show that literally gave me the willies every time one of the actual chefs approached a terrified contestant.

The audience chairs were arranged in a series of rows and I imagined the front row was reserved for winery dignitaries, magazine mavens, and the media. The three judges had their own table, set on a platform adjacent to the horizontal tables. Huge placards spelled out their names and their positions.

Looking at the horizontal tables, a pit formed in my stomach. Unlike the three judges' seats that were clearly marked, there was no indication of which chocolatier was going to be at which table. Crap! How was I ever going to pull off my plan without knowing where my suspect was going to be working?

I crossed my arms, tapped the floor with my foot, and stood there. I hadn't come all this way just to have my little scheme fizzle in front of me. I'd improvise. That was all there was to it. It would be a small adjustment in the overall scheme of things, but I reasoned the plan would still work. But only if I could sneak into the room prior to the actual event.

Chapter 32

There was no doubt in my mind that the main door would be locked until it was time to let the audience inside. However, most ballrooms had side exits that lead to who knew where and that was exactly what I was about to find out.

You're not the only one climbing into bell towers, Nancy.

In the case of this ballroom, there were three exit doors. One directly in the back and two off to the sides. I walked to the nearest one on my left and realized it was a small kitchen area with no visible egress. I moved to the door directly in the rear, where a small foyer led to a narrow stairwell that only went one way from where I stood—down. I took my chances and walked down the single flight of stairs. Hallelujah! It ended in a large utility room that opened to a hallway. I figured I could easily access that stairwell tonight but only if the door was unlocked and that wasn't likely. Unless I could do something about it.

I'd only seen this done in movies, but what other choice did I have? Without wasting a second, I opened every single drawer in that utility room until I found a roll of duct tape and used enough of it on the door lock to prevent it from doing its job. And, I had completed the task in such a way that the duct tape wasn't obvious. *Move over, MacGyver.* Satisfied I'd be able to pull off my grand plan, I walked down the hallway as if I was taking a midday stroll on a beach.

That was when my phone rang and I nearly jumped out of my skin.

"Norrie. It's Cammy. We thought you'd be stopping by the tasting room."

"Um, oh, I didn't think it would be that busy today."

"It's busy all right. But that's not why I called. There are rumors floating all over the place that Stanislav Vetro is being charged with murder."

"Geez. I should have left you a message or something. He was escorted out of Port of Call last night by Deputy Hickman and, according to Gladys, he's only being held for questioning." *I hope.* "Between you and me, I think someone's setting him up."

"Too bad Bradley Jamison can't help him out. Which brings me to the next reason I called. Bradley's been trying to reach you. He left you a message on your landline and on your cell. He'll get to the event tonight, but he'll be late. He's stuck in a meeting and doesn't expect to get out of Yonkers much before two thirty."

"It's a five-hour drive under perfect conditions and Route 17 is anything but. Thanks, Cammy. I'll call him back."

Now it was my turn to leave a message on Bradley's cell. I told him I'd save a plate of food for him and to drive safe. I sounded like my mother.

The first thing I did when I got home was check the status of those spiders. Still vertical. At least that was a relief. The three earwigs were still dead. In case I'd been mistaken about them.

With a few hours of uninterrupted work time in front of me, I grabbed an apple from the fridge, a few Oreo cookies, and a Coke. I told myself that this time, no matter what, I'd get moving on *Beguiled into Love.* There was literally nothing I could do for Stanislav and, besides, didn't Allete say she was going to call the Russian embassy?

At least we wouldn't have to witness God knew what kind of display Earvin would put on if indeed Stanislav got released. Earvin was all but guaranteed a spot between the two women chocolatiers.

At a little past six, I called Don and Theo to see if they'd heard anything since last night but like me, they were only privy to rumors.

"Guess we'll have to get to Geneva on the Lake to find out who's on first, huh?" Theo said. "I just hope Allete doesn't start sobbing into the tempering machine. Water ruins the chocolate, you know. Hey, weren't you going to tell me about evidence pointing to another suspect? Other than Anika or Hortensia?"

"It can wait. I might be off."

"Okay. See you in a bit."

Last thing I needed was to second guess myself and that was exactly what I would have done if Theo heard my plan and ixnayed it. I needed to stay focused. Even if it meant keeping something from the people I trusted the most.

The chocolate event dinner at Geneva on the Lake was to begin promptly at seven thirty, with a wine bar in the ballroom lobby at seven. By six forty, I was dressed and ready to go, with one exception—the bell jar. It would be impossible to carry something so cumbersome in a small handbag and the thought of walking into the place with something that resembled a satchel was out of the question. I had to improvise.

The only thing I could think of was a Ziploc bag large enough to accommodate my menagerie. Like I'd done with the bell jar lid, I poked tiny holes in the plastic bag, and then folded it into my purse, hoping I wouldn't crush the ammunition I needed for tonight.

When I arrived at the hotel, I was astonished at how far out I had to park. It might as well have been in the next county. To make matters worse, the front driveway was totally blocked by a long row of limousines and the area adjacent to that was taken up by news vans from the local stations.

I clutched my purse and headed to the entrance. Once inside, I was asked to show my ticket at the reception desk and then directed to the corridor where the ballroom was situated.

"Um, I need to leave two other tickets for guests who haven't arrived yet. Dr. Godfrey Klein and Mr. Bradley Jamison."

Without hesitation, the gentleman took the tickets and wrote down the names. "There's a bank of coat racks in the corridor by the foyer. Please feel free to put your wrap there."

Is that his way of telling me to take off that hideous coat of mine?

"Dr. Klein should be here any minute," I said, "but Mr. Jamison may be an hour or so late. He's driving from Yonkers."

"He may be later than that," the man said. "My sister lives in Roscoe on Route 17 and they're getting some icy rain that's expected to move farther west."

Drivers could prepare for most anything in upstate New York with the right snow tires and studs, but there was no remedy for icy rain, except to wait it out. I figured if Bradley didn't show in the next hour or so, I'd call or text him.

I thanked the receptionist and walked toward the ballroom. The large foyer that opened into the dining area was filled to capacity. Two wine bars were set up against the walls, and the hotel had added a few bistro tables. I recognized several attendees, including a few of the women from WOW and their spouses, as well as Leandre, Rosalee's winemaker.

Out of the corner of my eye, I caught a glimpse of Rachael Ray with a man who looked surprisingly like Guy Fieri. Yep, the place was teeming with culinary bigshots. I'd better start milling around and making conversation or I'd look like a star-struck teenager on a movie set.

Just as I started to approach the bistro table where Henry Speltmore was seated, Stephanie tapped me on the shoulder. "Can you believe this crowd? The tension is almost palpable. Looks like the contenders are going to be Allete, Anika, and Earvin. I overheard one of the judges speaking with Henry. Stanislav is still in the Yates County Public Safety Building, even though no charges were made."

"By the time they let him out, it'll be too late for him to compete."

"That certainly changes the odds for Allete. She and Stanislav had a two-thirds advantage. If one of them won, they'd be sharing the windfall with the other to start their own company. Now, he's probably facing trumped-up charges and she's got a one-third chance of winning. *If* she can concentrate."

"So, you don't think Stanislav's the killer, either. The man's got decoy written all over him. I think I can flush out the real murderer tonight."

Stephanie widened her eyes and took a step back. "You're not thinking Hortensia, are you? She's over by the wine bar on the left."

I looked over my shoulder and caught sight of Hortensia chatting with someone. "There's definitely something *off* about her, that's for sure."

No sooner did I finish my thought than an announcement was made to enter the ballroom for the gala dinner event preceding the chocolate competition.

"Come on, Norrie," Stephanie said. "We'd better find our tables."

"Our tables? We have assigned tables?"

"Yes. Check your ticket."

Sure enough, Godfrey and I were assigned to table twelve. I had no idea who we'd be seated with, but I had to make sure that no matter what, Bradley Jamison would also be at my table. Awkward or not.

"Thanks Stephanie. I need to find Rosalee. Right now."

Before Stephanie could answer, I elbowed my way through the oncoming crowd to find out what table the wine trail assigned to Rosalee. I didn't think quarterbacks worked as hard as I did.

"Rosalee!" I shouted the moment I spotted her. "What table are you at?"

Rosalee looked at the ticket in her hand. "Twelve. They better not have seated me with a bunch of boring old coots or worse yet, one of those celebrities who's always talking about themselves."

For once I understood the expression "flooded with relief."

"I'm at your table. With Godfrey and Bradley. I don't know who else we've got." I peered into the ballroom. Fancy white tablecloths, red and white floral centerpieces, and more stemware than the wedding department at Macys. "Looks like the tables are meant for six."

"Might as well get this fiasco over with," Rosalee grumbled as she made her way into the ballroom.

Godfrey waved from across the room, and I waved back. He was the only one seated at our table and, like Rosalee, I, too, hoped we wouldn't be saddled with anyone boring or self-involved. As it turned out, we were joined by Don and Theo, so all of us could relax.

"What's with these cards?" Rosalee seated herself next to Don and flipped a small card over. "They've got a green dot on one side and a red one on the other. Don't tell me we're going to be forced to play some idiotic game."

Don laughed. "It's a Brazilian steakhouse-themed event. In a few minutes, servers are going to approach the tables with all sorts of meats and poultry. Keep your green dot face up if you want more, turn it to red if you need a break. Theo and I went to one of those restaurants last year when we were in Toronto."

"Good," Rosalee said. "Then maybe you'll know what the stuff sitting in front of me is."

"Polenta," Don and Godfrey replied simultaneously.

"And caramelized bananas," Theo added.

And a price tag the wineries will be paying well into the next century.

"I don't see the chocolatiers anywhere in the ballroom," I said. *And please don't tell me they're already at their prep tables on the second floor.*

Theo picked up a piece of the polenta and took a bite. "According to the contest rules, which were sent to us weeks ago but only recently read in our household, the chocolatiers aren't allowed in the contest area until the competition begins. Their names will be announced and they'll walk to their tables. I imagine none of them are in the mood to stuff up on assorted meats and poultry. By the way, where's Bradley Jamison? Isn't he supposed to be joining you, Norrie?"

I smiled at Godfrey and my cheeks got warm. "Um, yeah. He was. I mean, he is. But he's in Yonkers. He's on his way."

Then I turned to Godfrey and whispered, "I should have mentioned it but—"

Godfrey gave me a wink. "It's okay. I haven't been living under a rock. Only going there occasionally to look for specimens."

I laughed and reached over to give his wrist a quick squeeze. Then I motioned for the server with the bacon-wrapped morsels of chicken to put a few on my plate. So far, so good. If what Theo said was true, I'd be able to execute my plan in plenty of time. Two slices of filet mignon later, along with ancho beef and parmesan-crusted pork, I was more than satiated. Finger Lakes wines were featured and, although I was tempted, I decided to stick with ice water.

When the servers cleared the tables and set-up the coffee service, I excused myself under the guise of needing to call Bradley. That part was true, but I omitted the real reason I needed to hightail it out of there. I had to follow through with my plan.

Chapter 33

The door to the utility room opened without a glitch. I made a mental note to buy stock in duct tape and walked up the stairwell to the reserve ballroom. Everything looked the way it did earlier in the day, with one exception. Sheets of block chocolate had been placed on each of the preparation tables.

Since I had no idea which chocolatier would be assigned to a particular table, I had no choice but to take my chances and select two tables for the spiders, hoping one of them belonged to my suspect. As for the dead earwigs…well, I really wasn't sure why I grabbed them in the first place. It was like impulse shopping at its worst. Still, a properly placed dead earwig might suffice, should the spider-less table house the killer. Without giving it further thought, I concealed the dead earwigs on each table directly underneath the linen cloth that covered the tray of dipping forks.

The spiders were my real concern. I worried they might scurry off. Then again, maybe I could place them under something where they weren't as likely to escape. I stood directly in front of the tables and tried to figure out how I was going to do that when I heard voices coming from the small kitchen off to the left. I had to move fast.

Each table had some large spoons on it. Face up. Quickly, I placed a spider under the largest spoon at the first two tables and then overturned the spoon at the third table so everything would look identical. I was about to retreat when I heard footsteps. Not heavy thudding footsteps but the sound that high heels made on wooden floors.

There was no time to bolt out of there, so I did the only thing I could. I crawled under the table and prayed the skirting would hide me. I held my breath as the footsteps got closer. The skirting was about four inches from the floor. Enough space for me to crouch to the ground and take a peek. Sure enough, I stared at a pair of women's stiletto heels, complete with a tiny strap and rhinestones. Definitely not the kitchen staff.

It felt as if my every single breath got louder and louder. Whoever was at the table took their time. Overhead, I heard rustling. I wouldn't put it past Anika or even Allete to sneak over to their table and do what? Cheat? It wasn't as if they were hiding answers to a midterm exam.

A quick movement from the stiletto-heeled woman and she left with a click-click echoing across the floor. Setting a world's record for exhaling, I crawled out from under the table and studied the set-up. I seriously doubted the woman had messed with my table embellishments or she would have made some sort of sound. Even a tiny gasp. Nope. Whatever it was she did, or didn't do, wasn't noticeable.

To be on the safe side, I tiptoed across the room and back to the utility room. That was when the second the door opened from the other side and I was face-to-face with Stanislav. His hair was untamed and he was in dire need of a shave. I opened my mouth to speak and he immediately cupped it with his hand.

"Not a word. Understand?"

I nodded like a bobble-head doll and he removed his hand. My heart beat fast and my hands began to shake. "I thought you were under arrest."

"Ha! Those buffoons got the evidence wrong. It wasn't antifreeze they found in that flavor marinator. It was a mixture of corn syrup and blue food coloring. Someone went to a lot of trouble to get me out of the way but it didn't work. I have a plan of my own to find out who it was. That's why I snuck up here. Staying at this hotel has its advantages. Allete and I could watch the comings and goings of the staff. That's how I knew that the competition would be in this ballroom and not downstairs."

I gulped and bit my lower lip. A stream of saliva rolled down my chin. At least I hoped it was saliva and not blood. Stanislav reached into the pocket of his black trousers and handed me a cloth handkerchief. "Please. Do not be alarmed. My plan does not include murder."

Again, I nodded like a ridiculous bobble-head doll. "Um, okay, then. I really need to get back downstairs."

"Not a word. Agreed?"

"Agreed."

I figured what the heck. If my plan didn't work, then maybe Stanislav's would. I retreated down the stairs and leaned against the wall. I had to call Bradley. And I had to compose myself.

Bradley's voice sounded as if he was standing right next to me. It had to be the Bluetooth service. "I'm on Route 14 north. I should be there in less than twenty minutes. Don't save me any food. I ate at the Roscoe Diner."

"The competition hasn't started yet. It's on the second floor in the reserve ballroom. Go in there. I'll look for you."

"Can't wait. The drive's been hellish and Yonkers was worse. See you in a bit."

I got back downstairs as everyone was finishing their dessert. Some sort of cheesecake that looked fantastic.

"We didn't know what kind you wanted, so we ordered the chocolate and vanilla swirl for you," Godfrey said. "Everything all right with Bradley?"

"Yes. He ate on the way. Said the drive was awful but he'll be here in less than a half hour. I told him to go directly to the competition on the second floor."

"How did you know it was on the second floor?" Theo asked.

"Um, er, uh…"

"Because it's on the program," Rosalee said. "Didn't any of you bother to read it?"

I spooned the rich cheesecake into my mouth and shut my eyes. It was a moment I wanted to savor, but if all went well, I'd soon have another.

Again, an announcement was made, only this time the speaker directed everyone to the upstairs reserve ballroom. As we stood from the table, Theo gave me a poke. "You still haven't told me about this evidence you have."

"Actually, it's more like a plan."

He shot me a look. "A plan as in something you're considering or, God help us, something you've already set in motion?"

"The last thing you said."

The six of us exited the table and followed the crowd to the second floor, waiting our turns at the elevators.

"This plan of yours," Theo whispered as we got in the elevator, "it won't disrupt the chocolate competition, will it?"

Not anymore than Stanislav's. I crinkled my nose and shook my head. "Nah."

Magazine editors and publishers, along with famed chefs and media moguls, were already seated in the row of honor when our little entourage made its way into the reserve ballroom. Rosalee thundered into the first available row that had six adjacent seats. Our row was fourth or fifth from the front, and I made sure there was an empty seat at the end for Bradley. Godfrey was on my other side, with Theo next to him.

Reporters flanked both sides of the room and snapped photos of the preparation tables as well as a few shots of the first row. I clutched my purse next to me and prayed my hunch was right.

A few moments later, Henry walked to the front of the room and introduced the program. He asked that the audience remember Jules Leurant with a moment of silence and then thanked everyone for their support. When the judges were introduced, the audience rose and gave them each a thunderous applause. Then the chocolatiers were summoned from the small kitchen area to the center of the room where they were introduced with a similar amount of fanfare. Henry explained that "due to circumstances beyond anyone's control, Stanislav wouldn't be able to participate in tonight's competition and Earvin Roels would be taking his place."

There was so much rumbling from the audience that Henry had to clear his throat at least three times. Then, shouts from the reporters.

"Was Stanislav arrested for murder?"

"Was Stanislav killed?"

"Was Stanislav abducted?"

Henry ignored all the questions and wiped his brow with the back of his hand. I seriously doubted the White House Press Secretary would have been able to pull off that announcement without a hitch.

The chocolatiers, who were dressed in black chef coats with red and gold trim, stood motionless behind Henry. Allete and Anika had their hair pulled back and both had chosen to use ribbons to hold it in place. Earvin looked like the proverbial cat that had eaten the canary. Without prompting, he took a bow and positioned himself at the second table. That was one of the tables where a spider was hiding under the large spoon. But who knew where Stanislav was lurking.

Allete was given the first table and she strode behind it with a look of sheer determination. Only Anika seemed a bit wary as she made her way to the third presentation table. Once the chocolatiers were standing directly behind their tables, the editor-in-chief of *Food & Wine* told the audience what the chocolatiers were about to create. In no uncertain terms, the three of them had ninety minutes to create a chocolate castle complete with its own royal family.

My sister and I once insisted on making a gingerbread house for Christmas when we were little and my mother, not wanting to disappoint us, agreed to let us try. The end result, although edible, looked like a structure that had been condemned and slated for demolition.

Next, the editor explained the criteria for judging the piece and welcomed everyone to enjoy the process. I leaned back and wondered how long it would take before I knew for certain who the killer was. Of course, I had no idea what Stanislav had in mind, but I was fairly certain it wouldn't interfere with my arthropod plan. As things turned out, it didn't matter. No amount of foresight could have prepared me for what happened next.

I'd seen numerous tennis matches on TV during which one of the players went ballistic at the referee, even going so far as to smash an expensive racket on the ground and let loose with a series of expletives. But nothing, absolutely nothing, compared to the plan I loosely set in motion. If I could have walked back to those tables and returned the earwigs and spiders to the Ziploc bag in my purse, I would have done so without hesitation.

Unfortunately, it was too late.

At first, the chocolatiers seemed to be fixated on the same process. They had to introduce the block chocolate to the tempering machine. Then, it happened. Allete lifted the cloth from her tray of dipping forks and bent down to take a closer look. Immediately, she grabbed a small spoon, scooped what I knew to be the earwig from the tray, and flung it directly at Earvin, who was otherwise occupied at his table.

"*Mince!*" she shouted, followed by "*Punaise!*"

I had no idea what those words meant, but I knew I wasn't likely to find them on Rosetta Stone. Next, Earvin, who hadn't yet realized he, too, was in possession of a dead insect, not to mention a spider that still had some life in it, returned the favor by shouting, "*Gaot eroep zitte, joeng!*" Again, I didn't expect to find that retort in a guide to conversational Dutch.

The only person not embroiled in the mudslinging was Anika. She continued to temper her chocolate and set out a series of molds. Then she lifted the cloth from the tray with the dipping forks and looked down. A second later, she stabbed her earwig with one of the forks and marched it over to Earvin, where she waved it under his nose. "I have every right to be here, you sniveling, self-centered, chocolate turd! Your childish antics won't deter me."

"My antics?" he shouted. "You two women are insane."

With that, Earvin went back to his table, muttering in Dutch or maybe even German. Anika returned to her table, but only after flicking her index finger at Earvin. Whatever *that* meant. Meanwhile, Allete poured some of her tempered chocolate into a series of small molds as if nothing had happened.

"What was that about?" Rosalee leaned forward in her seat.

"Artistic differences," I replied.

I watched Allete and Earvin carefully, hoping they'd notice the spiders I placed under their large spoons. With my gaze oscillating between the two of them, I didn't see Anika unwrap another block chocolate, presumably for the tempering machine. By the time I figured out what was going on, Anika was at Earvin's throat, pointing the prongs of a dipping fork directly under his chin.

"Will someone kindly remove this madwoman?" Earvin shouted. "She's lost her mind."

"And you're about to lose this contest, you murderous scoundrel," Anika replied. "Next time you want to send me a message, use Facebook and not my chocolate. You think I don't know about that incident in Amsterdam? Jules's assistant used to work for the same chocolate company I did in Denmark before he signed on to assist your miserable uncle."

"I never went near your precious chocolate. I don't know what you're talking about."

At that juncture in time, cameramen and reporters rushed to the front of the room to capture, what I imagined would be, the next big news story. And Stephanie rushed over to where I was seated and motioned for me to follow her.

I kept turning my head to the presentation area as I inched my way out of the row and over to a corner of the room, where Stephanie stood against the wall.

"What's going on? From the looks of things, this could be explosive," I said.

"That's what I wanted to tell you. I might have had something to do with it. This idea sort of popped into my head really late last night and I knew I had to act on it."

"Idea? What idea?"

Stephanie bent her head down and kept her voice low. "When you told me about the breakdown Allete had over some message in the block chocolate, I got the idea to re-create the scenario during the competition. I figured it would unnerve the killer, who I think might be Earvin, and he would give himself away. I sneaked into that small kitchen area, found the block chocolates and carved KILLER messages in all three of them. I wanted to substitute them for the chocolate that was already there. Unfortunately, I only got to one table. I could have sworn someone was watching me so I got the hell out of there before I could substitute the other two."

I looked at the floor and groaned. "That was you? The clicking of your heels could be heard in Baltimore."

"You were there? You were the person who was watching me?"

"Shh! Yes. I had an idea, too. Only mine was a bit more graphic."

"What do you mean by 'graphic'?"

I told Stephanie about the earwigs and the spiders and her jaw dropped. "Geez, Norrie, you know what this means, don't you?"

I shrugged. "What?"

"Health inspectors. I bet money someone's going to notify the Ontario County Health Department."

"It wasn't like I flooded the place with roaches," I muttered. "But you're right. In retrospect, maybe it wasn't the best idea."

"You think?"

"Listen," I said, "I read that pamphlet about the chocolatiers from cover-to-cover yesterday. And I paid a great deal of attention to the family photos."

"What are you getting at?"

"I think I know who killed Jules."

Chapter 34

Suddenly, we heard a commotion coming from the hallway in front of the ballroom.

"You have thirty seconds to remove him or I'll do it myself!"

I recognized the voice immediately. It was Stanislav's and, before the other parties in the hallway could respond, he charged through the doors, past the rows of attendees, and onto the presentation area. Without so much as stopping to catch his breath, Stanislav lifted Earvin from the man's waist and proceeded to dump him in front of the judges' table. But that didn't deter Earvin. He kicked Stanislav in the shins and the ankles, all the while bellowing in a language none of us understood.

The shock on Allete's face was a dead giveaway. I was positive she never expected Stanislav to be released from the county lock-up, given the incriminating evidence against him.

I whispered to Stephanie, "Her. Allete. And if Stanislav isn't careful, he'll be next."

"Stanislav? That's her boyfriend or lover, or whatever you call it these days."

"That's what she wanted everyone to think, but it was a trap so she could get her dirty work done and then take the winnings to bail out her ex-husband's company. And Stanislav fell for it."

"What does any of that have to do with your dead insects and those spiders?" she asked.

"Hold on, I'll get to that."

Just then, Stanislav shouted to Earvin, "I'm removing you to save your life, you insignificant little worm. There's a brown recluse spider on your table and if it touches you, you'll need at least a dozen skin grafts to save your flesh."

I turned to Stephanie. "A brown recluse spider? Oh my God! I thought I put house spiders on the tables. And how does he know?"

Stanislav then marched over to Allete. "Sorry, darling. I have a bad habit of reading other people's diaries. And how you got that thing past customs is beyond me."

Allete began to sob, insisting she didn't do it.

"Save your theatrics for the deputies. When the lab report came back about corn syrup and blue coloring, there was no doubt in my mind you were the culprit. That was the mixture you were working on for one of your chocolate fillings. When I realized that, I snuck a peek at your diary. Imagine my surprise when I read you and Daan were never divorced."

Allete continued to cry, muttering about "a misunderstanding" when Earvin grabbed a hand towel from Anika's table and threw it at Allete's face. "You tried to kill me, you little she-witch! Just like you killed my uncle!"

By now, the media was all over the room. Cameras flashing, reporters jostling for positions, and news anchors hurriedly making phone calls. I sat there wide-eyed with my jaw dropping.

Anika, who had, up to this point, remained fairly calm, strode over to Allete and screamed, "Earwigs! Filthy, disgusting earwigs. What did you do? Read that interview I gave for *Culinary Masterpieces* about my phobia when it came to those things? Well, I've got news for you. I've gotten over it. As Earvin can attest."

Earvin shuddered and rolled his eyes as more and more reporters raced to the front of the room.

Godfrey ran over to where I was standing. "Those insects…Please don't tell me you're the one responsible for this mess."

"Only partially."

In a voice that all but shook the room, Earvin bellowed, "Will someone please arrest that French woman for murdering my uncle and attempting to kill me?"

"I swear, I wasn't the one who poisoned that bonbon," Allete shrieked. "What was I going to do? Buy a gallon of antifreeze and stash it somewhere?"

Then, a voice no one expected, Hortensia Vermeulen's. "No, not the antifreeze. You left that for your husband. And no purchase was required. Daan Langbroek is the son of a mechanic and knows his way around car engines. It was no problem for him to dip into the little reserve on some poor unsuspecting vehicle and help himself to the poison. Antifreeze is sweet so it would have gone undetected in Jules's mouth, especially after drinking wine."

Good. Wine. A nice generic term and not Cabernet Sauvignon from Two Witches Winery.

"My husband?" Allete croaked. "Why would he do such a thing?"

"To salvage his business with the prize money. The stock plunged and he was desperate. He's been on Interpol's radar ever since the murder of Puccini Zinest's CEO in Amsterdam. A murder your husband committed. Too bad he slipped out of the country before an arrest could be made. With the CEO out of the picture, it was "a go" as far as the international chocolate competition went. And you, my dear Allete, were virtually assured of being one of the finalists."

Allete dabbed her face with a napkin. "And how could my husband accomplish such a thing?"

Hortensia glared at Allete. "Daan was able to get into the CEO's room and spray Ambien on the man's toothbrush. It was enough to make him woozy and slip under water. It worked once so Daan did it again with the wineglass that Jules used. You had to get Jules out of the way because he was the only person who stood between you and a fortune. And if you wonder why no Ambien spray bottles were ever found during the intense searches the local deputies made after Jules's death, it was because Daan was clever enough to soak off the label on the spray bottle and replace it with the label for Flonase. The spray bottles are similar in size and shape."

Theo leaned over and poked my elbow. "Didn't I say that about the Flonase?"

"Yes, yes, you did. But you were convinced Stanislav had it. But forget the Flonase for a minute. Since when do horticulturalists conduct crime investigations?"

"Shh!" he said as Hortensia continued.

"Puccini Zinest's CEO was the only obstacle against a merger, which would have meant no contest and no prize money. Daan was desperate so he pretended to suffer from insomnia so he could be given a prescription from a health clinic."

"I'm confused," Theo whispered. "What does this have to do with Anika sneaking around at the opening reception?"

"The opening reception?" I asked. "Where does soil maximization fit into any of this because the last time I looked, that's why Hortensia Vermeulen is in the United States to begin with."

Then Earvin spoke again. Only this time he walked directly in front of Hortensia, put his hands on his hips, and groaned. "Fine. Fine. Will you please arrest Daan Langbroek along with Allete Barrineau so we can get on with the competition? And maybe now you'll stop bugging me about my uncle's death. I got a nasty cut over my eye, thanks to that humungous ring of yours. Not to mention the fall I took. I don't even think my professional chef's jacket can be cleaned. And, for your information, it's missing a button. Those things cost a fortune. How the hell was I supposed to know who you really are? I thought you were a crazed chocolate aficionado."

Hortensia patted Earvin on the arm. "I said I was sorry. You were in a rush to avoid my questioning and when I followed you to the car, I slipped on the snowy ground. I was flaying all around and my hand accidently brushed against your forehead. The head bleeds quite a lot, you know. I didn't think the sharpness of the gold filigree would do that much damage. And I certainly didn't expect you to fall. Unfortunately, I do not have the authority to arrest anyone. As I told you in the parking lot, I retired from the General Directorate of Judicial Police in Belgium and now work as a detective serving Belgium, France, and the Netherlands. Much more lucrative."

Stephanie cleared her throat. "No wonder she can afford that ring."

"As you've surmised," Hortensia said, "I'm not Hortensia Vermeulen. I'm Margot Jansen. However, I bear a strong resemblance to Hortensia and that's when I was contacted by Puccini Zinest to pretend to be the famed horticulturalist so I could unobtrusively track Daan Langbroek's moves in New York. The real Hortensia was more than glad to assist with our little operation. Of course, that meant collaborating with law enforcement from two countries, but with an employer who wields as much clout as Puccini Zinest, it was no problem."

"That explains why she didn't answer any questions at her canned lecture. She knows as much about soil as I do," I muttered. "The real Hortensia must have put that PowerPoint together."

Margot looked at the audience and took a breath. "The company was convinced there'd be another murder, and unfortunately, they were right. Daan's a clever killer, and I was too late to prevent Jules from ingesting that bonbon."

Suddenly, Daan Langbroek shot out of his chair and bolted to the door. "You won't be able to prove anything."

"That's what you think," Margot replied. "When you had that little tussle with Stanislav during his chocolate demonstration, you mixed antifreeze into the chocolate that you threw on him. Like a magician, you substituted your own concoction for the tempered chocolate he was working with and when he taste-tested the mixture, it was too late. Thanks to Deputy Hickman, the jacket Stanislav was wearing went to the Yates county lab for testing. I contacted the deputy as soon as you darted out of the winery. So, indeed, I can prove attempted murder."

Daan leaned his body against the door. "How did you know my plan for Stanislav?"

"I didn't. Not right away. But I overheard one of the guests at the hotel complaining to the management that someone broke into her car and left a gooey mess on the hood. I put two and two together and got over to Gable Hill Winery as soon as I'd had my little conversation with Earvin that day."

"You still can't prove a damn thing!" Daan shouted and raced out the door.

Allete began to sob again. "I swear, I had nothing to do with any of this. I came here to compete with the best intentions."

"Like leading me on and pretending to be interested in starting our own chocolate company?" Stanislav asked from the other side of room. "What's the American word for that? Ah yes. A Jezebel!"

"A Jezebel?" Don couldn't stop himself from laughing. "The last person I heard use that word was my great-grandmother."

In that instant, we heard a loud crash in the hallway. Then another. Before any of us could get to the door, Bradley walked in. Completely covered with red wine. He looked absolutely dazed but adorable, as usual. The room went completely quiet and Bradley looked around. "Um, uh, sorry if I disrupted the program. A big guy came racing out of here and nearly knocked me over. I darted to one side just as a server came by with a wine cart. The big guy crashed into it and hit his head on the corner of the cart. It must have stunned him because he lost his footing and he's on the ground. I missed toppling into the guy but couldn't avoid getting splattered with wine."

"Quick!" Margot shouted. "Someone detain Daan Langbroek and call the local deputies!"

In a flurry of excitement, Henry led the charge as he and a few attendees left the reserve ballroom for the foyer.

"I didn't think Henry could move that fast," Rosalee announced. "I thought he only had two speeds—slow and slower."

The reporters who had fixed their attention on the presentation tables now moved to the foyer. The room resembled a football field—with everyone running every which way.

The three competing chocolatiers, Allete, Anika, and Earvin, remained at their positions, with Allete weeping, Earvin fussing over his table, and Anika standing with her hands on her hips.

Chapter 35

It was no surprise that Deputy Hickman arrived on scene in a most foul mood, along with two Ontario County deputies.

"There'd better be a good reason for this," Grizzly Gary shouted as he got off the elevator and stormed into the ballroom. "It's barbeque night at the Elks Club, and I'm missing some spicy ribs. Whoever's in charge here needs to call Maintenance. Looks like one of your servers made a huge mess of things in the foyer, and that crowd of lookie-loos isn't helping."

"That crowd of 'lookie-loos' is holding down one of Jules's killers," Margot said. She removed her auburn wig and shook out her shoulder-length blond hair. "We've nabbed him, Deputy Hickman." She took a napkin from one of the tables and wiped off her makeup, revealing a much younger woman in her forties perhaps, not sixties. Suddenly, Deputy Hickman's entire demeanor changed right in front of us. He turned to the two Ontario county deputies and motioned for them to follow him back to the foyer.

"Well, they won't have too far to look for the other killer," I said to Theo, Don, and Godfrey. I stood and made my way over to Bradley, turning my head to finish my comment. "Allete's only a few feet away, and I knew it was her when I plowed through that program booklet Henry sent us. My God. That thing could rival *War and Peace*. Anyway, there were family photos of Allete dangling little spiders at her brothers. The instant I saw them, I knew she was faking all along. Kids who play with spiders and insects don't grow up to freak out over harmless house spiders."

Bradley rushed toward me and gave me a hug. "Was the guy who knocked into me the killer? Geez. Talk about timing."

With the ballroom doors wide open, I got a good look at Deputy Hickman, Margot Jansen, Henry Speltmore, and the two Ontario County deputies huddled around Daan Langbroek. Too bad it was short-lived. Within seconds, a sea of reporters engulfed the entire area, leaving me no choice but to return to my seat, along with Theo, Don, Godfrey, and Bradley.

Nothing changed at the competition tables except that Allete's sobs were getting louder.

"Oh brother," Theo said. "This is a disaster. They can't hold the competition now. Who are they going to remove?"

Within minutes, the reporters fanned out and I got a birds-eye view of Daan Langbroek with his hands behind his back being escorted out of the hallway and into the elevator by Deputy Hickman and the Ontario county deputies.

"I'm surprised Allete isn't right behind him," I said.

Theo shook his head. "She's no fool. She still thinks she has a chance to compete for the grand prize. Stanislav's accusations were simply that. Accusations. He'd need to press charges."

When the commotion died down in the hallway, Henry stepped to the front of the room. "Our apologies for a most unsettling evening. Please give me a moment to confer with our judges regarding the status of our competition."

With that, he walked to the judges' area and the four of them looked as if they were deeply involved in prayer. Heads bent down and no sign of movement. The reporters snapped photos of that little "powwow" as well.

Earvin continued to fuss with the accoutrements on his table, but Anika strode over to where Allete was standing and motioned for her. The two of them stood face-to-face against the wall nearest to the utility room door.

I jumped from my seat and virtually shoved Bradley into Godfrey as I stumbled forward. "Gotta go. Nature calls."

With that, I took off like a madwoman for the door and the stairs leading to the other entrance to the utility room. Whatever conversation Allete and Anika were having, I needed to hear every single word. My feet felt as if someone had planted lead weights on them as I pushed myself to reach that utility room in time to hear what those two women were saying. Then I made sure to push the recording app on my cell phone. Once inside the utility room, I wedged the door open a sliver and held out my phone. It was enough space for me to see the women without them noticing I was there. Or so I thought.

"Your husband promised me three hundred twenty Danish krone if I followed Jules outside when he left that opening reception at the hotel and saw to it he wouldn't get up easily if he fell. Where's my money?"

"Shh! Quiet! Our voices can carry. You'll get your miserable fifty thousand dollars as soon as I win this contest and post bail money for my husband."

Oh my God! The third killer is Anika. That's why she pretended to be one of the servers at the event.

"What makes you so sure you'll take the prize?" Anika demanded.

"Because Earvin's a buffoon and if you don't let me win, I'll tell the authorities it was you who came up with the idea to kill Jules. I'll tell them how I overheard you boasting about it when we were in Munich. You needed to get Jules out of way so you'd be guaranteed a spot in the finals."

"Liar. We were both in on it. You were desperate to save your husband's business. Desperate from day one when Daan made sure the CEO would drown in his bathtub."

"I'll deny everything," Allete said.

Anika's voice got louder. "I can do that, too. In fact, if push comes to shove, I'll admit to trying to save Jules by moving the body but when I realized he was dead, it was too late. I can cry too, you know."

"Fire up the tears because I don't think we're alone."

This was always the scene in the movies where someone said, "We've been made," only there was no "we," just me, and I knew I was in trouble. Of course, by the time I realized it, it was already too late. Anika shoved the door backward and lunged at me. "Give me your damn cell phone if you know what's good for you."

"Like hell." *I'd need to write a whole new screenplay to afford another one.*

"Don't make it hard on yourself." Allete closed the door that separated the utility room from the ballroom, while Anika grabbed me by the wrist and twisted my arm. The pain seared through me. I dropped my phone but managed to kick it under a table so one of those witches would have to bend down to retrieve it. I waited to see which one of them would make the move. My money was on Anika since she was closer and, sure enough, I was right. Without waiting to see what Allete had in mind, I let out a bloodcurdling shriek and jumped on Anika's back, yanking her hair with every bit of strength I had. Granted, it was a move Nancy Drew never would have made and one my mother certainly wouldn't have condoned. Francine and I were taught hair-pulling wasn't considered fair fighting.

Then again, Nancy Drew and my mother weren't fending off a maniac.

"Do something, Allete!" Anika shouted, only Allete was no longer in the room.

By now, Anika and I were embroiled in a genuine scuffle. I rolled off her back and resorted to a more civilized means of self-defense—kicking and punching. The stainless-steel bowls and kitchen utensils on the table fell to the ground and Anika wasted no time grabbing a large slotted spoon which she aimed at my head.

The only thing within my reach was a metal colander, but with a quick thrust, I landed it against her cheek and screamed at the top of my lungs. The sound must have caught someone's attention because I heard a voice shouting, "Norrie, are you all right?"

The door to the utility room flung open and, from my vantage point on the ground, I saw men's shoes. At least two pairs. My arms pressed down on Anika's shoulders and I yelled, "Don't let her get away!"

It was Bradley and Godfrey who managed to pull me off her while she insisted I had "lost my mind" and attacked her "like a rabid dog."

"Rabid dog?" By now, I really *had* lost my mind. I got down on all fours to scrounge for my cell phone all the while gasping "She's the other killer. And Allete was in on it, too!"

"Allete? She's the one who ran into the ballroom from the foyer. She said Anika attacked you. Said Anika is as unstable as they get."

And Allete is as unbalanced as they come.

I retrieved my cell phone and played the conversation I'd taped. At least ten more people, including Theo, Don, Cammy, and Margot Jansen, crammed into the utility room and listened to my recording. Too bad it didn't include the under-the-table melee between Anika and me.

"Guess Deputy Hickman won't be biting into any of those spicy ribs tonight, huh?" Theo said.

"And we won't get to watch famed chocolatiers create fantasy castles," Don said. "Not tonight anyway. No doubt Allete will be brought in for questioning once those deputies finish processing Daan Langbroek's arrest. And with Anika's phone confession, Earvin can't very well compete against himself."

"I'm not so sure about that," I said. "He's got quite the ego."

In a matter of minutes, everyone returned to their seats and Henry, along with the judges, rendered their decision regarding the status of the competition.

Henry stood in front of the room looking like the images I had seen of General Lee surrendering to General Grant. "It is with great sadness and duress that I announce the Chocolate Extravaganza Competition has been cancelled. Our sincere apologies to our ticket holders, our sponsors, and, of course, our esteemed guests from the culinary magazines and institutions. The Seneca Lake Wine Trail Association thanks you for your unwavering support and promises to continue our fine partnerships."

"That's blatantly unfair!" Earvin bellowed. "I've had to put up with all sorts of trauma, including the death of my dear uncle Jules. I should be awarded that prize by default."

The editor and chief of *Wine Spectator* stepped toward Earvin. "Please accept our apologies, but the rules clearly indicated no one would receive the prize via default. We wish you the very best in your endeavors."

Earvin muttered something in Dutch, or perhaps German, and stormed out of the ballroom, colliding with Deputy Hickman, who had just gotten off the elevator.

"Someone in here called my office to tell them the killer is at large in the ballroom. Will someone please tell me what's going on? If I'm not mistaken, we have the killer in custody. Daan Langbroek is sitting in the backseat of an official Ontario County van as we speak."

"You can arrest two more people." Earvin pointed to Allete, who was standing by the door, sobbing into a wadded-up handful of tissues and then to Anika, who was cornered by Theo, Don, Godfrey, Bradley, Cammy, and Margot.

"I'm afraid that's true, Deputy Hickman," Margot said. "Thanks to Norrie Ellington, we have recorded evidence that can implicate both women."

Deputy Hickman walked toward me and held out his hand.

"It's my only cell phone," I said. "I can't part with it."

"It's evidence, Miss Ellington. It will be returned to you once the case is closed."

"Once the case is closed? There are cases in both counties that have been going on for over a decade!"

I handed him my cell phone and felt as if I severed my arm.

"Walmart's open twenty-four hours," the deputy said. "You can buy a pre-paid one for the time being." With that, he slipped my phone into a plastic evidence bag and walked toward the elevator.

Chapter 36

"Are you all right, Norrie?" Bradley asked once Deputy Hickman left. "I can drive you to Walmart if you want."

"And I've got an old flip phone you can use," Cammy said.

"Nah. I'll be okay. I'll go tomorrow. I still have my laptop and my iPad at home. By the way, who called Deputy Hickman?"

Stephanie, who stood between Cammy and Godfrey, waved. "I get the blame for that one. Once I figured out what was going on, I didn't want either of the murderesses to get away with anything."

"Guess that's it for the Chocolate & Wine Extravaganza," I said. "No sense hanging around here. We can go downstairs, grab comfortable seats at the bar, and chalk this off to another great winery event."

"I'm in!" Don said, followed by a chorus of "yeahs."

Except for Rosalee, who said she'd had enough excitement for the day, the rest of us traipsed off to the bar, only to find it was jam packed with reporters who had followed Earvin Roels there.

"What do you suppose that's all about?" Cammy asked.

"Earvin's the 'man of the hour,'" I said. "He's the only surviving chocolatier who won't be indicted for murder."

"And who will be going home with an empty pocket," Theo added.

I looked at the growing crowd of reporters. "I'm not so sure about that. He'll get interviews, press conferences, photo ops. Mark my words. Earvin Roels will be the next big thing."

"What I'd like to know," Godfrey said, "is how you and Stephanie thought you could lure out the killers with dead bugs and a carved message in the chocolate."

I laughed. "My part's easy. I knew Allete was bluffing, but I needed all of them to turn against each other until one of them lost it and confessed. It almost worked. Come on. Let's grab those chairs near the corner before someone takes them."

A few minutes later, when all of us were seated comfortably, Stephanie brushed a long strand of hair from her face. "When I found out about the alleged death threat in the block chocolate, I figured the same thing. Let them think one of the other chocolatiers knew what they were up to. Naturally, they'd suspect each other. Too bad I couldn't come up with a more cryptic message."

Don leaned back and poked me in the arm. "Hey, speaking of cryptic messages, what was that whole deal with the note you found in Hortensia's, I mean, Margot's trash?"

"I'm not sure," I said. "Not without asking Margot. But I think the note was written by her for Earvin. Remember, she'd been tailing him for information ever since she got here. And as for the stationery, well, it was no surprise. She was working for Puccini Zinest. She probably has scads of their notepaper."

"And to think I missed all of this while I was stuck in Yonkers," Bradley said. "I hate working on mergers."

As soon as he said the word "merger," I froze. "Yonkers. You were in Yonkers."

"Norrie, are you okay? Of course I was in Yonkers."

I took a slow breath and tapped my teeth. "Yonkers is the headquarters for Bomboni Americano Chocolates. Please don't tell me that's the merger you were working on. I thought you were dealing with a complex settlement case. And I thought you worked on family law."

"It is. I mean, it was. A complex settlement case. And it was a family matter. Bomboni Zinest and Bomboni Americano are from the same family. Unfortunately, the family patriarch didn't share the same philosophy as his progeny. When he was found dead over a year ago at that hotel in Amsterdam, the family became convinced, more than ever, that they needed to work together lest another one of them suffer the same fate. It never dawned on them that the death had more to do with outsider greed over a competition than a power struggle. Anyway, it looks as if the perpetrators will get their due. Too bad it all had to unfold in the Finger Lakes."

"No kidding," I said. "And too bad they had to pick a glass with our wine in it. At least we were vindicated and people can enjoy our Cabernet Sauvignon without worrying that it will be the last thing they taste."

"Which reminds me," Don said. "Where is that server? I could use a glass of something right now. We all could."

Bradley gave my hand a squeeze and I looked over at Godfrey, wondering if he noticed. At some point, I needed to figure out how I felt about each of them, but right now, all I cared about was getting a good night's sleep and putting the Chocolate and Wine Extravaganza behind me.

* * * *

I had no intention of getting up at the break of dawn, but apparently that didn't matter to Deputy Hickman. A familiar pounding on my door a little before eight shook me out of bed like an earthquake.

Once again, I tossed an old sweatshirt over my pajamas and slipped into jeans. I don't even remember if I bothered to comb my hair before answering the door. If I looked like hell, the deputy either didn't notice or chose to ignore it. He gave me a nod and I motioned for him to come inside.

"Are you here to return my iPhone?" I asked.

"Not as yet. It's evidence. I'm here because we had a confession regarding the marijuana incident at your winery. It happened late last night while we were interrogating Daan Langbroek, Allete Barrineau, and Anika Schou. True, it's a rather minor and seemingly inconsequential matter, considering the three of them were involved in a murder, but still, I felt as if you deserved an answer."

"Who did it? Which one of those scoundrels?"

"It was Allete's plan. She smuggled in some marijuana oil, for lack of a better term, and her husband put it in Earvin's tea during the demonstration at your winery. She knew there would be a huge crowd, so chances of him being caught were virtually nil. Naturally, she laced her own drink."

"What about Stanislav's coffee? It was in that, too. Wasn't it?"

"Nope. Not at all. He pretended it was and dumped the coffee. Allete convinced him to be part of the ruse. She told him she paid someone to spike Earvin's tea. Stanislav never suspected it was her husband. The whole premise was to rattle Earvin so he would be a bundle of nerves for the competition."

"Oh brother. Talk about being burned. But he wasn't the only one. Margot Jansen had us fooled, and I actually sat through her boring lecture on soil when she pretended to be Hortensia. I was positive she could have been the killer."

"Perhaps that will be a lesson to you, Miss Ellington. To let law enforcement do its job. Unless, of course, the soil lecture was pertinent to the winery."

I shrugged. "I still don't understand why she couldn't have investigated as herself and not used a fake identity."

"She had to establish a persona that would allow the chocolatiers to be off-guard. Trust me when I tell you, her planning was meticulous."

"Not that meticulous. Jules still wound up dead as a doornail."

"But his legacy will live on, I imagine, through that nephew of his. Anyway, Miss Ellington, I must be on my way. Have a nice day."

I thought about what Deputy Hickman said regarding Earvin and then dismissed it. In fact, I didn't think about Earvin much at all—until a month later when the winery copy of *Time* magazine came in the mail. Cammy called me the minute it arrived.

"Norrie, you're not going to believe this, but Earvin Roels is on the cover of *Time* magazine as chocolatier of the year!"

"Does the article make any mention of the fact that we solved those murders?" I asked.

"Um, no. In fact, it refers to our region as "Upstate New York.""

"That's it? 'Upstate New York?' Upstate New York could be anywhere."

And that was only the beginning. Earvin appeared on the covers of *Saveur, Food & Wine, Wine Spectator,* and a zillion other culinary and wine magazines. The man reached such celebrity status—it was as if he was responsible for discovering chocolate instead of the Aztecs.

Cammy told me I needed to move on. In fact, she was quite adamant. "Let it go, Norrie. We've got bigger fish to fry."

"What do you mean?"

"I mean, in a few months, we'll be celebrating the acclaimed Wine and Cheese Event. You'll forget all about chocolate. I guarantee it."

Suddenly, I felt that familiar pit in my stomach.

This better be a simple event. Grilled cheese, cheese balls, and cheese puffs. Most of all, it better not include the words "murder," "dead body," or "corpse." I have enough on my plate.

Dressed Up For Murder

If you enjoyed SAUVIGONE FOR GOOD
be sure not to miss
the next book in
bestselling
J.C. Eaton's series
A SOPHIE KIMBALL MYSTERY
DRESSED UP 4 MURDER
will be available
in March 2020
Turn the page for a peek at this exciting story!

Chapter 1

Harriet Plunkett's House
Sun City West, Arizona

"Isn't he the most adorable little dog you've ever seen?" my mother asked when I walked into her house on a late Wednesday afternoon in October. Signs of autumn were everywhere in Sun City West, including pumpkins on front patios, leaf wreaths on doorways, and someone's large ceramic pig dressed like a witch. Of course, it was still over ninety degrees, but that wasn't stopping anyone from welcoming the fall and winter holidays.

My mother begged me to stop by on my way home from work to look at Streetman's costume for the "Precious Pooches Holiday Extravaganza" for dogs of all ages and breeds. And since her dog was a Chiweenie, part Chihuahua part Dachshund, he certainly qualified. The contest made no mention of neuroses.

I tried to be objective, but it was impossible. "He looks like an overstuffed grape or something, if you ask me. And what's he doing? He's scratching at your patio door. Does he need to go out?"

"He's not a grape. He's going as an acorn. He'll look better once I get the hat on him. When he stops biting. And no, he doesn't need to go out. We were just out a half hour ago."

"Maybe he's trying to escape because you're about to put the hat on him."

"Very funny. It's not easy, you know. There are contests in three separate categories, and I've registered him for all of them—Halloween, Thanksgiving, and Hanukkah/Christmas. And just wait until it comes time for the St. Patrick's Day Doggie Contest in March. The prize for that one is almost as good as a pot of gold."

St. Patrick's Day? That's months away. And what's next, dressing him up as "Yankee Doodle Dandy" for the Fourth of July?

"Like I was saying, Phee, Shirley Johnson is making the costumes. You're looking at the Thanksgiving one. I can't make up my mind if I want Streetman to go as a pumpkin for Halloween or a ghost. Goodness. I haven't even given any thought to the winter costume. Maybe a snowflake…"

"Right now, I think he wants to go. Period. Look. He's frantically pawing at your patio door."

"He only wants to sniff around the Galbraiths' grill. A coyote or something must've marked the tarp because, ever since yesterday, the dog has been beside himself to check it out. I certainly don't need him peeing on their grill. They won't be back until early November. I spoke to Janet a few days ago. She really appreciates Streetman and me checking out her place while they're up in Alberta. You know how it is with the Canadian snowbirds. They can only stay here for five months or they lose their health insurance. Something like that."

"Uh-huh."

"Anyway, how are you and Marshall managing with your move? That's coming up sometime soon, isn't it?"

"Not soon enough. I feel as if I'm living out of cardboard boxes, and Marshall's place is no different. We won't be able to get in to the new rental until November first. That's three weeks away and three weeks too long."

Marshall and I worked for the same Mankato, Minnesota, police department for years before I moved out west to become the bookkeeper for retired Mankato detective, Nate Williams. Nate opened his own investigation firm and insisted I join him. A year later, and in dire need of a good investigator, he talked Marshall into making the move as well. I was ecstatic, considering I'd had a crush on the guy for years. Turned out it was reciprocal.

"Do you need any help with the move?" my mother asked. "Lucinda and Shirley offered to help you pack."

Oh dear God. We'd never finish. They'd be arguing over everything.

Shirley Johnson and Lucinda Espinoza were two of my mother's book club friends and as opposite as any two people could possibly be. Shirley was an elegant black woman and a former milliner while Lucinda, a retired housewife, looked as if she had recently escaped a windstorm.

"No, I'll be fine. The hard part's done. I can't believe I actually sold my house in Mankato. Other than autumn strolls around Sibley Park, I really won't miss Minnesota."

"What about my granddaughter? Did she get all nostalgic?"

"Um, not really. In fact, she had me donate most of the stuff she had in storage to charity. She's sharing a small apartment in St. Cloud with another teacher and they don't have much room. Besides, Kalese was never the packrat type."

My mother had turned away for a second and walked to the patio door. "Maybe you're right. Maybe he does need to go out again. Hold on. I'll grab his leash. We can both go out back." Except for the people living next door to my mother and busybody Herb Garrett across the street, the other neighbors were all snowbirds. Michigan. South Dakota. Canada.

"Dear God. You're not going to take him outside in that outfit, are you?" I asked.

"Fine. I'll unsnap the Velcro. Shirley's using Velcro for everything."

At the instant in which the sliding glass door opened, Streetman yanked my mother across the patio and straight toward the Galbraiths' backyard barbeque grill.

"I should never have taken the retractable leash," she shouted. "He's already yards ahead of me."

"Can't you push a button or something on that leash?"

"I haven't learned how to use it yet. It's new."

I was a few feet behind her, running as fast as I could in wedge heels.

Her voice bellowed across the adjoining yards as she approached the Galbraiths' grill. "Streetman, stop that! Stop that this instant!"

The dog zeroed in on the tarp and had gripped the edge of it with his teeth. My mother stood directly behind him and fiddled with the retractable leash.

"Now see what you've done," she said to the dog. "You've gone ahead and uncovered the bottom of the grill. I'll just shove those black boxes back a bit and put the tarp back down."

"Don't move, Mom!" I screamed. "Take a good look. They're not boxes. They're shoes."

"What?" My mother flashed me a look. "Who puts shoes under a grill where snakes and scorpions can climb in them?"

I bent down to take a closer look and froze. Streetman was still tugging to get under the tarp and my mother seemed oblivious to what was really there.

"Um, it's not shoes. I mean, yeah, those are shoes, all right, but they're kind of attached to someone's legs."

"What??"

If I thought my mother's voice was loud when she was yelling at the dog, it was a veritable explosion at that point. "A body? There's a body under there? You're telling me there's a body under that tarp? Oh my God. Poor Streetman. This could really set him back."

Yes, above all, the dog's emotional state was the first thing that came to my mind, too.

"Mom, step back."

At that moment, she scooped Streetman into her arms and ran for the house. "I'm calling the sheriff. No! Wait. We must find out who it is first. Once those deputy sheriffs get here, they'll never let us near the body."

"Good. I don't want to be near a dead body. Do you?"

"Of course not. But I need to know who it is. My God, Phee, it could be one of the neighbors. Can't you just pull the tarp back and take a look?"

Streetman was putting up a major fuss, squirming in my mother's arms and trying to get down.

"Okay, Mom. Go back to the house. Put the dog inside and come back here. I won't move until you do. Oh, and bring your cell phone."

My mother didn't say a word. She walked as quickly as she could and returned a few minutes later, cell phone in hand. "Here. Take this plastic doggie bag and use it as you pull the tarp away. Don't get your fingerprints on the tarp."

"I'll pull the tarp back and take a look, but I won't have the slightest idea if it's one of your neighbors. I don't know all of them."

"Fine. Fine. Oh, and look for cause of death while you're at it."

"Cause of death? I'm not a medical examiner." I bent down, put my hand in the plastic bag and gingerly lifted the tarp. I tried not to look at what, or in this case, who, was underneath it, but it was useless. I got a bird's eye view. Male. Fully clothed, thank God, and face up. Middle aged. Dark hair. Jaundice coloring. Small trickle of blood from his nose to shirt. No puddles of blood behind the head or around the body.

My mother let out a piercing scream. "Oh my God. Oh my God in heaven!"

"Who? Who is it? Is it someone you know?"

I immediately let go of the tarp and let it drape over the body.

"No, no one I know."

"Then why were you screaming bloody murder?"

"Because there's a dead man directly across from my patio. A well-dressed dead man. Here, you call the sheriff's office. I'm too upset. And when you're done, give me the phone. I need to call Herb Garrett."

"Herb Garrett? Why on earth would you need to call Herb?"

"Once those emergency vehicles show up, he'll be pounding at my door. Might as well save us some time."

I started to dial nine-one-one when my mother grabbed my arm and stopped me. "Whatever you do, don't tell them it was Streetman who discovered the body."

"Why? What difference does that make?"

"Next thing you know, they'll want to use him for one of those cadaver dogs. He's got an excellent sense of smell. Don't say a word."

"You're kidding, right? First of all, the law enforcement agencies have their own trained dogs. *Trained* being the key word. No one's going to put up with all his shenanigans. And second of all, how else are you and I going to explain how we happened to come across a dead body under the neighbors' tarp?"

My mother pursed her lips and stood still for a second. "Okay. Fine. Go ahead and call."

The dispatch operator asked me three times if I was positively certain we had uncovered a dead body. I had reached my apex the third time.

"Unless they're starting to make store mannequins in various stages of decomposition, then what we've discovered is indeed a dead body. Not a doll. Not a lifelike toy. And certainly not someone's Halloween decoration!"

Finally, I gave her my mother's address and told her we were behind the house. Then I handed my mother the phone. "Go ahead. Make Herb's day. Sorry, Mom, I couldn't resist the Clint Eastwood reference."

My mother took the phone and pushed a button. "I have him on speed dial in case of an emergency."

All I could hear was her end of the conversation, but it was enough.

"I'm telling you, I had no idea there'd be a body under that tarp. Sure, it was a huge tarp, but I thought it was covering up one of those gigantic grills. Uh-huh…Really? A griddle feature? No, all I have is a small Weber. Uh-huh. Behind the house. Fine. See you in a minute."

"I take it Herb is on his way."

My mother nodded. "Do you think I should call Shirley and Lucinda?"

"This isn't an afternoon social, for crying out loud, it's a crime scene. No, don't call them. It's bad enough Herb's going to be here any second. Maybe we should go wait on your patio. We can see everything from there."

Just then I heard the distant sound of sirens. "Never mind. We might as well stay put."

My mother thrust the phone at me. "Quick. While there's time, call your office. Get Nate or Marshall over here."

"Much as I'd like to accommodate you by having my boss and my boyfriend show up, I can't. Marshall's on a case up in Payson and won't be back until the weekend. I think he took the case so he wouldn't have to be stepping over cartons. And as for my boss, Nate's so tied up with his other cases, he certainly doesn't have time to interfere with a Maricopa County Sheriffs' Office investigation."

"Humph. You know as well as I do those deputies will be bumbling around until they finally cave and bring in Williams Investigations to consult."

Much as I hated to admit it, my mother was right. Not because the sheriff deputies were "nincompoops" as she liked to put it, but the department was so inundated with drug-related crimes, kidnappings, and now a highway serial killer in the valley, that they relied on my boss's office to assist.

"Look, if and when that happens, I'll let you know."

The sirens were getting louder and I turned to face my mother's patio.

From the left of the garage, Herb Garrett stormed across the gravel yard. "Where's the stiff? I want to take a look before the place is plastered in yellow crime tape."

"Under the tarp." I failed to mention the need for a plastic bag.

Herb made a beeline for the Galbraiths' grill and lifted the tarp. "Nope. Don't know him. Damn it. I forgot my phone."

"Don't tell me you were going to snap a photo. And do what? Post it on the internet?"

Herb let the tarp drop and positioned himself next to my mother. "How else is poor Harriet going to sleep at night knowing some depraved killer is depositing bodies in the neighborhood? If I post it, maybe someone will know something."

My mother gasped. "Depraved killer? Bodies?"

"Herb's exaggerating," I said. "Aren't you?"

Suddenly it seemed as if the sirens were inches away from us. Then they stopped completely.

"Oh no," I said. "This can't be happening. Not again."

My mother grabbed my wrist. "What? What's happening?"

I took a deep breath. "Remember the two deputy sheriffs who were called in to investigate the murder at the Stardust Theater?"

"Uh-huh."

"Looks like they're back for a repeat performance. Deputies Ranston and Bowman. I don't know which one dislikes me more."

Well, maybe *dislike* wasn't quite the word to describe how they felt about me. Annoyed might have summed it up better. Over a year ago, when my mother and her book club ladies were taking part in Agatha Christie's

The Mousetrap at the Stardust Theater, someone was found dead on the catwalk. And even though I wasn't a detective, only the accountant at Williams Investigations, I sort of did a bit of sleuthing on my own and might have stepped on their toes. What the hell. They're big men. They needed to get over it.

"Miss Kimball." Deputy Ranston's feet crunched on the yard gravel as he approached us from the side of my mother's house. "I should have taken a closer look at the name when I read the nine-one-one report. Seems you're the one who placed the call."

"Nice seeing you again, Deputy Ranston." I turned to his counterpart and mumbled something similar before re-introducing my mother and Herb.

"So, was it you who found the body?" Ranston asked.

I honestly don't know why, but for some reason, the man reminded me of a Sonoran Desert Toad. I kept expecting his tongue to roll out a full foot as he spoke.

"Um, actually it was my mother's dog. Streetman. He found the body." Deputy Bowman cut in. "Just like that? Out of the blue?"

My mother took a few steps forward until she was almost nose to nose with Bowman. "For your information, Streetman and I cut across the Galbraiths' yard every day while they're still in Canada. We keep an eye on the house for them. Usually the dog is more concerned with the quail and the rabbits that hide under the bushes. He never as much as made a move toward the grill. Until yesterday afternoon. That's when he started whining to go over there. I thought a coyote might have marked it or left a deposit there."

"So, you lifted the tarp up to check?" Bowman asked.

"Of course not. The dog was on a retractable leash and got to the grill before I did. He nuzzled the tarp aside, and that's when we saw the body."

Bowman gave his partner a sideways glance. "How big a dog is this Streetman that he could lift an entire tarp off a body?"

"He's less than ten pounds," I said, "but very strong."

Bowman wasn't buying it. "Look, Miss Kimball, I know you have a penchant for unsolved crimes and I'm more likely to believe it was you who lifted the tarp."

My mother responded before I could utter a word. "Only for a split second and only because she happened to see someone's legs attached to the shoes that were beneath it. And she used a plastic bag so she wouldn't get fingerprints on the material."

Then the deputies turned to Herb and Ranston spoke. "Were you here as well when the ladies discovered the body, Mr. Garrett?"

"No. Harriet called me after dialing nine-one-one."

"I see."

Ranston wrote something on a small notepad and looked up. "The nine-one-one dispatcher gave us the Plunkett address. Would any of you happen to know the Galbraiths' address?"

"Of course," my mother said. "Something West Sentinel Drive. It's the small cul-de-sac behind us."

I could hear both deputies groan as Bowman placed a call.

"In a few minutes," he said, "a forensic team will be arriving as well as the coroner. I suggest you all return to your houses and stay clear of this property until further notice."

"Will you at least tell us who it is?" Herb asked. "For all we know, it could be one of our neighbors. Or a cartel drug lord who was dropped off here."

"Here? In Sun City West? That's what we have the desert for," my mother said.

Deputy Bowman forced a smile and repeated what he had told us a second ago. "Please go back to your houses. This is an official investigation."

"Will you be contacting the Galbraiths?" I asked.

Bowman gave a nod. "Yes."

I tapped my mother on the elbow and pointed to her house. "He's right." Then I whispered, "If you hurry, you can call the Galbraiths first."

Meet the Author

J.C. Eaton is the wife and husband team of Ann I. Goldfarb and James E. Clapp. Ann has published eight YA time travel mysteries.

Visit their website at www.jceatonmysteries.com

Printed in the United States
by Baker & Taylor Publisher Services